Chasing Orion

Chasing Orion

KATHRYN LASKY

CANDLEWICK PRESS

Copyright © 2010 by Kathryn Lasky

First edition 2010

Library of Congress Cataloging-in-Publication Data
Lasky, Kathryn.
Chasing Orion / Kathryn Lasky. — 1st ed.
p.   cm.
Summary: In 1952, When Georgie is eleven years old, her family moves to a new Indiana neighborhood where her teenaged neighbor has polio and is in an iron lung.
ISBN 978-0-7636-3982-2
[1. Poliomyelitis — Fiction. 2. Neighbors — Fiction.
3. Indiana — History — 20th century — Fiction.]   I. Title.
PZ7.L3274Cg 2010
[Fic] — dc22   2009007327

10 11 12 13 14 15 MVP 10 9 8 7 6 5 4 3 2 1

Printed in York, PA, U.S.A.

This book was typeset in Granjon.

Candlewick Press
99 Dover Street
Somerville, Massachusetts 02144

visit us at www.candlewick.com

Chapter One

Silver glinting behind leafy trees—that is the first thing I noticed as I stood in the backyard of our new house that hot summer day. Like a glistening metallic eye, the silver winked through the deep green leaves. A creepy feeling stole over me. It was as if I were being watched. Weird! But then again, everything seemed weird in this new neighborhood.

Look in the other direction, and you could see our just-landscaped yard, sweating in the July heat. A few new shrubs and young trees crouched beneath the Indiana sun. Mom refused to put down grass seed yet. She said it would burn up. We'd wait until spring. I hated this new neighborhood, this new house, and this new yard. The "lawn" looked naked and raw. Ripples of heat rose up and turned the air wavy. Our old yard was small, but it was nice and shady.

There was only one really big tree in our old yard, but that was enough. That space, the space defined by the tree and its shade, became the first small world I ever made. Making scenes in boxes was my hobby. But they were more than just scenes; they were stories. Just about as soon as I got my first dollhouse, I decided to try and make my own, except I didn't want a dollhouse exactly. I wanted a whole world and a good story put in a little box. I didn't care that much about all the dollhouse stuff: tiny refrigerators, minute sewing machines, and little beds and chairs—all the same things that you outfit a real house with.

I knew I would never make a small world of this stupid backyard. Never! I did have a thought, though. Backyards might change, but the sky doesn't. I was under the same sky here in this new ugly neighborhood as I had been in our old shady one. At night, the stars, the constellations, were the same. I found some comfort in that thought. My older brother, Emmett, was an amateur astronomer. He had even built telescopes, and we did a lot of sky watching at night. Why not make a small world of the sky, maybe a small universe?

I was staring back at the metallic eye, maybe slightly hypnotized, when I heard a car pull into our drive. It was Mom. Her Buick shimmered darkly in the heat. It didn't look quite real, as if it might just up and evaporate.

"Georgie!"

"Yeah, Mom."

"You water those trees yet?"

"No."

"Well, why not?"

"Too hot." Mom walked over to my lawn chair— I'd been reading my comic books under an umbrella we'd stuck into a crack in the patio.

She sighed. "Too hot? Georgia Louise Mason, you've been complaining all summer about not going swimming, and now's your chance to get wet and cool and you don't do it."

"Mom, everyone else gets to go swimming up until August. You wouldn't even let me go to Susie Grenelle's birthday party, and it was in June! At a private pool!"

"Honestly, Georgie, are you going to hold Susie Grenelle's birthday party against me for the rest of my life?"

"But Mom, I have no friends in this neighborhood. I have to go to a new school, and we are the only family in the whole state that had to stay out of swimming pools all summer. Even on the Fourth of July!"

I took the Fourth of July personally. It was not just a national holiday. It was my birthday. In fact, my mom and dad had considered, for about two minutes, calling me Georgia Liberty Mason, but then decided to slide in Louise for the middle part, a kind of nothing name if you ask me. Ever since I could remember, or at least ever since I had known how to swim, I had had a splash party for my birthday at the local swimming pool. But not this year. Not now that there was polio. I took this so personally that I refused to have any Fourth of July stuff on my birthday cake, as I usually did. I guess it was a matter of offend me, offend my country—we share a birthday. So there!

"Georgie, sweetheart." Her voice changed. It wasn't scolding anymore. It was kind of soft and wavy like the ripples of heat. "You don't want to end up like her." She nodded toward the trees where the silver glinted.

"Who?" I was getting a queasy feeling in my gut.

"That girl over there, our new neighbors, the

Kellers. I met them yesterday. Their daughter, Phyllis, is the same age as Emmett. She got polio and she's . . ." I think I knew what was coming. "She's in an iron lung."

I dropped my comic book on the patio, rose up from the chair, and looked at the glints of silver. It had seemed weird but at the same time almost magical when I had looked through the trees. Now there was nothing magical. It was simply and horribly unbelievable. I had seen iron lungs, but only pictures of them on television and in newsreels in the movie theaters— where we were now not allowed to go in the summer, along with the swimming pools, because of the crowds and the fear of catching polio.

"You mean right next door to us there's an iron lung?"

"I do indeed."

"But I thought you had to be in the hospital if they put you in one of them."

"Mr. Keller is a very important scientist for the Eli Lilly drug company, and I suppose like most of those Lilly big shots, he's got plenty of money. So they can afford to have one at home. It's all very sad. So let's not talk anymore about swimming and swimming pools."

"And the state fair," I added in a dull voice.

I had always loved the Indiana State Fair. Here's what I loved about it: the goats, the freak shows—even though Emmett said they were fake freaks half the time—and the cotton candy. In that order: goats, freaks, cotton candy.

In my opinion there was nothing better than goats. Goats are the most companionable of farm animals. That's what my grandma always said, and she should know because she was a farmer's wife and had a mess of goats. They are fun because every goat has a different personality. I knew goats that had more personality than many people. At the state fair they had goat exhibitions. And that was my idea of heaven. Just a whole mess of goats frisking around in the arena, showing off their goatiness. I wanted to have a goat at our old house, but Mom said the yard was too small. And then when we moved into this new house with a big huge yard, I asked again, but Mom said the neighborhood was too fancy to have goats pooping all over the place. Goats wouldn't be "tolerated." Imagine moving into a neighborhood where they wouldn't tolerate goats. Emmett said there were a lot of things not tolerated in Indianapolis—like Negroes at the swimming pool and Negroes at the amusement park and Negroes in neighborhoods like ours. So I guessed that Negroes were having an even more boring summer than I was.

"I don't know why you want to go to that old state fair, anyhow. It's hot, dusty, and dirty," Mom said, and plopped down into the lawn chair next to mine.

"Because." It was too hot to explain any more.

"Sure hope your dad doesn't go this year."

"He's got to," I said in a shocked voice. "Mom, he's head of the Indiana Poultry Association. Who will judge the chickens?"

"Let someone else do it. He doesn't get paid a nickel for that durned job." My mom could never bring herself to say *darn,* let alone *damn.* I could never figure out how slipping that *u* in there made *darn* less of a curse word.

"Well, he has to," I said quietly. Mom just grunted. My dad was a poultry broker. It's a fancy name for buying chickens and eggs in huge quantities and selling them to grocery store chains and restaurants and hotels and stuff like that. But it was *not* being a chicken farmer, as Darrell Caufield said, and for which I beat him up in the second grade. Anyhow, Mom was right. Dad didn't get paid a nickel for being the head of the Indiana Poultry Association or for judging the chickens at the state fair. He just did it because it was what he called a "civic-minded" thing to do, and besides, at one time there had been a lot of what he called "corrupt practices"—in other words, cheating—in the poultry world. I know it's hard to think of poultry as attracting gangsters. But there had been, according to Dad, "hanky-panky" with health regulations and shipment of hatching eggs.

"You know, Georgie, instead of sitting around complaining about the heat, you could go to the library. There's a brand-new one here. It's close enough to walk to."

"It's too hot to walk."

"It's air-conditioned once you get there. They have it up full blast. I was just there."

"Is that what you got in those bags—books?" I asked.

"Yes, and other stuff for school."

"School doesn't start for way over a month. Why are you getting it now? The books will be overdue by the first day of school."

"They have a special policy for teachers. We can keep them for six weeks and just call up to renew."

"What else do you have? It looks like you've been to the five-and-dime."

"Yes, the extra-fat crayons came in and they are perfect for kindergarten kids, and I knew they would sell out in a flash." My mom was a kindergarten teacher. "Come on, sweetie, get up and start watering these trees. It looks like a durned desert around here."

"Can I read my Archie comic while I do it?"

"I'm sure he won't mind." She laughed.

No, Archie wouldn't mind, I thought, but would the gorgeous blond Betty or the raven-haired Veronica be standing in a dried-up yard watering a spindly little tree? They didn't use the words *raven-haired,* of course, in the comic books. But I liked that word for black hair. It sounded dangerous and beautiful at the same time. They talked about movie actresses or heroines in old-fashioned books having raven hair or, better still, raven locks. I was not raven-haired. I was brown-haired. Muddy-water brown. And my hair was too stubby to be considered locks.

I decided to water the tree closest to the small grove that separated our yard from the Kellers' and see if I could catch a glimpse of the iron lung. I had done a report for school on the polio epidemic. Starting in January, the National Foundation for Infantile Paralysis had sent out 1,225 iron lungs to all the epidemic states. There were twenty-one epidemic states.

Indiana was not one yet. But our next door neighbor, Ohio, was. Philip Drinker had invented the iron lung, and then this other guy, Emerson, improved upon it. They were both probably millionaires by now. Even though not every polio person had to go into an iron lung—plenty didn't—they still couldn't make them fast enough for the really sick people whose lungs didn't work. At least not this year. 1952. The year was only half over, and I had read in the newspaper that health officials were anticipating more than 50,000 new cases. Holy cow! I kept track of these things. I was sort of a list maker. I did a fantastic graph of all this stuff for extra credit in math and got an A++. And I still kept track of the new cases in a little notebook in my desk and wrote down the numbers. These statistics were published every day in the newspaper, and sometimes they showed pictures of polio wards crammed with iron lungs. I kept a folder with stuff that I had cut out from the newspapers about polio. And now I could hardly believe it—there was an iron lung right next door with a girl in it.

I wondered who the girl looked like—Veronica or Betty. I had this notion that any girl who was a teenager had a very good chance at being beautiful and glamorous—even, I guessed, if she were in an iron lung. Something happened to girls when they became teenagers, I believed. And when I became one, in just two more years, when I would be thirteen, I too would stretch out. My legs would lengthen, my waist would drop, my eyebrows would sweep like minnows swimming in a stream, and my stubs of hair would become glossy locks. In fact, I would be able to flip my hair around with barely discernible yet coy movements of my head. And I would wear real lipstick, and not that awful Tangee orangy stuff that smelled good but looked like nothing.

Chapter Two

I was edging closer and closer to that stand of trees between our yards, and as I did so, I could hear a whooshing sound. I moved right into the middle of the small grove, dragging the hose with me and forgetting about the little shrimp of a dogwood behind me. The water began to pool around my feet, but I hardly noticed. What I did notice was that there were not just glints of silver; the trees themselves were suddenly spangled with bouncing light.

I couldn't imagine what was causing this, but I felt sure that the glints and the spangles were all part of the same thing. It felt as if I had entered some strange borderland. This border didn't simply separate our yard from theirs; it was a border between two realities, and I was suspended in the fragile space where they met. I began walking with the hose deeper into the grove. I wanted to get closer.

The whooshing continued to pump through the leafy shade. It was as if the grove were inhaling and exhaling. But intermingled with this sound was the hissing sweep of a sprinkler. My eyes adjusted, and I could see now straight through to their yard. There was a big fancy stone patio, and on it was the machine. A long silver cylinder. From its sides, several metal attachments projected that bent every which way like a tangle of arms and legs. In fact, it all reminded me of a huge insect that had been flipped onto its back, helpless and scratching at the sky. The sprinkler suddenly shut down, and now through the whooshing I could hear a voice—a clear, very fine voice that might have belonged to a grand actress:

"By the margin, willow veil'd
Slide the heavy barges trail'd
By slow horses; and unhail'd
The shallop flitteth silken-sail'd
Skimming down to Camelot:

But who hath seen her wave her hand?
Or at the casement seen her stand?
Or is she known in all the land,
    The Lady of Shalott?"

I heard footsteps behind me. It was my brother, Emmett! He had followed the hose straight into the grove of trees.

I put a finger to my lips to hush him and cocked my head toward the sound of the voice that threaded through the whooshing. The voice was no longer reciting poetry and was harder to hear.

"Georgie," he whispered, "what the devil are you doing?"

"Nothing," I whispered back. But I was mad at this interruption. I had been concentrating on the poem. I hadn't understood half the words, like, what is a *casement*? Still, it seemed beautiful to me. I liked poetry. Miss Gilbert, my fourth-grade teacher, had loved poetry and we had what she called poetry festivals, where we would get up and recite stuff. I won more than once. I wanted to hear more of this poetry, and I deeply resented my brother's intrusion. He was always telling me to get out of his room and stop butting in. So why did he think he could do that to *me* now? "What does it look like I'm doing?" I whispered.

"Watering your feet?" I looked down and muffled a giggle. I was indeed standing in a spreading puddle.

"Oh, that. I got distracted. Look next door. Squint your eyes like this," I said. "Doesn't it look kind of like the Thing?" *The Thing from Another World* was Emmett's and my favorite movie. It was about scientists at an Arctic station who at first think they've just found an unusual plane, but it turns out to be an alien being. Emmett had seen the movie fifteen times. Me, about eight. Not this summer, though. No movies, because there was something worse than the Thing. It was the Polio.

"What is it?" Emmett asked, squinting.

"Iron lung. There's a girl in it. Kind of like living next to a freak or something!"

"Georgie! Don't call her a freak! She's sick." Emmett seemed shocked.

I felt myself blush. I don't really know why I said that, except at that moment in my mind, what was next door was really just this monster machine thumping away. I didn't even connect it with a person.

I couldn't imagine that the voice I'd been listening to could have been coming from inside the machine.

The sprinkler turned back on with a loud sputtering and then the hissing sweep. The grove was flooded with new noise, and I forgot about being quiet. I think to hide my shame, or to distract from what I said, I turned the hose and sprayed Emmett. But Emmett was quick and tall. He played center forward on the Westridge varsity basketball team. That was no small potatoes, as my dad would say, because this was Indiana basketball we were talking about. Indiana produced the best basketball players in the country. Emmett quickly blocked the hose nozzle and turned it back on me. I chased him out of the woods. By the time we were in our yard, I was screaming and trying to tackle him.

Soon enough we were tussling on the ground and water was spraying all over the place and we were laughing our heads off. By the time we finished, we were drenched.

Chapter Three

"So I guess you got cooled off," my mother said, laughing at us, when we came up to the house.

"Not the way I like to," I replied.

"As I said before, you can always go to the library. It's air-conditioned, and when we go to Grandma and Grandpa's, you can swim in their pond. Now, go up and dry off." There were no humans, of course, in Grandma and Grandpa's pond. They lived on a farm. Just cows came to drink, and I guessed that there wasn't any chance of catching polio from a cow. But there were zillions of mosquitoes and worst of all, snakes. I might be a goat person, but I was definitely not a snake person.

"There's a surprise in your bedroom," Mom called out after me.

When I walked into my room, I saw it immediately. A brand-new princess vanity dressing table with the heart-shaped mirror! I couldn't believe it. I knew how much it cost: fifty dollars! It had been advertised in the newspaper from Block's department store. And it came with this pouffy pink tulle skirt with silvery dots on it that hung down to the floor. There were two little built-in compartments on either side of the mirror, lined with purple velvet, that you could put jewelry or barrettes in. I had a million barrettes, but fat lot of good they did me. Terminal cowlicks was my problem. You could hardly figure out which way to put a barrette in. If I parted my hair in the middle—a near impossibility—and put them on either side of the part, the barrettes sort of looked like warring troops lined up on a battlefield. The battlefield being my hair. But still it was something that Mom and Dad had bought the vanity for me.

"What do you think of it?" My mom was leaning against the door to my bedroom.

"It's great, Mom. I can't believe you and Dad bought this for me."

"It's not like we've never bought you a present."

"I know, but still." I was thinking that they must really feel sorry for me.

"We had to take down the Thing and *Revolt of the Zombies* posters because the mirror got in the way."

"Oh, don't worry. I can move them over to the left side," I said.

Mom did her little crooked smile, which meant she was perplexed.

"Somehow it seems funny—horror movie posters with the princess vanity."

"Bride of Frankenstein!" Emmett called in as he went past my door down to his own bedroom. Mom and I both laughed at this. Emmett was so quick. He didn't talk all that much, but he really got off some funny ones.

"And maybe we'll think about the daisy wallpaper."

"The daisy wallpaper!" I was so excited. My friend Carol's teenage sister had daisy wallpaper. In fact a lot of girls had it, or the forget-me-not wallpaper. It was beautiful and made your room look like a spring garden all year round. It was made by an Indianapolis wallpaper company, the Victor Franken Company, and it was sort of expensive. But it was so beautiful.

"Well, you have a real boudoir now," Mom said.

"What's a *boo-dwar*?"

"Sort of a fancy place for a lady to get dressed in, do her makeup."

I was not going to bring it up—or as they say, look a gift horse in the mouth—but I didn't have any makeup. Just that awful Tangee orange lipstick that didn't show. So when you really thought about it, I wasn't much of a candidate for a boudoir. So I might get very bored in my boudoir at my princess vanity dressing table. It didn't matter. I still wanted it. Maybe I would make it sort of like a desk too, even though I already had a desk. And the mirror was really good. It had little teeny-weeny light bulbs outlining the heart-shaped frame. I could keep a sharp lookout for pimples. That was my one beauty blessing so far. No pimples.

I was finally cool after my hosing down by Emmett. So I decided to have the perfect afternoon in my boudoir, even if it meant that I had no real equipment to boo with. It was just when I had this thought about nothing to boo with that I thought of a great joke: a boo-dwar—a dressing room for witches!

I went full throttle into the Georgie Mason heat-reduction program. This meant putting on just my underpants and an old undershirt of my dad's that came down to my knees. I lowered the blinds, turned on the fan, and went downstairs and got the ice bucket that my parents used for cocktails. I filled it with ice and stuck in four Popsicles—two orange and two grape. Those were my two favorite flavors. I hated green, and so did Emmett. But they always came in the package, and Mom said it was wasteful to throw them out. So she ate them, even though I knew she didn't like them. I often thought how I would most likely grow up to be a lousy mother, because I was pretty sure that I would never eat a green Popsicle and give up the grape and orange ones for my kid. Maybe you got less selfish with age.

Anything beyond being a teenager sounded very old to me, and getting old didn't sound so great. I mean you had to be selfless and economical, you got age spots—Mom had a couple—and worst of all, you got sick. Heart stuff, joints freeze up on you, all that. But then I suddenly thought of the girl next door. She hadn't even gotten a chance to use up all her selfishness tickets yet. Polio had changed all that. She hadn't even had a crack at age spots before she got polio.

I sucked on my Popsicle some more. I had brought up the newspaper to see what movies were playing that we were not going to be allowed to see. There was a ritual, however, to the way I read the newspaper. First I went directly to the community news page. I checked the list of all the hospitals and the newly reported polio cases. This was so scary to read. But I sort of had to do it. Saint Vincent's had had four cases in one day. That was a lot. Then I read the box called SYMPTOMS ALERT!

Phase 1: Mild symptoms occur in most cases:
- Mild fever
- Headache
- Sore throat
- Vomiting
- Malaise

Recovery within 24 to 72 hours
Most patients do not progress to Phase 2 symptoms.

Phase 2: More severe symptoms including *meningitis* may occur after several days:
- Meningitis—see *symptoms of meningitis*
- Fever
- Severe headache
- Stiff neck
- Stiff back
- Muscle pain

Very severe symptoms:

- Muscle weakness
- Muscle paralysis
- Difficulty swallowing
- Nasal voice
- Difficulty breathing
- Respiratory paralysis

Phase one was easy to check for. I mean, basically, throwing up is not a subtle thing. You do it, or you don't do it. I did keep a thermometer, an extra one Mom had, in my bathroom and would check my temperature a lot, but no matter how hot I felt, my temperature was always a steady 98.6. The tricky one in phase one was "malaise." I had to look up the word in the dictionary. The definition was truly a slippery slope. Mr. W.—that was what I called *Webster's,* or sometimes Noah—described it as being "a condition of general bodily weakness or discomfort." That was the first definition. I could live with that. It was the second definition that always got me: "an unfocused feeling of mental uneasiness or discomfort." Now I ask you, what in Sam Hill is that? I felt mentally uneasy about twenty times a day, especially with the thought of going to a new school where I had zero friends.

I was very malaised. Sometimes I got so malaised that I really wanted to get in an ambulance and go straight to Saint Vincent's. But what if I only came in with malaise and not the rest of it, the phase two stuff, like difficulty swallowing? A nasal voice (that seemed very weird to me. Bugs Bunny has a nasal voice, for crying out loud). I could imagine the nurse or doctor saying to me, "What hurts?" or, "What are your symptoms?" and I would say, "Malaise, real bad malaise." Where do they go from there? It would be kind of embarrassing if I didn't have polio. So the question was, how long would I suffer from malaise before I'd turn myself in? Or would I die of embarrassment? Truly terminal embarrassment, I thought.

The other symptoms of phase two were easy to check for. Stiff neck, muscle pain, high fever. I did this now as I read the list, which I didn't really have to read, because after reading it for two years, I had memorized it.

But it was hard now to read these symptoms without thinking of the girl next door. I wondered how it had been with her. What had she actually felt? Headache? Mild fever? Most of all I wondered how she caught it—at a swimming pool? A movie theater? To me the scariest thing about polio was that you never knew who had the live germs until it was too late. By the time someone had the disease and you knew that person was sick, the actual germ could no longer be transmitted. But that didn't mean that the sick person recovered, not the way a sick person did from, say, the flu. Those people recovered completely and went on to live their lives. Not the same with polio. Yes, some did recover, but for a lot of people who had polio, their lives were changed forever because the germ attacked the nerves in their spinal cord so they couldn't breathe on their own, or it might paralyze their legs. In the beginning they called it "infantile paralysis." They thought only babies got it. Not now. Anyone could get it. But oddly enough, I could not get it from the girl next door. She was no longer infectious. The germ had died in her and left her body as some kind of wrecked monument.

It was too depressing to think about, but I have to admit I had a kind of morbid curiosity. I wanted to meet her in the worst way. I was just tired of reading about polio, seeing the pictures in the paper, hearing the warnings on the news. Franklin Delano Roosevelt was the most famous polio victim ever. He became president. But he had never been in an iron lung, just a wheelchair. Still, he'd accomplished an awful lot.

I didn't think this girl—this Phyllis—would have a chance at anything. A woman in an iron lung, president? Ha! Then I felt really terrible. I shouldn't have made a joke. It wasn't a real joke. I guess it was a desperate joke. Still kind of mean.

I had had enough of reading about polio symptoms, so I flipped to the movie section.

"Omigod! Emmett, you're not going to believe this!" I yelled out.

"What?" he called from his bedroom.

"*Mrs. Randolph's Brain* is opening at the Vogue Theater."

He was in my room in a flash. "You're kidding!"

I shook my head slowly. "Nooooo."

"Ah, crap."

"You'll sneak out, won't you? You'll go with the guys from the basketball team." I shook my head again. It seemed so unfair. Emmett had a car. He had freedom. Teenagers could do anything, or at least a lot that their parents wouldn't ever find out about. But eleven-year-olds? It was too pathetic to even think about.

Emmett picked up the paper and started reading the review. "Rose Belton gives a subtle performance as Vivian Randolph, a Nobel Prize–winning scientist who works with her unfaithful neurosurgeon husband, played by Donald Crenshaw, pursuing experimental brain research. His wife is more highly regarded as a scientist than he is and it is his jealousy that triggers his infidelity. His mistress is played by newcomer Laura Nolton. When the two are returning from a weekend tryst, they are involved in a terrible car crash. The mistress is critically injured, but he emerges unscathed."

I held up my hand to stop Emmett. "Let me tell you what happens. He tries to save her, but she's going to die. So he gets the idea of saving her brain. He wants to put it in his wife's head, because he's so threatened by his wife's smarts but not his girlfriend's. But he's going to have to somehow get rid of his wife now."

Emmett looked at me over the top of the paper. "Not exactly, but pretty close. How'd you know? Did you already read the review?"

"No, I didn't read the review. It's the old-brain-in-a-jar movie with romance and murder added. But that doesn't mean I don't want to see it." I paused. "So if you sneak out to see it, would you take me?"

"I'm not sneaking out, and I wouldn't take you even if I did because that would get me into twice as much trouble. But hey, it gets better." He scanned the review. "You see, he doesn't exactly murder his wife, but he takes out her brain and puts the girlfriend's brain in her head."

I held up my hand again for him to stop.

"I've got it. But the brain doesn't work quite right, and it gets in cahoots somehow with maybe some leftovers from Vivian, the Nobel Prize–winning scientist."

Emmett's jaw literally dropped. "You're psychic. But it's not exactly leftovers—that makes it sound like a cold meatloaf sandwich or something."

"Well, it's the 'or something.' A spiritual thing, right? So that the wife and the girlfriend gang up against the evil surgeon."

"Wow! Georgie, maybe you should go to Hollywood and start writing movies."

"No, I just read a lot of science fiction like you. Oh, jeez, I really want to see it." I looked up at him with a pleading look.

"Don't do the puppy eyes thing with me, Georgie. We're not doing this. I don't want you to get polio."

"What about yourself? You want to get it?"

"Of course not. Don't be stupid."

Chapter Four

"You won't die, Nora, my love. You won't die. I swear, whatever I have to do, you shall live."

Dr. Randolph was saying this to his mistress, who was in a deep coma. The bleeps of an array of monitors became intermittent. The lines on the display screens began to flatten out.

An attending nurse enters the room and looks at the monitors, then to Dr. Randolph. "She's gone."

"I would like to be alone with her for a while, please," Dr. Randolph says.

The nurse leaves the room.

I leaned forward to tap my mother's shoulder. "It's coming, Mom. You better shut your eyes. He's going in for the brain."

"Oh, Lord!" Mom gasped and quickly assumed her standard position for watching the scary, gory parts of movies: hands clamped over her ears and eyes shut tight. Dad sat with his hands clutching the steering wheel, and Emmett and I were in the backseat of the car not getting polio. We were at a drive-in movie theater watching *Mrs. Randolph's Brain,* or right now it was about to be Nora's brain. In the next scene, we'd probably see Mrs. Randolph's gray matter when dear old Lester, Dr. Randolph, swapped them. This scene closed with the buzz of a surgical saw and a creepy shot of what looked like an oversize jelly jar waiting on a table.

"They would never use glass," Emmett said. "They have to use something that could be thermally controlled better and have a cryo-protectant solution."

"Picky, picky!" I muttered.

The fact that we were with our parents was certainly a sign of how desperate Emmett and I were to see it, because there was nothing, absolutely nothing on earth more square than going to a drive-in movie with your parents. Around us, car windows were steamy from couples making out like crazy. Some of the cars even shook a little! Emmett just kept slouching down farther in the backseat. Not me. I had to sit with my legs folded back underneath me to raise me up a little bit higher. I wanted to see everything: the brain in the jar, the teenagers smooching away.

I did think, however, if anything good came out of this experience, aside from getting to see the movie, it might jump-start Emmett's social life. Maybe he would be inspired to get an actual date to come to the movies, rather than his family. He was slow socially, to put it mildly. Smart as anything in school, but he'd never had a date, which bugged me. How was I ever going to learn anything about being a teenager if my big brother didn't start acting like one? I was tired of having to anticipate my entire future teenage life through Archie comic books.

"Is it over yet?" Mom asked from her see-no-evil, hear-no-evil position.

"There's hardly any blood, Mom," Emmett said.

"I don't want to see any," Mom replied.

"It's only catsup," I said. "Oh, that reminds me. Could we go to Northview for a hamburger afterward?"

"No!" Emmett barked.

"Sweet Jesus!" my father muttered. Dad hardly ever used the Lord's name.

From their reaction you would have thought that I had said, "Let's all go and have brain surgery just for the heck of it." But actually going to Northview, the drive-in restaurant, with your parents was just a fraction less square than going to a drive-in movie with them.

When we got home, Emmett brought one of his telescopes outside and we looked to see if we could find anything interesting.

"What's to look for, Emmett?" I asked. My Fudgsicle was melting faster than I could eat it.

"Neptune. Should be at its closest approach to Earth now, first week in August. You got to look for a little blue dot. Won't see much more than that—*if* that—with this telescope."

"Let me look?" I walked over.

"Eat your Fudgsicle first. I don't want you dripping all over my scope. Go rinse your hands in the hose. I don't want everything all sticky."

"Good grief," I muttered. Emmett was so bossy about his telescopes. Astronomy was Emmett's passion even before basketball. He knew more about the stars than anybody, even his high-school science teacher. Emmett was really smart in math and science and all that stuff. He'd read stuff by Albert Einstein and all sorts of scientists and astrophysicists.

I pressed my eye to the lens cup. People think that the night sky is just black and white. They don't realize that the brighter stars have color. It's very hard to see it, and only rarely can one ever see it with a naked eye. We both tried for the next hour to spot it. I yawned. "Let's turn in," Emmett said.

I couldn't fall asleep. I kept thinking about brain transplants. Then I thought about the steamy windows in the other cars at the drive-in. Then I thought about the car that was shaking. Then I thought about people doing it. Then I thought about my parents doing it! Oh, *ick*! Then I thought about the girl next door. The girl in the iron lung, and how she would probably never do it. Never ever.

I guess I finally did fall asleep, because something woke me up. It was the *thwup-thwup* sound of a basketball being dribbled. I guessed Emmett couldn't sleep either. I went to my bedroom window that looked out on our driveway. There he was, hammering down the asphalt, playing a game with phantom players. A shaft of moonlight poured down on the drive, and Emmett weaved in and out of it like liquid, like quicksilver through the moon's light. He was here; he was there, everywhere. He was so fast, and he could jump like nobody's business. He did that now, spiking into the night, at the top, with his red hair about to graze the moon; he rolled the ball to his shooting arm and then laid that ball into the hoop as softly as if it were a baby.

Chapter Five

The next day, it was 110 degrees. Mom agreed to drive me to the library even though it was only a half-mile away. From the outside, I have to admit, this library as heat retreat did not look promising. Our new neighborhood, on the northwest side of the city—although considered ritzy with its big houses, long driveways, and huge yards—had basically been built on what had been farmland. There were still cornfields. Indeed, one came right up to the edge of the library's driveway. It was almost noon, so there were no shadows. But in truth there wasn't much to cast a shadow. I felt something crumple in me when Mom said, "Look, Georgie, isn't it beautiful? Brand-new. So modern."

I thought it was ugly. Low and flat, the predictable one-story "ranch-house" style like a lot of the houses on this side of town. Who wanted to go to a library that looked like a ranch?

I imagined some darned librarian wearing a cowboy hat, chaps, spurs, the works. I liked my librarians to look like librarians. They should look like they read, not like they roped cows. There was even a short split-rail fence with a fake rustic sign that said NORTH SIDE BRANCH LIBRARY. But the wood ended there. The ranch house, or El Rancho, as I suddenly named it, was made of Indiana limestone, a pale grayish stone that a lot of the new houses were built of. And wow, did it look hot. I know that white is supposed to reflect and make things cooler inside. Like white cars are cooler than black ones in the summertime. But this ugly building looked like it was broiling. "OK, sweetie, have fun. I'll pick you up in an hour."

I stepped out of the car and felt like a hot iron was pressing down on me.

I might be walking into an oven! I'll be cooked. Barbecued! Hansel and Gretel, Hoosier style. I looked back at Mom. She was already pulling away. I missed our old library: a brick two-story building on a shady street with two big maple trees by the front steps. There wasn't a breath of wind here. Just the glare from the sun, merciless on this rambling pile of limestone. Calcium carbonate—that's what Indiana limestone is. I had done a report on it for social studies. I could name the three most important quarries in southern Indiana. Tell you all about the marine fossils that had decomposed from the inland sea. Yes, once upon a time in the post-Cambrian but pre-cornfield era, this had all been a sea. I walked in a heat daze toward the door. "It better be cool in there," I muttered.

I walked through the door and felt a blast of ice-cold air. "Aaaaahh!"

"Nice, isn't it?" A voice came out of the shadows. Then a woman padded silently toward me. She wasn't wearing chaps, no spurs in sight. Gads, she was a sight for sore eyes. She had a shawl, an actual shawl, around her shoulders, and she was carrying an armload of books. Not only that: she wasn't wearing shoes—just golf socks with those mini puff-balls on the heels that kept them from sliding down into golf shoes (had she been wearing them). That's why her steps were so quiet. "I've made some lemonade. Help yourself. It's over there on the round table in the corner."

"Thanks," I whispered.

"And if it gets too cold, I have extra sweaters."

It had not simply been the air-conditioning that made me want to go to the library but a new idea I had had for a small world—the small universe one. I had decided that my idea of making a diorama of the sky was not such a bad one at all. Maybe call it a sky-o-rama instead of a diorama. I was amazed that I had never thought of this before. I had often put the moon and stars into my small worlds, but just as background details. I would use Day-Glo paint or glitter on glue for those. But now I had decided to actually use real electricity. Emmett said I could power it with dry-cell batteries and use those teeny-weeny bulbs that are in flashlights. It could really be beautiful. So I had spent a lot of time thinking about the electrical details, but then I realized that I didn't actually have a story. Somehow my mythology book had gotten lost in the move. And I needed to figure out a good story. All the constellations had mythological stories connected to them. It was just as if ancient people looked up into the night and saw some kind of picture and then decided they had to make up a story to go with it. It was like their religion, and they figured the gods must have put all that glitter up there. None of it Christian, of course, but they had as many gods and as many versions of gods getting mixed up with people and animal stories as there are kinds of religion today. I only knew the basic outlines of most of the myths.

I asked the librarian, who was still padding around in golf socks, where the Greek mythology section was. She pointed toward the opposite corner and said turn left at the poster of—duh!—Zeus. So I did. I had to walk back through the rows of bookshelves, and when I got to the very last row, where the 290s were, I caught sight of something squashed in the corner. If the something had not been reading a book, I would have thought it was a bag of laundry.

How should I explain this? The laundry bag looked up when she heard me and blinked at me through round glasses with thin wire rims. Her hair sprung out in a dark electrified frizzle from her head, and she had the palest skin I ever saw. There was something about her shape, too, that suddenly reminded me of a mushroom. Her skin was maybe the color of one of those very white mushrooms—cultivated mushrooms, and not one of the wild ones that grow in the woods. *Yes, a mushroom exactly,* I thought.

"Hi," she said softly, in a voice I instantly thought of as very mushroom, if indeed they ever spoke.

"Hi," I said, and turned back to looking at the books on the shelf. I looked for maybe a minute, and then I heard the soft voice again.

"If you need one of the ones I'm using, feel free." I looked over and saw that she had a huge stack of books on the floor beside her. She was sitting on one of those beanbag things, more or less growing out of it rather than sitting. "What are you looking for?"

"Myths about the sky."

"Oh, yeah, here's one." She held out a book. The title was *Myths and Constellations*. "It's not altogether accurate."

"It isn't?"

"No, it claims that the earliest references to the mythological significance of constellations are in the *Iliad,* seventh century BC. But actually there are cuneiform references from six thousand years ago."

"Oh!" I said. What else could I say? I wasn't sure what cuneiform was, but I certainly had the feeling that I was speaking to a form of life that was higher than fungal. Then she smiled. It was a fragile smile, and it made her face pretty. "There's another beanbag right there, if you want to sit down."

"Thanks," I said, and dragged the beanbag over so I would be closer to the pile of books. Then I sank down into the fake leather puffiness and opened the book she gave me. I began reading the story of Callisto and Arcas. Not exactly a jolly tale. Callisto has been romanced by Zeus, who had to disguise himself because his wife, Hera, was jealous. She gives birth to a son, Arcas. Hera finds out and is so ticked off that she turns Callisto into a bear. One day her son sees her and doesn't recognize her as his mother. He raises his bow to shoot her. But Zeus, looking down from Olympus, sees what is about to happen and saves the day and magically turns Arcas into a little bear. Then he grabs both mother and son by their tails and hurls them out into the sky.

The Mushroom looked over at what I was reading. "Oh, Callisto. Sad. Matricide always is . . . intentional or not."

"You mean killing his mother?"

"Yeah, but luckily he didn't." The Mushroom sighed.

I looked at her more closely. "What's your name?"

"Evelyn Winkler. What's yours?"

"Georgia Mason, but everyone calls me Georgie."

"Me too?" There was something so pathetic about her question. It was almost as if she had never had a close friend.

"Of course. I said everyone, Evelyn." I would never think of her as the Mushroom again. And actually a slight blush rose in her pale white cheeks. She smiled and looked pretty again.

"Why are you interested in myths about the sky?" she asked.

I began to explain about my small worlds and why I was looking for a good star story. We talked and talked. Evelyn was very nice and very smart. Both her mom and her dad were doctors. I had never heard of a lady doctor before. "What kind of doctor?" I asked.

"My mom's a gynecologist."

I wasn't really sure what a gynecologist was, but I asked, "Does she ever have polio patients?"

She looked at me kind of funny. So I said really quickly, "Just wondering, because the girl who lives next door to us is in an iron lung."

"Gee whiz, is she pregnant or something?" Evelyn asked.

This really threw me for a loop. "No, why?"

"Well, when you asked if my mom did anything with polio and told me about this girl, I thought maybe she was going to have a baby. That's the other part of being a gynecologist. She's an obstetrician, too. She delivers babies. But have you met this girl in the iron lung?"

"Oh, no. We just moved into the neighborhood."

"I never heard of a person at home in an iron lung. Boy, kind of weird, isn't it?"

"Sure is."

"I wonder if you'll ever get to meet her," Evelyn said.

"I don't know."

"Well, if you do, you don't have to worry about catching anything. It's no longer infectious after the person has come down with it."

"I know. Not transmissible. I read a lot about polio."

"Did you know that they used to think it was a poor people's disease? But that was all wrong."

"Really? I never read that."

"Yep. The virus spreads through people not washing their hands after pooping and other bodily secretions." I wasn't sure what the word *secretions* meant, but I could take a pretty good guess—pee, possibly. I thought of how when I was really little I had often peed in swimming pools, rather than taking the time to get out and walk all the way to a bathroom. "But it's actually the poor people with bad sewers that built up an immunity to those viruses."

"So it's rich people with better sewers who get it now."

"Yep," Evelyn said, and blinked.

Of course, now we had moved into this new fancy neighborhood that probably had much better sewers than our old neighborhood. Not that I ever noticed anything wrong with the plumbing. It turned out that Evelyn and her family had just moved, too. They had lived closer to the downtown of Indianapolis before and she had gone to a special school for really smart kids, an exam school where you had to take a test to get in. But now her parents felt it was too long a drive to that school. So she would be going to the same new school as I would. This was some consolation. At least I would know someone.

Before I knew it, the hour was up and Mom was coming in the front door of the library. But Evelyn and I made plans to meet there the next day. We exchanged phone numbers. I checked out a whole mess of books. Just before I was going out the door, Evelyn came and said, "You never told me what your favorite constellation is, Georgie." She smiled when she said my name. It was as if she just enjoyed the sound of it.

"Orion! It's so beautiful. The jeweled sword, the club, the lion skin that he drags across the winter sky. But it's a really sad story."

"But if you love it, you should do it."

"Maybe so," I said softly.

I did love the Orion story, and there were as many versions of that as any of the rest. The problem with myths is that there are a lot of contradictory things, irrational parts, pieces left out and unexplained. I like reasons for stuff. There were a lot of gaps in the Orion story and a lot of things you had to take on faith. I was even thinking of a two-level diorama because Orion's story begins in the sea. He was the son of Poseidon. Underwater filtered light—I could use an aquarium for part of it. We had two in the basement. I realized I would literally have to build this story from the seafloor up to the sky, or more accurately, from the basement up.

I went there as soon as I got home and found the aquarium. I had been thinking about the "seascaping." I was pretty good with clay. I knew I could model a great seafloor. But then I had a really brilliant idea. In that stand of trees between our house and the polio girl's, the only shady place in our new neighborhood, I had seen some moss. It would be really neat if I could get some and stick it in the clay. I had once made a moss garden and kept it alive just by spritzing it twice a week. I liked the idea of having something living in this diorama. Live plants and real electricity. This might become my masterpiece—truly a small universe!

Chapter Six

The temperature had dropped ten whole degrees since I had come home. But in the shade of the grove, it was even cooler. Maybe the arctic nineties. Even from the edge of the grove I could see the shimmer of the iron lung. By the time I was right in the grove, I could hear it pumping away. Then I heard Mom calling me and Emmett's voice much closer.

"Mom wants to know if you want to go with her to the Hoosier Twirler thing."

Just at that moment there was another voice. "Is somebody there?" Emmett and I looked at each other as a woman walked through the trees. She was wearing

Bermuda shorts and had gardening gloves on. She held a pair of shears in her hand. "Oh, my goodness. You must be the Mason children. I've been meaning to come over and introduce myself. I'm Roslyn Keller. I would love it if you would come over and meet our Phyllis. We just wheeled her out, now that it's cooler. She loves to be outside, even on the hottest days." She said this as if it were the most ordinary thing that people got wheeled around in iron lungs.

"Sure," I said. I quickly forgot my mission of collecting moss.

"What's your name, dear?"

"Georgie."

"And yours?" she said, turning to Emmett.

"Emmett."

"Oh, you look like you're about to be a senior. Just Phyllis's age. This will mean so much to her."

I ran home to tell Mom to go without me and then followed Mrs. Keller through the trees and into the long shadows of their yard, which was beautiful, with lush green grass and really big trees. We passed a flower bed thick with violets and inky green lilies of the valley. None of the lilies had their little white bells. "These lilies in May were always Phyllis's favorite." It made me shiver when Mrs. Keller said that. Was she

* 48 *

talking about the flowers being dead and gone by, or Phyllis? It was as if we were being brought to meet a dead person. I was scared. I kind of wanted to hold Emmett's hand. But I thought that would look really dumb. Suddenly a terrible thought struck me: What if Phyllis was wearing a diaper? In the newsreels and in the newspapers, they were always showing people in iron lungs, grown-up people, wearing baby diapers with their skinny ugly legs sticking out. I could not meet this girl if she was going to be in a diaper. And what about Emmett? Emmett was seventeen years old, and this girl was supposed to be a teenager. This would be so embarrassing. *Oh, good Lord!* I thought. I tried to imagine Veronica or Betty in diapers and Jughead and Archie looking at them. This was just too awful. I could hardly move my feet forward.

There was no turning back now. The machine, huge and glinting, was just ahead. Like some monster insect in a horror movie, its arms were reaching out toward us. We were suddenly caught in a radiant cross fire of reflected beams bouncing off the iron lung. I had to squint. It was as if she had been swallowed by this mechanical multi-eyed bug, every bit of her except for her head and neck. She was completely enclosed in the belly of this shining, glittering creature. The shell of the beast must have measured at least ten feet long and maybe a yard wide. So after I got by the metallic body and the shock of not seeing a human one except for this weirdly disembodied head, I saw Emmett's and my faces crowding into mirrors. There were mirrors on almost every arm of the machine, and they all seemed to be reflecting us. Some mysterious force was rotating them, turning and tracking our movements. It was like an ambush of mirrors, and we were caught in a web of reflections.

"Hi. I'm Phyllis," a voice said. But I wasn't sure where it was coming from. The whooshing mechanical monster seemed to be sucking in almost every sound, swallowing up every whisper of the true wind and every birdsong from the trees. "Oh, hi." Emmett laughed nervously. I followed where he was looking. A head with a mass of white-blond curls protruded from the opening of the glistening metal shell and rested on a pillow. A thick rubber collar encircled her neck.

Beneath the gusty whooshing of the machine there was another sound, sharper and hissing, still a part of the monster's breath. I felt my chest tighten as if I might have to struggle for my next breath.

"What's your name?" Phyllis asked. The mirrors all rotated to reflect just me.

"G-G-Georgie . . . Georgie."

"And I'm Emmett," Emmett said.

"I know the sound of the Creature breathing sort of takes your own breath away. Don't worry, Georgie. You can breathe fine. Just relax. Sit down. Mother, get some lemonade for them."

"Certainly, dear."

It was kind of strange when she asked her mother to do this. It wasn't like a kid speaking to a parent, exactly. It was as if she were giving an order military style, the way one would if one were the captain of a ship or the pilot of a plane, or spaceship for that matter. This might as well have been a spaceship. She was certainly in a space that none of us had been. I noticed that although she was talking to me now, it was only Emmett's face in her mirrors.

"Some people, when they get around this thing, it makes them short of breath. Just remember, Georgie, you've got all the air in the world, the whole sky up there." Emmett's face slipped out of the mirrors. They mysteriously swiveled and tipped up, capturing clouds and blue sky. "I have eighty-seven cubic centimeters of air, but you have the world."

I wasn't sure what she was talking about. And it wasn't exactly the air that was getting stuck in me.

It was the words. I looked hard at Phyllis. She could talk. But there was an unvarying rhythm to Phyllis's speech. It was the rhythm of the machine. She and the machine were one. The Creature set the pace, which was always the same. Neverthless I had this sudden thought that Phyllis in a sense was a kind of stutterer, but instead of words clotting for her, it was air. Phyllis was a stutterer of air.

For a brief time in the first grade I stuttered. I got over it very quickly, but I can still remember that there was this terrible sense of isolation because the words just dangled out there in front of me in a kind of half-light. I would reach for them, and a wind would blow them away or a shadow would pass over, and they would vanish into some dark empty place. I was always left with the horrible feeling that I would never be able to find the right word. It was a kind of death, a bunch of little deaths I suffered every day. And the loneliness was the worst part because I felt so disconnected. But, thank goodness, it ended.

I stepped closer to the machine. There were all sorts of dials and gauges.

"You can touch it," she said.

I put out my hand. It felt hot from the sun reflecting on its shiny surface.

"Is it hot inside?"

"No. There's a cooling system. My own private air-conditioning." She laughed, but it sounded more like a hiccup. I looked slowly now over the machine. This was her world. She was the largest thing in that world. Nothing would change within that world. This thought unnerved me plenty. I stepped away. I didn't want to touch it. I had unthinkingly called it a beast before, but now I realized that it had with my touch become just that to me: a hideous beast. I imagined the mirrors turning into arms like those of a huge, gleaming, panting spider. I could see them reaching out to drag me into that unchanging place.

Phyllis could turn her head a little bit to see us, but she didn't need to because the mirrors rotated again and tipped down while the sky slid away, and now once again I could see only Emmett's face filling one of the larger mirrors.

"Are those Spiegelman mirrors?" Emmett asked.

"Yes, how'd you know? No one ever asks that."

"I'm interested in mirrors."

This was so typical of Emmett! I know I was getting caught up in the machine because it was the strangest thing I had ever seen in my life. But Emmett should have seen beyond it and seen what had to be one of the most beautiful girls ever! With her shiny blond hair and the bluest eyes and dimples! She was the perfect high-school girl. She was prettier than Betty or Veronica. She could have been a cheerleader. No. She could have been a movie star! She was movie-star gorgeous. But, of course, she wasn't going to be any of those things.

Emmett just kept studying the mirrors and not really looking into them, where my face and Phyllis's and some of his face were reflected. He kept trying to sort of dodge out of the mirror. But she caught him! I don't know how. She did something with those mirrors, tilted them some way, somehow, and then bingo! There was his face filling up the whole mirror. I was out of the picture. But Phyllis had Emmett just where she wanted him.

"An expert in mirrors. Don't tell me you're a narcissist! I don't need any more narcissistic males."

Narcissistic? Never heard of the word. Did it matter? Not at all. I couldn't believe how she was zeroing in on Emmett. I guess maybe this was flirting, but it actually seemed halfway between flirting and a guided missile strike. I don't think Emmett knew that *nar* word either, but he laughed as if he understood exactly what she was talking about. And that moment, Emmett's face creased into deep lines that ran from just below his cheekbones to his jaw, and his dark red hair suddenly flashed in the sun, and his deep blue eyes radiated smile crinkles fanning from the corners.

But I saw all this in the mirrors, just the way Phyllis saw it. And for an instant he wasn't my brother. He had been transformed into someone else. Someone that I didn't quite recognize, but Phyllis did.

"Naw," Emmett was saying. "I just fiddle around with telescopes."

"He's building a big telescope, and he's already built three others. But this one's going to be really big," I piped up. I wanted to get in on this conversation even if I didn't know what the word *narciss*-whatever meant. I sensed that something was happening, and I wanted to be in on it so badly.

But no such luck, because just at that moment the mirrors swiveled and I was cut out of the picture. It was the two of them again.

"I bet you're good at math, Emmett," Phyllis said, and narrowed her eyes as if she were thinking about something. There was a kind of sly sparkle behind the incredible blueness.

Emmett blushed. "Pretty good," he said.

"Ah, come on," Phyllis said. "I bet you're better than pretty good."

"He's great!" I blurted out. "He got 800 on his SATs, the math part."

"Oh, good Lord." More hiccuppy giggles from Phyllis, and I was still not in the mirror. "I won't even tell you what I got. Let's just say my talents lie elsewhere." A cunning look slid across her face.

Poor Emmett got all flustered. "I'm sure they weren't that bad."

Wrong thing to say, Emmett. Wrong!

"Oh, yes, they were." She giggled again. If Phyllis had been a normal girl with a normal body, I could have just pictured her shoulders kind of doing a little shimmy. As it was, the hiccuppy giggle sent a tremor through her blond curls.

Then she whispered something to Emmett. But I couldn't hear. And he couldn't either. "Come over here. I'll tell you," she said, meaning Emmett and not me. Emmett walked over to where her head poked out of the machine. He had to maneuver around some of the things sticking out from it. "Now bend down," she said. "Put your ear close to my mouth."

Oh, my word! I thought. What was I about to see? Emmett was blushing right to the roots of his red hair. There was now absolutely no difference between his hair color and his skin color. I was too afraid to look, so I studied a small ant colony that I had discovered emerging from between the stones of the patio. I wondered what would happen if an ant got into the iron lung. Would it live? If a male and female ant got in there, could they reproduce? Could the female lay eggs in an iron lung, or would the concentration of the eighty-seven cubic centimeters of air crush everything somehow? Then Emmett backed away. He looked incredibly pleased with himself, and I don't think it was just because of his SAT scores.

Then suddenly she swiveled the mirrors and I was caught.

"Tell me about Nubian goats, Georgie."

"What?"

"Your T-shirt."

"Oh," I said.

But then Emmett interrupted. "Hey, how come you can read that? How come it's not backward?"

"My special reading mirror! My dad invented it. But he's made improvements. A whole new model that will make it even easier for me."

"Wow!" Emmett whispered.

"Come on, tell me about the goats," Phyllis urged.

I stood up and came a little closer to her head, sticking out from the machine. It was weird to talk to someone this way. It felt as if her head were just sort of floating there, attached to nothing.

"Uh, I just like them, that's all."

"Why do you like them? Tell me all about goats. I know nothing."

"Well," I began, "you've got your dairy goats, your pygmies, your Nigerian dwarf goats, and dozens of others." I paused and looked at her in the mirror. She still seemed interested. So I continued. "It's my true belief that there is a goat for every kind of person. And goats are very affectionate. They love it when folks scratch them. They are the most companionable of farm animals—that's what my grandma says."

Phyllis made another little hiccuppy sound. It sounded like a sputtering waterfall, except instead of water, it was air.

"Now, turn around," she said. "I caught a glimpse in the mirror of something on the back of your shorts."

"Oh," I said. "My mom sewed a cut-out poodle on them."

"So you like poodles and goats, I see."

"I don't really like poodles that much. I think

they're kind of silly. They just make a nice decoration, you know."

"They are supposedly among the smartest of dogs," Phyllis said. I kind of shrugged.

"Maybe, but goats aren't nearly as dumb as people think."

Just then Mrs. Keller came out with a tray of lemonade and a plate of cookies.

"Now, let's see," she said, setting down the tray. One of the glasses was special and had a straw in it about a foot long. She set this glass into a metal claw that stuck out from the iron lung, then put the straw into Phyllis's mouth. I was fascinated as Mrs. Keller put the glass in the claw and then somehow the claw automatically brought the glass, straw and all, closer to Phyllis. Mrs. Keller had been talking while she was doing this stuff with the glass and the straw. I was thinking about how beautiful Phyllis was, and I was thinking that when her face and Emmett's had been trapped in the mirror together . . . well, they looked really nice. If that mirror had been heart-shaped, it could have been like a Valentine card.

"Georgie! Georgie!" Emmett gave me a nudge.

"Yeah!" I jerked back to attention.

"Mrs. Keller was asking you where you are going to school."

"Oh," I said, and straightened up. "I used to go to Peter Stoner Elementary School, but now I'll go to Crooked Creek since we've moved into this neighborhood." I wanted to tell them how this was a stinking rotten deal that I had to change schools and Emmett didn't.

"And you're going to Westridge, I assume," Mrs. Keller was saying to Emmett.

"Yes ma'am, I've been there all along." Then he turned to Phyllis and leaned forward a bit. Both their faces crowded into the mirror. "Where did you go, Phyllis? North Tech?"

"Oh, no," Mrs. Keller said quickly. "Phyllis went to Tudor Hall School for Girls." *They must be rich,* I thought. I had never met anybody who had gone to a private school.

Now I could never figure out how Phyllis could do the next thing she did, because as far as I could see, my face wasn't in the mirror, but somehow she must have seen my expression. "You're surprised, Georgie?"

I didn't know what to say. So I just shrugged and said, "Only girls?"

"Only girls," she repeated, and she gave her head a very small shake and the white-gold curls shivered.

"Do they have proms?" I was fascinated by proms. It killed me that Emmett, who was about to be a senior, had never invited a girl to a prom. Emmett didn't care about anything except basketball and astronomy. His life was nothing like Archie's and Veronica's and Betty's. Imagine a comic book called *Emmett*. People would fall asleep. Emmett was not my idea of a true teenager. He might as well have been forty.

"They call them proms, but they're pretty pathetic, if you know what I mean." Instantly I knew she was talking to me. And then my face was in the mirror with hers. Just the two of us! There was a quick flash of blue in the mirror that was like a little secret message to me. She had actually winked at me when she said, "if you know what I mean." It was that feeling I would get when I would see the first shooting star on a summer night. I wanted it to happen again. There was something so personal about her wink and what she said. It was just like I was her equal and she was sharing a secret. A high-school girl and a sixth-grader sharing a secret! I was actually tempted to wink back at her and say, "Oh, yeah! I know what you mean."

Six little words, but they meant so much. It was as if these six little words had been put in a bundle and tied up with a pretty ribbon. A gift for me—just for me.

Well, I knew what she meant—sort of, even though I had never been to a prom. I felt this deep thrill inside me. I was really being included in a way I had never thought of. This floaty feeling would happen to me when I got really excited about something. I know exactly the first time it happened. I was actually floating. I was in a swimming pool learning how to swim. It happened when I was finally able to pick my feet up from the bottom of the swimming pool and not sink. It was this wonderful, indescribable feeling. Maybe a baby bird felt this way when it first flew. I don't know, but I definitely felt floaty at this moment with Phyllis, as if I had passed into another element—water, air, and I was part of it, no longer outside it.

When we got home from Phyllis's, I went in and fixed myself a second lunch—two Popsicles and a slice of ham. I realized I hadn't read the paper that day. It was still on the counter. I never missed a day reading the reported new cases. They listed them county by county. Marion County was our county now. So far this year, there had been fifty-one cases. I looked at the numbers, and the hospitals where the nameless victims had been admitted. So far only two friends of my parents had contracted the disease. But they had recovered. And neither of them was in an iron lung. But now I knew someone who was not nameless, not just a Marion County statistic. I felt in a weird way special.

I had to call Evelyn.

She answered the phone on the second ring. "The Doctors Winkler residence."

"It's Georgie, Evelyn. Guess what?"

"What?"

"I met her."

"Who?"

"The girl next door. The iron lung girl! She's beautiful. So beautiful. And you talk to her sort of through mirrors."

"What?" Evelyn was dumbfounded—this was not a natural state for Evelyn. So I explained all about the mirrors, and all the gizmos that stuck out, and the automatic claw that her mom put the drink in. She was impressed. She said she hoped that I would make friends with her so she could come over and visit her, too. I wasn't altogether sure I wanted her to meet Phyllis. I mean, now that I had met Phyllis—well, she wasn't a freak anymore. And I remembered how she had said those six little words—just to me. "If you know what I mean." It had been so personal—like a gift, and it was one I didn't exactly want to share. I guess it could be called selfish. Maybe it was, but on the other hand, I didn't want Phyllis to be a sideshow for my friends either.

Evelyn said just before we hung up that she couldn't meet me at the library the next day because she had just found out that she had to go someplace with her mom and younger sister.

When I went to bed, I felt a little bad about my selfishness—wanting to keep Phyllis just for me. It seemed wrong. When Phyllis winked, she had reached out to me in one of the very few ways she could, and I was hoarding that wink. The way a miser would hoard gold. Was I going to dole out Phyllis to my friend Evelyn in little small snippets told over the phone?

I closed my eyes tight and saw the gleaming carapace of the Creature. I could hear its mechanical inhalations and exhalations. Phyllis had called it a monster, but it was a miser as well. And the realization made me shudder. It doled out the breaths to her in a monotonous rhythm. It had locked her into a single position for the rest of her life. Change it, and she'd die. Her eyes always had to look up. But the worst thing of all was that for Phyllis and any person inside of an iron lung, nothing would ever change. On the most basic level this was true. You're not getting taller in there. If anything, you might be shrinking because you never use a muscle for anything. Phyllis's life was totally changeless, and that to me was the most frightening thing imaginable: to know you are never going to change, ever!

But then I thought of how Phyllis had been with Emmett, and I began wondering what would happen if maybe Emmett and Phyllis started liking each other, just a little bit. Could this make for a change in a life doomed to never change? This could be good for Emmett as well because he'd never been on a date or anything. I mean it would be like training wheels. I giggled to myself. Then I felt a little bad comparing Phyllis to training wheels. But then again I thought it could be nice for Phyllis too in a way. I mean, her life must be pretty boring.

As I lay in bed that night, Phyllis's voice came back to me, the six words in their pretty package of a smile and a wink. I tried to recapture that floaty feeling. But I couldn't. I guess there are certain feelings, sensations that you only get to experience once in life and only at the time when they happen. And now I couldn't even exactly picture Phyllis. I tried to imagine us both in the mirror, but the details of her face just kept slipping away or there would be something slightly off about the way I remembered her. It was like pieces of a puzzle that didn't quite fit.

Chapter Seven

When I got up the next morning, I began work on my small world. I first washed out the aquarium and then measured out the second level where the sky part would go. The aquarium was a rectangular glass box, but I wanted the sky to be a vault that would fit on top. I had fiddled around with trying to draw what I wanted. It didn't look that great. I had this idea that maybe I could use mirrors in some way and create a kind of optical illusion so that the figure of Orion could actually be reflected onto the sky. I couldn't help but wonder if Phyllis's beast had in some way been the inspiration for this. There was a lot to work out. I got bored with making the clay seascape. I had picked up some moss in the grove on our way back from Phyllis's. I have to say, it looked pretty good stuck in the swirls of green-and-blue clay that made up the sea floor; however, I decided to save most of it to use for the forest floor when Orion became the mighty hunter. I wanted this small world to look really fabulous. I had never tried lighting before, special effects! This should look as good as a movie set. I couldn't quite figure out what to do next.

Emmett could help me, but Emmett, I suddenly remembered, wasn't here. He was at dumb preseason basketball practice. Lucky Emmett. Emmett not only had friends, he had a whole team! He didn't have to change schools. Life was easy for him. He could do what he loved—basketball. Basketball courts, unlike swimming pools, were not considered breeding grounds for polio infection. So I went downstairs to get a Popsicle and feel sorry for myself. "A Popsicle now, Georgie? You'll spoil your lunch," Mom said.

"This is my lunch," I answered grumpily.

"That's not very healthy," my mom said as she read the paper. Something just ticked me off about the way she said this. She didn't even look up from the newspaper. "What, am I going to get *po-li-o*? Huh?"

There was a high sass level in my voice, and you better believe it, Mom put down the newspaper, took off her glasses, and blinked at me and then opened her eyes very wide. Maybe this was threat behavior. Wolves open their eyes when they get angry and try to show rank. Mom was definitely pulling rank here.

"What in the world is wrong with you?"

"Everything! I hate this house. I hate this neighborhood. I have no friends."

"What about that lovely girl you met at the library? I thought you were going back to meet her there."

"She can't meet me. She has to go with her friends someplace." This of course was a lie; it was her mother and sister she had to do something with. "She canceled," I said with emphasis. *Canceled* described my feelings. It sounded like some sort of execution.

"You don't want to go to the library, even if your new friend can't be there today?"

"Mom, I've only known her for an hour. I can't exactly call her my friend yet."

"OK, OK," my mom said wearily. "Have you tried Susie?"

"I'm embarrassed. I didn't go to her birthday party. I can't just go call her up now."

"What about Carol?"

"She's at Bible school," I replied sullenly.

"You mean it hasn't been closed? I thought all summer camps had been closed."

"Maybe if you just sit around reading about God and Jesus all day, you can't get polio."

Mom looked at me narrowly this time. Normally she would have really scolded me hard about talking this way. Instead she just said, "It's not that easy, young lady! If it were, more people would be in Bible school."

"Mom!" I stood up, gripping my Popsicle. Those two words, *young* and *lady,* just set me off. "I have to tell you something." I spoke in a very serious voice.

"What's that?" she asked.

"I absolutely hate it when grown-ups call girls my age 'young lady.' You know why I hate it?" I didn't give her time to answer. "I hate it because they never mean it. They use it as a way to put you down. To remind you for yet the millionth time that you, or in my particular case, me, that I am anything but a young lady. That I am a minor and I have no rights whatsoever and exist for big ladies to boss around." By this time I was standing in a pool of grape Popsicle. I tossed the stick in the sink and stomped out of the kitchen. Mom didn't say a word. But the look on her face was impressive, as in she was impressed with my little speech.

"What about Laurie and Wendy?" she called after me. I was already on the stairs going up and yelled back.

"Mom, stop it. You're making me feel worse than I already do. Don't you get it? They're all on the other side of town. They don't even call me anymore." I look forlornly at the telephone. In my previous life—for that was indeed the way I thought of it—I had spent hours on the telephone with friends. It was a major part of my social life. My parents even had put a timer by the phone limiting me to fifteen minutes. But now it was like out of sight, out of mind, and definitely off the telephone line. I had called my old friends a few times but it was as if there was so little to talk about, what was the point? I wasn't in the thick of it anymore. What I'd ask about was already ancient history. Boring.

She came to the bottom of the staircase and looked up at me. "You know, Georgie, you act as if we've moved to Siberia. We're less than two miles from our old house. They're still your friends."

"Mom, it might as well be Siberia. I'm going to a different school. They're all getting ready for the fall festival. I don't even know if my new school has a fall festival. I was on the planning committee. I was *elected* to the planning committee for it. You have to be popular for that. And now I'm just gone. I have nothing to plan. I have to start all over again. It's just all different, and you don't understand. You'll never understand."

I knew I was going to cry any second. I felt not just my eyes but my whole face swelling up with tears. I raced the rest of the way upstairs to my bedroom, slammed the door, threw myself on the bed, and started sobbing. I heard my mother's footsteps coming up the stairs and then these timid little knocks on the door.

"Go away." I sobbed.

"Georgie, really!"

"Really go away!" I yelled back.

Nothing was fair. Life was so unfair.

Almost as soon as I thought of the word *fair,* I thought of Phyllis.

Phyllis was out on the patio. I could tell when I walked into the grove of trees. Those silver shimmers wove through the green leaves like a bright thread. I wanted to figure out how close I could get before she caught me in the mirrors. I walked slowly across the lawn. The day before, when Emmett and I had come, it was late afternoon, the time when shadows stretch. I had a sense that somehow the interplay between the shadows and the mirror reflections tipped Phyllis off. But now it was late morning, the short-shadow time. I watched my own stubby dark shadow spring to life as I emerged from the grove. I kept my eye on it as it slid across the lawn at an angle slightly to the left of me. That shadow song that Dad always sang began winding through my head. Something about him and his shadow strolling along.

"Hi, Georgie," Phyllis called out. "I was hoping you might come by." I had actually gotten a bit farther this time before she trapped me in the web of reflections. It must have had something to do with shadows, but she still caught me before I could logically be within the range of the mirrors or her vision. There was something magical about it.

"This is Sally," Phyllis said. "She's one of my nurses." And now my face floated into the mirror with the smiling one of a pretty Negro lady. She wasn't dressed like a nurse, though. She had on flowered pedal pushers and a bright pink blouse. "Sally, this is Georgie."

"Hello, Georgie," she said. She had withdrawn her hand from a kind of hole in the middle section of the iron lung. She was holding a washcloth.

"Hi."

"Sally, you don't have to stay out here now. I've got company. Stuff I want to discuss with Georgie."

I felt that deep thrill again. "All right, I'll leave you two to yourselves. Send Georgie in if you need anything."

As soon as Sally left, Phyllis did something with the mirrors so that we were both crowded into every single one. It was sort of neat. I mean, it was just the two of us, but all over the place. And if you didn't know that from the neck down the rest of Phyllis was in an iron lung, you would have thought this was the healthiest person in the world. She could have been a Breck shampoo girl. She had that same luminous skin and glistening hair. The Breck girls were illustrations in pastels. And even though Phyllis was every bit as beautiful as a Breck girl, there was really nothing pastel about her. I think it was her eyes that made the difference. The Breck girls' eyes were always downcast in a very modest, shy way. Not Phyllis. Her eyes were bold. They crackled with a sort of energy, well, maybe a fury—a startling blue fury.

Phyllis had a kind of wildness. And yet she was caged as no animal had ever been caged. It made me almost weak to think about this. It was as if on one hand I knew what I was seeing. But knowing and understanding weren't really feeling. And feeling would come in waves, waves that would just engulf me, pull me down into some terrible undertow. It would be Phyllis's seeming normalness that would pull me back.

"Now, you've got to tell me all about Emmett," Phyllis said in a low, conspiratorial voice.

"Me?"

"Well, you're his sister, aren't you?"

"Yeah, but what do you want to know?"

"Can I ask you something, Georgie?"

"Sure, anything, Phyllis."

"Does Emmett have a girlfriend?" I was stunned and sort of confused. I wasn't sure why she was asking me this. Maybe she was beginning to like Emmett, and maybe she really did think I was in some way her equal and that it was the most perfectly natural thing in the world to ask me about Emmett's love life. Love life! I nearly laughed out loud.

"Are you kidding? No, never."

"Never?"

"Uh-uh." I could feel my heart beating faster.

"It's hard to believe, never. He seems like such an attractive young man."

Attractive young man? That sounded to me like something a fifty-year-old woman would say, certainly not a pretty teenage girl, even if she *was* in an iron lung.

"Well, he hasn't, and that's that," I said.

"Why do you say it that way?" She looked at me slyly. "Come closer." She moved the mirrors again as if to beckon me.

"Say it what way?" I moved the stool up a little bit.

"So final, like there's not a chance for him ever having a girlfriend."

"I don't know. It's just hard to imagine. I mean he's never been on a date, never been to a prom. He's kind of dumb. I mean in that way. He's really smart and all in school, but, well, you know what I mean."

"But I bet you think about your big brother going on dates. Come on, don't you think about some of that stuff?" She certainly had my number!

"Phyllis! Why are you going off and asking me these questions?"

"Georrrrgie! Why are you blushing?"

It was kind of odd, but I was actually enjoying

this conversation. "Come on, don't you think about all that stuff? Tell me."

"Well, I read Archie comic books."

"Oh, I love Archie and Betty and Veronica and Jughead. Have you seen Archie's dad's new car?"

"Yeah, and Jughead wants to borrow it, and you know what's going to happen!"

"Who would you rather look like, Veronica or Betty?" Phyllis asked.

"I keep going back and forth," I said.

"I don't. I'd like to look like Veronica, with all that black hair." Phyllis sighed. "I guess you always want what you don't have." She stopped and looked at the confusion on my face. "I mean in terms of hair, you know, 'cause I'm a blonde, black hair seems like, well, you know, the grass is always greener." She laughed, a kind of high shrill cackle, then there was a small gasping hiccup. "Oh, dear, I'm mixing my metaphors."

Now I was completely mixed up. What in the heck was a metaphor?

Next she swerved sharply. "What about you?"

"Me?"

"Yeah, you. Don't you have any crushes?"

Suddenly Archie, Veronica, and Betty were history.

"I'm too young to date."

"But not too young to have a crush. Come on. There must be somebody."

"Well . . ." I said slowly. I couldn't believe I was saying this. I hadn't even told Carol or Wendy or anybody. "There's this cute guy. His name's Tim, and he and I were both elected to be on the planning committee for the fall festival at my old school."

"Well, that's neat."

"No, not really. See, I have to go to a new school now. No fall festival, no planning committee. No Tim." We both sighed. Well, Phyllis didn't exactly sigh. It sounded more like a little one of those hiccups. I looked at her. "Phyllis, you promise you'll never say anything."

"Don't worry, Georgie. Never. Trust me." She said the words very clearly, with a lot of force. It made me feel so good. It was almost like that wink.

"Hey!" she said suddenly. "Want to try on makeup?"

"Try on makeup? I don't wear makeup." I laughed.

"Neither do I. Not anymore. And I got a whole box full of stuff. Come on, Georgie, I bet you wear that Tangee stuff. How about trying on some real lipstick?"

"You mean it?"

"Of course I mean it. Go in and ask Sally. She'll show you where it is in my bedroom."

When I walked into Phyllis's bedroom, I almost gasped. I had never seen such a beautiful bedroom, and yet it was like nothing I had ever even dreamed of. First of all, the color of the walls. No daisy wallpaper. No Victor Franken wallpaper at all. The walls were painted a very pale green, the color of celery, and the woodwork was silver—not shiny silver but a soft, old silver look. There was a four-poster bed with a canopy. But it wasn't one of those ruffly ones. It was made out of something that looked like very elegant mosquito netting, gauzy, and it was swirled around like clouds. There was a dressing table, but not with a pouffy tulle skirt. It was a stiff fabric, the same celery green as the walls, and it was pleated, hundreds of pleats. How did someone even think up this stuff, something so different, so unique?

On the wall were pictures of all her friends. It wasn't a bulletin board, either. Instead, the pictures were arranged in a large beautiful frame with clear glass edges! Where did a person get a frame like that? Everything in the room, from the canopy to the picture frame, were in one sense ordinary yet somehow special. I just stood in the center of the room in absolute awe and suddenly wondered why I was such a boring person. I almost wanted to run home that very instant and tell Mom to not order the stupid daisy wallpaper, and why had I ever thought that a vanity with a tulle skirt that looked like it was made for a two-ton ballerina was neat? Maybe that was exactly the problem: *neat, cool, square.* Maybe stupid fads, word fads, fashion fads, ruled our lives too much and wound up making us all boring. Not just boring, but like carbon copies or rubber stamps, sort of blurry and not at all distinct.

I snooped around up there for a while. There were a lot of pictures of a really cute guy, and one of Phyllis sitting on his lap in a bathing suit beside a swimming pool, and another one of them at a prom. She had on a beautiful dress with what looked like a rosebud corsage pinned to her waist, and he was in a white dinner jacket. A lot of teenage girls kept their old corsages. They kept them pinned to their bulletin boards. Not Phyllis! Hers were in a huge glass vase that been made into a lamp! And she must have gone to absolutely squillions of proms because that vase was stuffed with them. Then there was another picture of her with a bunch of really cute girls all piled up on the hood of a car.

But the bedroom had a strange quality. It was sort of like a time capsule of a very short life. I had read a book that summer about the lost city of Pompeii. They had described it as a place where time had stopped. Where bodies of people had been found almost perfectly preserved in hardened volcanic ash at the moment of death. There was even a photograph of a chained dog gasping for air as it suffocated in the surge of falling ash and poisonous gases. That is what Phyllis's room reminded me of—a lost city, like a city we have never seen, nor could imagine, that had been inhabited by the ghosts of a previous life, her life before she got sick, and the ghost of Phyllis herself seemed to fill the room. I found the box of makeup and got out.

"Did you like my room?" she asked when I came back.

"Yeah, it's really pretty." Understatement of the year.

"Did you see the pictures?"

"Yes."

"Did you see the ones of me and my boyfriend?"

"That was your boyfriend?" She nodded.

"What did you think?"

"He looked pretty cute."

"Pretty cute? Raymond—he's gorgeous!" *Is?* I thought. *Is he still her boyfriend?*

"Do-d-do—" I began to stutter.

"Do I still see him?" Her voice was almost sharp.

"Yeah."

"No. He's got another girlfriend now." She didn't even sound especially bitter. But I was shocked.

"He does?"

"Well, it's not exactly surprising, Georgie, now, is it? I mean it's not like we were married. It's not like in sickness and in health."

"B-b-b . . . but were you going steady?"

"Yes, but that is not being married, you know." She spoke in an offhand way.

"I know," I said in a low voice. I hoped she didn't think I sounded stupid.

"Come on, let's get out the makeup."

It was fun; I have to admit. And Phyllis had every color and brand ever displayed on the drugstore lipstick rack—Hazel Bishop, Max Factor, and on and on. The first one I tried on was called Red as

All Get Out! Needless to say, we didn't have to get a mirror.

"Overpowering," Phyllis declared. "The only person who could wear that is Lucille Ball. My mother saw her in person once."

"Oh, the *I Love Lucy* show. That's my favorite."

"Yeah, too bad color television isn't here yet. She's got incredibly red hair according to my mother."

"But people say color television is coming."

"I'm not holding my breath."

I froze when Phyllis said this. She started to laugh in that hiccuppy way. "Don't look so shocked. It's a joke, Georgie!" Then she paused and her face became serious. "Of course, I'm the only person who can make breathing jokes. Etiquette, you know."

"Huh?"

"You know—like it's not polite to make jokes about Jews if you're a Christian or colored people if you're not colored."

"Oh," I said. I didn't quite get it because I had never wanted to make jokes about Jewish people or colored people.

But in any case, I went on with the makeup. She even let me put some on her lips. There was perfume in there, too. The expensive one called Evening in Paris. But the best thing of all was a lipstick holder that was a little stand with two holes and a poodle in between.

"You can have that," she said, casual as anything.

"Really? Are you sure?"

"Yes, and pick out two lipsticks to go in it."

I picked out one called Peachy Keen and another one called Cherries in the Snow.

"I'll tell you a beauty secret: if you put white lipstick over the Cherries in the Snow, it's absolutely gorgeous. There's a white lipstick in there someplace. You can have it, too. Just paw around for it. You'll find it."

When Sally came out, Phyllis asked her to bring down her jewelry box. As I opened it up, Phyllis said, "You won't find a pop-it bead in there." I could see that right away and I immediately felt embarrassed. Last year the pearly finished beads that popped together to make strands were the rage for seventh-grade girls, and Susie Grenelle and I both saved our money and bought some. "You must promise me, Georgie"— Phyllis looked at me very seriously in the mirror—

"that you shall never wear pop-it beads. They are just so cheesy."

"Oh, I promise," I said solemnly.

"If there is one thing I had back before I got sick, it was style."

Style, I thought. *That's it exactly.* That's what Phyllis had—style. It went way beyond fads or fashion. It was just out there—not for the future, not from the past. It was timeless and completely unique.

"You know," Phyllis was saying, "as soon as Raymond started going out with this other girl, I heard he got a flattop. Not all boys can wear flattops. His head looks like a box, I'm sure. He should have stuck with a crew cut."

"Yeah," I said softly.

I was completely in awe of Phyllis. When I went back home, walked into my bedroom, and sat down at my princess vanity in front of my heart-shaped mirror, I could hardly look in it. My only thought was *I am soooo ordinary!*

I heard the phone ringing and then Mom called upstairs, "Georgie, it's for you!" There was an unnatural brightness in her voice, or maybe it was a camouflage for her desperation. There would definitely be no timer for this call. I ambled to the phone hoping it was Wendy.

"Hi . . . it's me." I have to confess that my heart sank just a little bit. Her voice sounded even more mushroomy over the phone.

"Oh, hi, Evelyn."

"We got back early, but I think it's too late to go to the library now."

"But we can talk!" I said. I wanted to tell her about my conversation with Phyllis.

"Sure!"

"You're never going to believe this!"

"What?" Evelyn asked eagerly.

I got into my most comfy telephone-talking position, which is lying on the floor with my feet propped up against the wall. "So," I continued, "I was over at Phyllis's and guess what?"

"What?"

"Well, she starts asking me all about my brother, Emmett—like does he have a girlfriend, has he ever had a girlfriend . . . and I'm thinking, gads, am I hearing this right? Or am I imagining it? Or does Phyllis actually have some kind of a crush on Emmett and is wanting me to play Cupid?"

"Hmmmm . . ." Evelyn said. If ever a mushroom sighed, that was the sound. I had expected a little more excitement.

"So what do you think? I mean, isn't it crystal clear?"

"Well, I'm not sure. Now, tell me exactly what you said and she said again."

So I repeated the conversation as best I could, then waited for Evelyn's response.

"OK," she said, a new energy in her voice. My hopes picked up that she would agree with me. "Now, here's what I think. You can't rush to conclusions."

"I don't think I'm rushing." I rearranged my feet on the wall. They had left sweaty prints with streaks of dirt. Mom wouldn't mind. She was desperate about me, after all. But I would try and clean them off afterward. I supposed that I should wash my feet as well.

"You're not rushing, but you must proceed in a logical fashion. This is the basis of scientific inquiry—hypothesis, exploration through testing the hypothesis, evidence, data, then conclusion. Has she ever used the word *date* as in, she would like to date him?"

"Evelyn!" I blurted out. "This is romance, not pea shoots." What she had just described sounded exactly like the science experiment I did last year with pea shoots growing toward light.

Evelyn started laughing so hard she finally, through gulps, gasped, "Pea shoots! I got to go before I pee in my pants." Then I started laughing, and so ended our second phone conversation. It had been the most fun I had had in a long time.

Five minutes later, the phone rang again. I picked up. It was Evelyn. I knew it would be. "My bladder is under control. We can talk."

Chapter Eight

For the women in our family, beginning with my grandmothers, baton twirling was not just a high-school activity, and never a "sport." It was an art form. For three generations the women had been baton twirlers and all members of the Hoosier Twirlers. Except me. I was too young. You had to be at least thirteen. When I got to eighth grade, I would be able to try out. I couldn't wait! Ha, ha. No. I was a freak of nature, genetically speaking. I didn't get the twirling gene or whatever it was that allows one to throw a silver stick high up into the air, catch it, flip it into a flutter twirl, and let it roll down her arm. In fact my one and only trip to the emergency ward was when I tried this and my nose got in the way of the baton and my hand. The baton broke my nose, and there was blood all over me, the baton, and all Mom's pals, old Hoosier Twirlers who got together for sessions with their daughters. But did that maybe give a teeny-weeny hint to Mom that I was not cut out for this sport? And yes, it is considered a sport. Don't ever say it's not a sport, or you'll get a twenty-minute lecture on all the muscle groups involved in baton twirling. But no, Mom was still convinced that I had the seeds, or whatever you call it, to become a great twirler. So in addition to terminal cowlicks, I had a crooked nose. It turned a little bit east. Thank heavens Mom wasn't pushing twirling this summer. I think Dad sort of discouraged her, what with the new house, the new school, and all.

But today was Mom's turn for hosting the alumnae of the Hoosier Twirlers.

And Velma, her best friend who had been the captain of the twirlers, was out there now setting the pace. I put my elbows on the windowsill and watched. It was so hot, I didn't know how they stood it. Gads, I couldn't believe it when I spotted Winona. Winona Beech was seventy-five years old. She was teensy even in her high-stepping boots, and until she was seventy, she could twirl three batons at once. Only a very few people could do that. I imagined that if I ever attempted it, I would not only break my nose but knock out both my eyes.

I put in earplugs to drown out the music and got my book. It was the newest Ray Bradbury. I was halfway through it now. But the first page was one of the best beginnings ever. I turned back to read the paragraph that I just loved.

Now, as George and Lydia Hadley stood in the center of the room, the walls began to purr and recede into crystalline distance, it seemed, and presently an African veldt appeared, in three dimensions, on all sides, in colors reproduced to the final pebble and bit of straw. The ceiling above them became a deep sky with a hot yellow sun.

Now that is what I call writing.

The book is about a man whose whole body is covered with tattoos, and these tattoos predict the future. I couldn't figure out how Ray Bradbury thought all this stuff up. He was so totally original. He was a genius. It was like Phyllis. She was original, too. Who else would think of painting a bedroom celery green with silver trim and making a lamp stuffed with prom corsages? I wasn't original at all. My princess vanity reminded me of this every time I looked at it and saw my stupid face in the heart-shaped mirror. It wasn't my face that sickened me now, not my stubby hair with its herd of stampeding cowlicks. It was the heart shape of the mirror. The vanity seemed so . . . so vain!

I looked up at the ceiling in my room. I wanted the walls to purr. The ceiling to dissolve into a deep blue. I wanted to be in a place before polio, a place where an iron lung had never been invented, never thought of, never needed. A place where an iron lung would be as strange as a flying saucer and polio would be science fiction. I remembered one graph in my polio folder that said in 1920 there were only something like 325 cases of polio in the entire country. I wondered what life was like then. There weren't families like the Rileys. The Rileys lived in one of the epidemic states—Wisconsin, I think. They lost four out of their six children in the space of seventy-two hours. The oldest boy was a basketball player. He came home from practice with a sore shoulder and then by the next day had died. That night his four-year-old sister also died, quickly followed by two more. This story haunted me. I suppose it was because the boy, Paul, was a star basketball player like Emmett. It was just too easy to imagine Emmett coming home with a sore muscle. That happened all the time, especially at the beginning of the season. But what if it wasn't a muscle? What if it was the polio virus attacking his spinal cord? And he'd get sick and die and then I would, and my parents would be left with no kids in a matter of hours. Like an extinction.

How could those stupid Hoosier Twirlers be out there with their batons flashing in the sun as if nothing were wrong? A John Philip Sousa march was blasting out across our nonexistent lawn. I know life was supposed to go on, but sometimes it seemed just plain wrong that it did. Nevertheless, life was going on to the accompaniment of a John Philip Sousa march! And there was no escaping. The summer was hot, and swimming pools and movie theaters and every place you could escape to was a breeding ground for this alien thing. So I put down *The Illustrated Man* and got up and decided to visit a real inmate. The Iron Girl.

When I arrived, they were just wheeling the iron lung inside. It took two nurses to do this. When Phyllis wasn't on the patio, she was in the family sunroom. There was a whole special panel with electrical stuff there just for operating the iron lung. There was a generator stashed in one corner for if the electricity went out. There was also a lot of other stuff that made it look sort of like a hospital room. It was as completely different from her bedroom as a place could be. Not very elegant. Lots of porch furniture with cushions covered in a sunflower print. I was looking around as they set Phyllis up again, and she must have seen me. Little escaped Phyllis's mirrors. "Pretty ugly, huh?" she said. There was that hiccup that was her way of laughing.

"No, not really." I mean, what was I supposed to say?

"Yes, really."

"Your mother offered to paint this room your favorite colors and get rid of the sunflowers," Sally said. "I don't know why you're so stubborn."

"You mean you could make this like your bedroom?" I asked.

"She sure could," Sally said.

"I don't want it like my bedroom. I'm not the same. Why should my bedroom be the same? Besides it's not a bedroom. It's an iron lung, for God's sake. Next thing you know, Mom will want to be wallpapering the lung."

"All right, all right, I'll shut up," Sally said, and walked out of the sunroom.

"Bitch," Phyllis muttered. Then she turned. "Me, not her."

"Maybe I should go."

"Maybe not?" There was no anger left in her voice, just a plea.

"Sure." I sat on the barstool and spun myself around slowly.

"So," Phyllis said, "I want you to tell me more about Emmett."

I went into super-alert status. My hypothesis was about to be tested. Would I find evidence?

"What's to tell?" I tried to sound casual. The idea here was to draw out as much information as possible—data!

"You really think that there's not a chance of him ever liking a girl? Going out on a date?"

This is it! Date data. Or data date. *Please, God,* I prayed, *don't let me think of pea shoots, because then I'll think of Evelyn peeing and burst out laughing and all will be lost.*

"Well, not never," I replied, cool as a cucumber. "It's just it's hard to imagine."

"Hard to imagine because you're his sister."

"Maybe," I said.

"Not hard for me." I stopped spinning on the barstool.

"What do you mean?" I asked. My breath caught in my throat.

"I mean I could imagine . . . you know . . ."

"Dating him? Really?" I couldn't wait to get home and call Evelyn.

"Yes, really, except for, of course, the obvious. Kind of hard to date a girl in an iron lung." She paused. I felt my heart pounding. It was louder than the beast.

"I . . . I don't know," I said softly.

"Don't know what?" Phyllis asked. The mirrors flickered.

"I . . . I don't know what. . . . I don't know." I laughed slightly.

"Do you think Emmett might like me a little bit?" Her blue eyes seemed huge. Was she about to cry?

"Are you saying that you kind of like Emmett and you sort of hope he likes you?"

"Yeah . . . but I'm kind of a freak, you know."

"So's he," I said. Phyllis laughed out loud at this, a really big two- or three-hiccup laugh.

"I'm sorry. I didn't mean that the way it sounds."

"Oh, Georgie, I love you!" Her eyes flashed with delight.

"You do?" I couldn't believe it. "I mean, we're both freaks, I guess."

"All three of us!" Phyllis added. Then she was quiet and her eyes were serious again. "So maybe you could find out if he likes me just a teeny tiny bit?"

I couldn't believe she was asking me to do this. This was too neat! I'd do this. I'd not only find out; I would make this happen.

But first, of course, I had to call Evelyn.

The Winklers had a special line for their kids since they were doctors and couldn't have their telephone tied up with their kids yakking when someone might be dying or having a baby. Evelyn picked up on the second ring. "I got data!" I screamed. "Date data!"

I began to recount carefully, word for word, my conversation with Phyllis. "She began by saying, 'Tell me more about Emmett.'"

Evelyn and I had been on the phone about five minutes or less. I got to the part when Phyllis asked me if Emmett might like her a little bit, and the dating questions, when she interrupted and said, "Hold on a second. I've got to go."

"Not your bladder again?"

"No. I'm getting index cards to enter the information on. I want to write it all down. Then I'll color-code it all."

Talk about taking the romance out of romance— index cards, color-coding! Pure Evelyn!

Chapter Nine

From the pantry, I heard them talking in their low kitchen voices. These were not the voices they used when they were talking about a disobedient Jell-O mold that had failed to unmold perfectly or how you could hardly whip cream with all this humidity. These were their other voices. The ones that children were not supposed to hear. I heard the words *iron lung,* and I had a feeling they might have been talking about Emmett and Phyllis.

We were out at Grandma and Grandpa's farm for Sunday dinner. I stayed in the pantry to listen and pretended to study the Holstein breeders' calendar that Grandpa had hung up there. For August they had a picture of an immense stud bull called Elandor of Eckbow. A caption underneath the picture read:

Sired Caprice. Winner of the Dairymans' High Yield Award three years running. Distinguished maternal pedigree. Extreme milk yield transmitter backed by two excellent dams with milk yields of over 38,000 pounds.

But I was really just listening and not concentrating on Elandor. "That is so sad. But at least she gets to be at home. Not in a hospital," Grandma was saying while admiring the three-flavored Jell-O mold with fruit suspended in the green part that had just exited most perfectly from its enamel fluted dish. They talked some more, and then Mom said, "You'll never guess what."

"What?"

"Velma's daughter is pregnant!"

"Oh, my word!" Grandma exclaimed in a loud whisper. "And she's captain of the Hoosier Twirlers!"

"Yes," Mama said.

"Well, she won't be twirling for long!" Grandma sort of snickered. "Babies do get in the way of a baton." My mom was well into her thirties when she had us, thank the Lord! I couldn't imagine anything worse than having a teenage mom. Some girl who hadn't even made it through algebra one. No matter how much teenagers impressed me, I did not want one to be my mother. And it would probably be a dumb teenager who would put Coca-Cola in my bottle, blow cigarette smoke in my face while she fed me, and never change my diapers. Ick! The whole idea made me nauseous. In fact, it gave me real bad malaise.

I was standing in the pantry thinking about all this when Grandma sailed in to get the dish for the butter beans.

"What're you doing, Georgia?"

"Nothing," I said.

"You've got a funny look on your face. It's just a stud bull up there on the calendar." She guffawed. "Why don't you go out and practice baton?"

"Too hot."

"Not under the beech tree, it isn't. Junior high's coming faster then you think. Got to be ready when tryouts come up for the Hoosier Twirlers. Can you do an arm roll yet?"

"Almost," I lied. Was she already thinking of a replacement for Velma's pregnant daughter?

"You're going to look so cute in those new skirts the girls wear now."

I was not going to look cute at all. The whole idea of me in the short sparkly skirt made me want to puke. I had very skinny legs and knobby knees and of course the stubby hair and let's not forget the nose that turns east. But it was especially when I thought of myself as a Hoosier Twirler that I began to have doubts about my legs lengthening and the other mysterious transformations that I dreamed about, most specifically my hair. All the twirlers wore their hair in either glistening pageboys that fell in straight orderly sweeps to their shoulders and then curved under perfectly or in wonderfully swingy ponytails. Stubby hair does not swing. It doesn't fall. It will not curve. It springs. I couldn't even make a part in my hair—that is how confused it was. To get rid of the cowlicks, I would have had to start all over with a new scalp, a new arrangement of hair holes in my scalp so the hair could grow in a straight, orderly fashion. What we were talking about was major scalp surgery. Once I had suggested to my mom and grandma that I could go down to the colored part of town and get the Madam Walker hair-straightening treatment. When I said this, you would have thought I had asked them if I could smoke a cigarette and a take a shot of whiskey on the side. In any case, I didn't argue with Grandma.

I went to the closet and selected one of about a dozen batons and headed for the beech tree. I wasn't really going to practice. I'd just climb up to one of the low-spreading limbs that joined the trunk at an angle that was perfect for reading. Of course, I didn't have anything to read. Well, I would just think. Maybe about that poem I had heard Phyllis's mom reading the first day I wandered into the grove and heard her voice threading through the mechanical breaths of the Creature. I wanted to find that poem. I had meant to ask Phyllis the name of it. But when she started talking to me about liking Emmett and could I find out, I was so excited I just forgot. I climbed up in the tree and reclined against the trunk. I looked up through the deep copper leaves as pieces of sky floated overhead. I was trying to remember some of the words from the poem, but other words, not the poet's, came to me instead.

"Remember what I said, Georgie: you've got all the air in the world, the whole sky up there. I have eighty-seven cubic centimeters of air, but you have the world." What had she meant exactly? I didn't want to ask Emmett, although I was sure he understood. But Emmett had been kind of weird ever since we met Phyllis. It was going to be hard asking him what he thought of her. I

think he'd been back over once or twice since we met her, but I wasn't sure.

Emmett was late now to dinner at Grandma and Grandpa's. He had said he had something to do and would drive himself out. I was getting hungry, so I hoped he came soon. I jammed my hand down into my shorts pocket and found a Tootsie Roll. I was just rearranging this big wad of Tootsie in my jaw when I saw something flapping in the air. I stopped chewing and looked straight ahead. Damn if that didn't look like a flamingo had slammed into Grandma's clothes-line. A flamingo in central Indiana? Impossible. I scrambled down the tree and began to walk toward the line.

"Oh, Lordy!" I whispered. It wasn't a flamingo. It was Grandma's corset, this pink contraption flapping in the breeze, snapping its elastic straps, silver garter buckles winking at the sky. I just blinked and thought, *What a fool I am,* and swore I would never ever wear one of those things in the dead heat of an Indiana summer no matter how fat I got or how much I began to sag and bag.

"Whatta ya staring at?" Emmett had sneaked up behind me.

"Grandma's corset."

"Is that what that thing is?"

"Yep."

"What's that next to it? They look too short for Grandpa."

There was a pair of pale pink satin chopped-off pants. "Of course they're too short for Grandpa." I giggled. "It's a girdle."

"How do you know about all this?" Emmett asked me. "Comes with the territory, I guess."

"What territory you talking about?"

"Being female and all."

I wasn't sure if I should take this as a compliment or not. I had almost decided not to, but then I realized that this was my opening for talking to Emmett about Phyllis. I thought for at least half a minute of a good way to get into it. "So what do you think about Phyllis?" I blurted out.

"What do you mean, what do I think of her?"

"I mean what do you think of her?"

"I hardly know her. She seems nice enough. Why are you asking me?"

"Uh . . ." I didn't know what to say. "Well, don't you think she's pretty?"

"Oh, yeah. She's beautiful!"

Beautiful! He didn't have to say that. He didn't have to go that far. I could see he was turning bright red again.

"I think . . . I think maybe she likes you a teeny bit." Emmett was pulling up clumps of grass and tossing them up toward a limb as if he were shooting baskets.

"You do?" He looked genuinely confused.

I hurtled ahead. "Emmett, you're so . . . so . . ."

"So what, Georgie?" His eyes turned hard.

"W-well," I began to stammer. I was so excited and the next thing I said was really a mistake. "She could be sort of like your starter kit."

"Starter kit. Jesus Christ, Georgie!" He turned and stomped off.

I shook my head. How could I have been so dumb? I was only trying to help. Starter kit! As if Phyllis were some crafts project!

"Wait up, Emmett," I called after him. "I didn't mean it that way! I really didn't!" I ran to catch up with him. "I'm sorry, I'm sorry. I didn't mean to say it that way." I reached out and grabbed his hand. "Stop walking, Emmett." He stopped and looked down at me.

"So what exactly did you mean?"

"She told me she liked you."

"She did?" He was surprised, I could tell.

I was not going to blow this. I nodded. "Yes, she really did."

"Hmm," was all he said.

I was ready to snore off during Sunday dinner. The conversation was incredibly boring unless you were a basketball star applying to college, hoping for a great basketball scholarship.

"So how many scouts been sniffing around so far?" Grandpa asked.

"None," Emmett said. "School hasn't started."

"But what about roundup? Don't they usually hang around for that?"

"Canceled," my dad said.

"Everything's getting canceled," I said.

"What else?" Grandma asked.

"Let's see." I sighed and leaned back in my chair and closed my eyes as I tried to remember the listing in that morning's paper. "The annual fish fry of the Order of the Eastern Star at Saint Joseph's Church, the Job's Daughters and Rainbow Girls summer picnic, the city swimming meet at the Riviera Club, the father-son golf tournament at Highland Country Club—"

"What in tarnation!" my grandfather blurted out. I stopped my recitation. Everyone was looking at me like I was some sort of freak.

"What's wrong?" I asked.

"Does she do this every day?" Grandma turned her head slowly toward Mom.

"Well, Georgie likes to keep up with things."

"Things like polio," Emmett whispered. "It's a little weird."

"Dorothy Jean." Grandma only called my mom by her full name when she was very serious. "Do you think this is healthy?"

What was not healthy in my opinion was people talking about you as if you were not there. Now I was really mad. "First of all, I am not dead. So quit talking like I'm not even here at the table. And second, it is unhealthy to go to public swimming pools, to go to the state fair, to go to movies, to not wash your hands after peeing or pooping." Everybody froze when I said this. "But it is not unhealthy to read about polio in the newspapers."

Grandpa now looked at me. "Georgia Louise, would you like to excuse yourself for a few minutes until you can behave at the dinner table?" I started to speak, but Dad gave me a fierce look.

"Sorry," I muttered, and got up from the table.

When I returned after about two minutes, my mom was talking. "The basketball roundup is just delayed until after October. After polio season. But Emmett's getting lots of letters—Indiana University, Purdue, Michigan."

"When are the commit dates?" Grandpa asked.

"End of November," Emmett replied. "But because I'm asking for more scholarship money, I don't really find out until spring."

"But Emmett can do what they call a C.C.," Mom said.

"C.C.?" Grandma asked.

"Commit with contingency," Emmett said. "If I get the full scholarship I ask for, I'll go. If not, all bets are off. That kid from South Tech, they say he's already been offered a thousand-dollar scholarship to Notre Dame."

"A thousand dollars! My goodness," Grandma said. "Mercy."

"No mercy about him," Emmett replied. "Cyril James. He's a beast on the court. He's seven feet tall."

"Tall, but short on brains," my mom said.

"Dumb as a box of rocks, but he's fast. He can shoot. But nothing compared to this freshman at Crispus Attucks," Emmett said.

"Who's that?" my grandfather asked.

"Kid named Oscar Robertson. He plays real smart. Great all-around player."

"But he's just a freshman," Grandma said. "Where's anyone seen him play?"

"Oh, Lil!" Grandpa said. "Where have you been all these years? This is Indiana. You don't wait until high school."

Even I knew this. Boys who liked to play basketball played anyplace. It didn't even have to be a real court. It could be a dirt lot as long as there was a hoop stuck to something.

"You mean down on the south side of town," Grandma said, and pressed her napkin to her lips in a nervous gesture.

"Yep," said Emmett. "We all go down there and have pickup games with those guys from Attucks." I knew what Grandma was thinking. Those guys from Attucks were colored boys. Crispus Attucks was the all-Negro high school. So Grandma thought they might be playing in a rough part of town. "He's just a plain great player. He can snap a ball like I've never seen. He invents moves. He does this head fake that leads into a driving layup that is phenomenal. And he can think midair like no one else."

"Sounds like he'll be getting a thousand-dollar scholarship."

"By the time he's a senior, it could be ten thousand dollars," Emmett said.

Ten thousand dollars! It was unimaginable. "Hey, do they ever give scholarships for baton twirling?" I asked. If they did, I might have to rethink my future as a twirler. For ten thousand dollars, I might manage to overcome my dislike of twirling. There was a sudden silence. Everyone looked at me, and then they started howling with laughter. You would have thought I had said the funniest thing in the world. You would have thought I was Jack Benny, Bob Hope, and Lucille Ball rolled into one. The answer was no. Scholarships were not given to baton twirlers. But nobody could stop laughing long enough to tell me this until about five minutes later.

"Look!" I complained. "All I did was ask an honest question. And what? Suddenly I'm the laughing-stock of the whole family? Har-de-har-har-har!"

Being eleven was indescribably awful. It's as if you're never really in on the joke. Not only that. You are the joke.

Chapter Ten

Here are the things I have begged and badgered my big brother for:

1. to go bowling with him and his friends at Alleys-A-Way
2. to go to Northwood, the drive-in restaurant, with him and his friends
3. to have his help with the electrical stuff on this new small world of the Orion story that I was attempting
4. to have a girlfriend—him, not me
5. to go to a prom—him, not me

I had been generally unsuccessful. Most of the things I had begged and badgered for meant including me. I didn't like being left out. Who does? Item number five was different. I wanted him to be a normal teenage boy and have a girlfriend and maybe even go to a prom. I would have been so proud of him all dressed up in a tuxedo, and I would have helped him pick out a corsage for his date. He wouldn't even have had to rent a tuxedo. Dad had one that would fit him perfectly, and a white dinner jacket, too. More and more boys were wearing white dinner jackets to spring proms. Well, guess what? Although I had still failed on the first three items, number four had a good chance of coming true. Emmett was over at Phyllis's a lot. And you know what else? I wasn't. Once again, I was feeling left out. Sidelined, as they say in basketball. I knew how awful Emmett felt when the coach did that to him. Couldn't he see how I might feel? Couldn't Phyllis see that, too? I mean, she asked me to find out if he liked her a teensy bit. I did. What thanks did I get? Zero.

Emmett would take his telescope over there. August might be boring on Earth in Indiana during polio time, but up in the sky it was purely exciting. The night simply flowed with stars. And Emmett and

Phyllis were out there on the Kellers' patio looking at it together.

In the meantime I discovered a new word that could have described me exactly. There was a picture in the paper of parents walking into a church behind two small coffins of two little twin girls who had both died of polio. I was looking at it when Mom came into the kitchen and began to read over my shoulder. She sighed. "That is so sad."

"It's sadder than sad," I said.

"Morose. Look at the parents' faces."

I had never heard that word before. I liked the sound of it. So I went upstairs and looked it up in my dictionary. The definition for *morose* surprised me. I had expected something sadder than sad. *Romantic* sad, maybe, because of the second syllable, *rose.* It was sad, all right, but in a different way, and not romantic at all. According to Noah, morose was "gloomily or sullenly ill-humored, as a person. Peevish, willful." I liked that. This wasn't just plain sad and mopey. This was sad with muscle. This was sad with teeth in it. This was sad that could bite. As morose as I was, I couldn't compare my situation to the parents of these two little twins. So I had to give that word up. It was only right. I went and got the diary that Grandma had given me for my birthday. I hadn't written in it since I poured out my heart to it saying how mad I was about not being allowed to go swimming and all that stuff about taking the Fourth of July personally. The diary was covered with pink-and-white checked fabric. It had a lock. I got the tiny key from where I kept it, unlocked the book, turned to the page with the right date, and started writing.

Dear Diary

    I saw a picture in the newspaper today of the parents of four-year-old twin girls who died of polio. They both died on the same day within the same hour. Usually unless it was a murder, they don't give the time of death, but in this case they did. There was an expression on the parents' faces that Mom called *morose*. I'm not feeling so hot myself these days. But I can't say I am morose. The twins' parents own that word, if you can own a word. And I have to tell you, Diary, I am starting to wonder about being Presbyterian and going to church and God. What happened to "God Bless America"? We've got polio all over the place. There are pretty girls and probably ugly ones too in iron lungs. I don't think God is blessing America. Maybe He doesn't get it. Maybe we should stop singing the song. It's sounding stupider every day.

Sincerely, Georgie

So, deprived of a really cool word, I went in search of another. Yes, as I have said, Indiana summers are boring. I went and sat in front of my dumb vanity. I leafed through the dictionary, looking for more sad words. It was pretty much what I expected. *Doleful*—sounds like pineapples. *Grumpy*—too cute, one of the seven dwarves. Then *broody* cropped up. No way. I wasn't a hen. But I started flipping back through the *b*'s, and I came across that word Mom had told me when I got the vanity—*boudoir.* My eyes almost popped out of my head. "Lady's bedroom or private sitting room." All right, that was to be expected. But the second part of the definition was unbelievable: "a sulking place," coming from the French word *bouder,* which means *to sulk,* as in boo-hoo. Tears just dripped from this word, and the dictionary went on to explain that the Latin suffix denoted a place. *Well, I'll be!* I thought. *Or I'll boo-hoo.*

It was a very starry night, and I walked over to the window. There was lots happening up there. It was very clear, and in another few hours the moon was going to whisk by Venus, the closest it would for the whole year. I knew that I couldn't beg or badger to go over to Phyllis's. But I really wanted to. Emmett and Phyllis were out there on the Kellers' patio, looking together. I thought that I could almost hear the iron lung from my window. It was like a ghost breathing, stirring the trees with its pulsing whooshes as it inhaled and exhaled for her all day, all night.

Just then I heard the phone ring, and Mom called up that it was for me. I ran down the hall.

"Hi. It's me, Evelyn." There had been many phone conversations, but we had actually only seen each other twice since that first meeting at the library. It seemed to me that she was always having to do stuff with her little sister or, most recently, go all the way to California for a medical convention with her parents. "Guess what?"

"What?" I asked.

"At this medical convention, they talked about how more than a dozen healthy babies had been born to polio moms in iron lungs in Los Angeles."

"Wow!"

"Yeah. Pretty neat, isn't it? You said that you thought that girl Phyllis might have a crush on your brother. So I just thought you'd like to know they could have a family." This was sort of jumping the gun, but I was touched that Evelyn had shared this information with me. I knew that she had really wanted to meet Phyllis and I had kind of held back. An idea popped into my head. "Hey, you want to come over and spend the night? Emmett's over there now and we could you know . . . sort of spy on them just a little bit."

Mom was so happy that I at last had made a new friend whom I actually had invited to a sleepover that she offered to go pick Evelyn up. But Evelyn's mom dropped her off. I had packed up some stuff for snacks: a thermos of lemonade, a bag of chips, and some Mallomars. Frozen Mallomars. I think I invented this, although Emmett claims he did. You stick a package of Mallomars in the freezer for at least three hours, and it revolutionizes a very ordinary cookie into something else.

I explained to Evelyn before we left about the mirrors and how she always seemed to catch your reflection way before you ever got there. But we could hear the machine almost as soon as we entered the grove.

"Jeez, I never thought it would be so loud," Evelyn said.

"Yes. When the wind is blowing from that direction, the direction of their house, the sound is louder right here. But if we can get pretty close to the house, I mean upwind of the iron lung, we'll be able to hear Phyllis and Emmett a lot better, I think." Evelyn just shrugged. I felt I owed her something more. "I think we might be able to see them." Then I added, "I think they maybe sometimes kiss." Evelyn's pale gray eyes glinted playfully.

"We'll have to crawl up on our bellies—like the pictures they show of those soldiers ·in Korea. You know, they slither up on their bellies and dig in their elbows to pull themselves forward. I've studied this," Evelyn said. It was my guess that there was not much that Evelyn hadn't studied. So we commenced soldier-style to drag ourselves across the Kellers' perfectly manicured lawn. We had to leave the snacks in the grove to do this. But it was very effective. It was not a full moon, luckily, and Evelyn—always a quick study—had advised when I told her about my shadow theory with the mirrors that we stay in the deep shadow cast by the Kellers' steep-roofed house.

This seemed to take us away from the patio, where Emmett and Phyllis were, but it turned out to be a great idea. Except for one thing: we were in the path of the sprinklers. It felt cool, however, and by the time we were close to the edge of the house, we were pretty well soaked. We then slithered along the foundations until we found a spot that had a perfect view of the patio. We could see them, but still it was hard hearing anything they were talking about.

In the patio light, the soft wind blew Emmett's red hair like licks of flame. "Oh, my God!" I mouthed the words when I saw the flames dip and obscure Phyllis's head entirely. Evelyn's eyes almost bugged out of their sockets. But more was to come! It wasn't five minutes after that I saw Emmett's arm reach down toward the middle section of the iron lung, and I knew what was coming. I cupped my hands over Evelyn's ear and whispered, "He's going to put his hand through the portal!"

Evelyn's lower lip jutted out as if to say, "Huh?" She looked bewildered. I cupped her ear again with my hand. "It's how nurses wash her, or sometimes I think they have to give her a shot or something. But she and Emmett are probably holding hands. It's the only way she can touch something." Evelyn's mouth pulled down into an inverted curve, an upside-down smile. "Yeah, kind of sad. But it still counts as data, right?" Evelyn nodded. I felt a little triumphant ping deep inside. We watched on in silence. I could see a smile on Phyllis's face. Her neck, protruding just a bit from the tight-fitting collar, seemed as fragile as a stalk. Her eyes closed. A slight wind ruffled her hair. Her head lost all definition. It could have been a flower on a slender white stem. That was all she was: a beautiful flower. I wanted to forget about the rest of her encased in the steel tube. This was romantic, data or not.

Everything was very still. There was Emmett at the midsection, his one hand swallowed by the Creature. His other hand stretched toward Phyllis's head with his fingers entwined in her breeze-ruffled hair. Phyllis's eyes were closed, but she had a radiant look on her face. It was a strange configuration of machinery and arms and heads, a confused anatomy of metal and human appendages limned in the moonlight of a hot summer night.

I knew that they were about to kiss when suddenly the lights in the house came on. *Shoot!* I thought. We heard a door slide open onto the patio and the sound of footsteps. We pressed ourselves closer to the brick wall of the house, for we were caught in a wash of bright light that poured through the windows, peeling back the shadows that had been our refuge. The light was scalding. We felt naked, exposed. There was some shrubbery near us, and I hoped that perhaps we could press up close to it and appear like another bush or two. We could clearly hear voices.

"Emmett, time for Phyllis to turn in," a deep voice said.

There was a harsh laugh. "I'm always in!"

There were the sounds of cables being moved and wheels turning. Evelyn and I were clamped against the side of the house, practically not breathing. The clouds cleared off, and the moon was sliding down the black dome of the night and beginning to spray light across the lawn in our direction, shaving the darkness from our shadowed refuge, nibbling away at its borders. It was a race between the Kellers and Emmett getting the iron lung into the house and the encroaching moonlight. Within a minute the dark would be stripped away entirely and we would be exposed, spies in the bleached night.

Just at that moment, we heard the thump of the

iron lung, all twelve hundred pounds of it, go over the threshold from the patio to the sunporch. We were revealed, but by that time the nurse, Emmett, and Dr. Keller were all occupied with rearranging the cables. No one noticed two small clumps huddled against the house. When the sliding doors shut, Evelyn and I were off like two shots. We didn't bother with the belly scramble across the lawn. We just raced for the grove, the lawn striped with our elongated shadows, which sprinted ahead of us. We grabbed the bag of snacks in the grove. When we were back in our yard, I went up on the patio and dragged down two lawn chairs. Five minutes later, I saw Emmett coming out of the grove.

"Hi," he said. "Whatcha doing?"

"Star watching. This is Evelyn, Emmett. Evelyn, this is my brother."

"How come you didn't bring down a telescope?" He paused "And how come you're soaking wet?"

Oh, jeez, I thought. *Think fast, dodo.* "We were hot and decided to turn on the sprinkler to cool off."

"And go in your clothes, not even a bathing suit? You're a strange one, Georgie—watching stars without a telescope and going in the sprinkler with all your clothes on."

"How was Phyllis?" I asked, trying to sound casual.

"Fine," he said. "Hey, you know, Phyllis would really like to see one of your small worlds."

"Really?"

"Yeah, really. How's the Orion one coming?"

"I need your help—I told you. I don't know how to wire it, and I need smaller bulbs then those little flashlight ones."

"Oh, you've started the Orion one?" Evelyn asked.

"Yeah, remember, you were the one who said I should do my favorite constellation, something I really loved."

"I could get you some really teeny-tiny lights. Doctors use them all the time. My dad and my mom are both surgeons. They need them to light up people's guts and stuff."

"That would be great."

"Just bring over one of your other small worlds," Emmett said. "She doesn't need to see a work in progress. Show her a finished one. She said you could come over tomorrow."

"Could Evelyn come?" I said quickly.

"I guess so. I can't stay all that long because I have basketball practice. But I'm sure she'd appreciate the company. It's a little weird at first, Evelyn. Have you ever seen a person in an iron lung? I mean, other than in pictures."

"Uh, no, can't say as I have," Evelyn said.

After Emmett went up to the house, Evelyn leaned over and whispered, "Do you think he suspected anything?"

"I don't think so."

"You were quick with that thing about running around in the sprinkler."

"Yes, but I hope he didn't notice that the grass wasn't wet."

"Oh, yeah, but thanks for inviting me to go with you to see Phyllis. Do you think we should just casually mention that there are recorded cases of healthy babies being born to mothers in iron lungs?"

"No! No way!" *Gads,* I thought. Evelyn, for all her smarts, was a bit clueless. "Want me to get some scopes so we can see what's up there tonight?"

"Sure."

I brought down two very light ones. "Will you be able to see Orion yet?" Evelyn asked.

I was dumbfounded. Everyone knew, or at least

I thought everyone did, that Orion was a winter constellation.

"Heck no! Orion only begins to rise in the fall. It's a winter constellation. Evelyn, didn't you know that?"

"Nope," she said simply. "I know a lot about microscopic stuff, microbiology. Cells, nerve endings. My dad uses an electron microscope all the time for his research. It's amazing what you can see. My dad has actually looked at the molecular structure of nerve endings through one. And he lets me look through it, too."

"Have you ever looked through a telescope?"

"No. I mean not through a good one. Not one where you can really see out into space."

"Well, you can take a look tonight."

It seemed sort of like an odd crossing of fates that Evelyn had never looked through a good telescope and I had only looked through crummy little kids' microscopes, the kind that come in science kits. It was as if we were both focused on different ends of a spectrum of life in our universe. She looked in, down to the teensiest particles of life on Earth, and I looked out toward the farthest reaches of time, to the very edge of the universe.

I brought back the best of Emmett's telescopes and set it up, pointing it east, where the stars begin to rise.

"So where is Orion right now if you can't see it?" Evelyn asked.

"Being chased by Scorpio," I said softly.

"What?"

"Scorpio killed Orion. Stung him in the foot."

"I didn't know that part of the story. I thought he went blind."

"He did, and then Scorpio chased him. So in summer, when Scorpio rises, Orion flees below the horizon."

"Scorpions are a kind of spider, you know."

"No, I didn't know that," I replied.

"Yes, they are arthropods. That's the class, but they belong to the same genus as spiders—arachnids, just different species."

"Oh," I said, and thought that Evelyn should be on a quiz show. Except for a lack in a very few areas, she had more information stuffed under that frizzled head of hair than anyone I had ever met.

"So where's Scorpio?" she asked.

I pointed to the Southeast. "It hasn't risen that high yet. But it's right over there. You can see his tail flicking up into the night, like he's dusting the other stars away." We were quiet for a minute. "Do you see his heart?"

"Heart?" Evelyn asked.

"Yeah, it's a red star, Antares. They say the name means 'rival of Mars'—because it's so red."

"Oh, wow, it really is red! No wonder Orion is running. When will he come back? Like, when is it safe?"

The question struck me as odd. I shrugged. "I'm not sure if it's ever safe. But starting in December and through March, that is the best time. When it's really dark. Orion is a thousand times lovelier than Scorpio."

That night when Evelyn and I went to bed, I set to thinking about which small world I should take over to Phyllis. There was one that my mom called my namesake small world: Saint George and the Dragon. Then there were my Nancy Drew houses. They were really just scenes from some of the books, like *Nancy Drew and the Hidden Staircase,* or *Nancy Drew and the Secret of the Old Clock.* But when I began reading science fiction, I started making these really weird landscapes and modeling creatures out of clay that had three eyes and pointy heads. My favorite small world came out of *The Martian Chronicles* by Ray Bradbury. He described this place that had canals that were the color of violets and ships with sails made of blue mist. And the Martians themselves had eyes like "golden coins" and transparent bodies through which the stars shone. There were ancient cities made of crystal and some of pink stone. It sounded more beautiful and fantastic than anything I could ever have dreamed of.

My first instinct was to bring all my small worlds. But that would have taken at least four or five trips to carry them over, even with Evelyn's help. Then I realized that if I showed them to her all at once, there would maybe be no reason for her to invite me back.

Chapter Eleven

So we went over the next day and I took the Saint George box. Emmett introduced Evelyn, and Phyllis seemed genuinely glad for the company. The first thing I realized was that Emmett had become an old hand at wheeling the iron lung around and checking its dials and pressure gauges and stuff. I had started to explain to Phyllis about the box and how I had made it all when Dr. Keller came out on the patio. He seemed like a jolly sort of person—very jolly.

"Hi, Dad," Phyllis said. "This is Emmett's sister, Georgia, and her friend Evelyn. Georgie brought over this neat little diorama she's made. Take a look. It's very clever."

"Ah yes," said Dr. Keller. But, in truth, he hardly looked, and I knew immediately that he didn't think it was all that clever. He was anxious to show what he had brought, which I guess you would say was definitely clever. "Look at this! Finally finished it!"

"Finished what?" Phyllis asked. Suddenly Saint George and the Dragon slid out from the mirrors, and then there were more mirrors, and instead Dr. Keller's hands were reflected.

"The new, improved double-reading mirror," he said.

"Of course," Phyllis said quietly.

"Well, honey, you should be excited. No more tiresome tongue-turning of pages." That was how Phyllis read. Emmett had told me. They put a book on a rack. Since she could turn her head a little and had full use of her mouth and tongue, she had a device that was like a long spoon which she could bite down on and turn the pages. But apparently it was tiring. So this was the answer, and Dr. Keller, who was an engineer, had invented it. "Got a patent pending. We're calling it the Phyllis. How about that?" He looked anxiously at Phyllis.

"Fine," she answered. Except I didn't think she sounded all that thrilled about it. I looked at Evelyn.

She blinked and sort of rolled her eyes as if she didn't think Phyllis sounded all that fine about it either.

"Hey, Emmett, help me set it up, won't you?"

"Sure, Dr. Keller."

"You know where I keep the power screwdriver down in my basement workshop, right?"

"Yes, sir."

I couldn't help but think that Emmett knew his way around the Kellers' house almost as well as he knew his way around ours. In no time they had the Phyllis attached to the gleaming cylinder. But the weirdest thing of all was that here I had come expecting to see a real romance blossoming between Emmett and Phyllis, and Emmett seemed almost indifferent to Phyllis. He was much more interested in talking to Dr. Keller about the iron lung. I tried to remind myself of the scene Evelyn and I had witnessed—Emmett sliding his hand through the portal—but right now it was as if none of that had ever happened and my brother had fallen in love with a machine. This horrid breathing creature was another problem for Emmett to solve. He had even brought over an old high-school textbook of his on basic mechanical engineering. Emmett was as about as romantic as a toolbox!

As they were working, Dr. Keller pointed out all the other little gadgets he had invented or devised and put on the iron lung so that it was absolutely "state-of-the-art."

"State-of-the-art" was a favorite expression of Dr. Keller. "Phyllis can do more, see more, perform more tasks than any other person in an iron lung. She has the most active, independent life of any respiratory poliomyelitis paralysis victim."

But she's still a prisoner in this cylinder, I thought, *with only eighty-seven cubic centimeters.* So what did it matter if she could have a baby? All those moms out in Los Angeles who had had babies—they could never cuddle them, hold them. I had read that in Japan's imperial family, the emperor and empress's babies were taken from them when they turned three years old and raised separately—away from their parents. This was what being a mom in an iron lung must be like. Like an empress mommy no longer permitted to hold or touch your child.

Emmett had explained to me that eighty-seven cubic centimeters of air was the volume the machine could contain. This air was somehow mechanically pumped into the iron lung through bellows. As it was sucked into the machine, the pressure increased, squeezing down on her body at the rate of fifteen pounds per square inch, pushing the air out of her lungs. She could not do this herself because her chest muscles didn't work. Then in the next whoosh, the pressure would decrease and her chest would expand automatically because of the low pressure, and allow her to take in a thin stream of air. And to this thin stream of air, while zillions of gallons of it gallivanted around in the sky, Phyllis was tied by a cable no thicker than a thumb. And if that cable broke or came unplugged, there were alarms that would sound and generators that would kick in so that the strange mindless mechanical whooshings would never cease; a breath would never be missed. So what did all the reading mirrors and the other gadgets mean or really matter? The iron lung was like a hateful insect with its gleaming carapace. I heard a taunt in its measured rhythmic breaths, a hiss beneath its whooshes, and all the mirrors gleaming and casting spangles of light glared with lies and deceptions of life.

The machine had totally swallowed Phyllis. Her parents believed in the iron lung and not in Phyllis. And now I was thinking that Emmett too believed in the iron lung more than in Phyllis. The unthinkable had happened. Phyllis had been sidelined! This was not the way it was supposed to be. I wondered what Evelyn thought.

"Come over here closer, Georgie," Phyllis said suddenly, interrupting her father. "And bring Saint George up here."

"But I got the reading mirrors all set up. Don't you want to try them?" her father asked in a pleading voice.

"I want to see Saint George and the Dragon, Dad."

I brought it close to the mirrors.

"How did you make the dragon?"

"I used a dinosaur mold and plaster of Paris, and then I stuck sequins on for scales."

"Oh, the knight is great, too! Look at it, Dad."

Dr. Keller's brow furrowed, and the jolliness of his face seemed to dissolve into a kind of confusion. "Of course, dear, of course." I could tell that Dr. Keller was not often confused. For his daughter, he would bear with anything. He would bring the whole world right to her. No, that is not accurate. With his clever mirrors mounted on gyros, he would bring the reflections of the whole world right to her. But right now she wanted to see the small world I had created.

Chapter Twelve

Phyllis made a sort of ugly little joke when I brought the Saint George diorama up close for her to see on the rolling table. "I guess you could say I am my own small world." I was the only one to hear the joke. She whispered it to me. Evelyn was a few feet behind me. In a way, the small worlds became my passport into Phyllis's world. She was clearly fascinated and wanted to see more. I went over a few more times. Just me, no one else, as basketball practice had started to crank up for Emmett, and Evelyn had to go to a family wedding out of town. I learned a lot about Phyllis's life in that small world of hers.

Here was what Phyllis could move aside from her head and neck: one muscle in her left foot and one in her thigh. She called that thigh muscle Ralph. I was formally introduced to Ralph on my next visit when I brought the little box world from *The Martian Chronicles*. I mean, she didn't show him to me, because she was wearing a long gown. She just said, "This is Ralph. You can't see his terrific tricks because my nightgown covers him but that is—how should I say it—where he resides with his mighty powers." The mirrors moved to catch a port that was near her thigh. I caught my breath because this was the port that I had seen Emmett put his hand through. He had touched Ralph! I almost wished at this point that Evelyn and I had never spied on them. In other words, there was getting to be too much evidence, too much data. I was feeling, quite frankly, overwhelmed.

Phyllis didn't have a name for the muscle in her foot. With Ralph, Phyllis could move something called a sensor that was taped to her thigh, and that's how she swiveled the mirrors. She was doing that to get a better view of *The Martian Chronicles* box.

"It's just a landscape really, kind of like a country in *The Martian Chronicles,* but I just call it the Beautiful Place."

"Oh, my goodness, it is beautiful."

"It's just like the way Ray Bradbury, the author, described the ancient city. I made it from rose quartz and crystal pieces that I got at a rock shop on our trip out west, summer before last."

"And what are those figures? How did you make them?"

"I molded them out of this kind of clear Plasticine stuff, and you see, I put little gold beads in for their eyes, 'cause Ray Bradbury said that the Martians had transparent bodies and eyes like gold coins and that the stars could shine through them."

"The stars could shine through them. How lovely."

She closed her eyes for a minute as if she were trying to hold on to this image, an image in her mind's eye and not a reflection in the mirror.

Mrs. Keller had come out, and unlike Mr. Keller, seemed to find the box genuinely clever. She also asked me a lot about the kinds of books I liked to read. Mrs. Keller taught English literature at a local college, so she knew a lot about books. She was so nice and friendly that I just thought I would ask her about that poem I first heard her reading.

"Now, what poem was that, dear?"

I couldn't remember all the words, but then I remembered the word I didn't know: *casement*. "It's something about some lady standing at a casement and waving her hand and—"

"Oh!" Mrs. Keller clapped her hands together. "'The Lady of Shalott.' A lovely poem."

"My poem," Phyllis said softly.

Mrs. Keller ran inside to get the poem and came out and read it. I couldn't believe it, but honestly it was the saddest, most horrible poem I had ever heard. It was about a lovely lady who lived in a tower under a terrible curse.

"There she weaves by night and day
A magic web with colours gay.
She has heard a whisper say,
A curse is on her if she stay
   To look down to Camelot.
She knows not what the curse may be,
And so she weaveth steadily,
And little other care hath she,
   The Lady of Shalott.

And moving thro' a mirror clear
That hangs before her all the year,
Shadows of the world appear.
There she see the highway near
    Winding down to Camelot;
There the river eddy whirls,
And there the surly village-churls,
And the red cloaks of market girls
    Pass onward from Shalott."

I felt a kind of panic begin to well up inside of
me. This was too much like Phyllis. The mirror that
hangs there all the year. Substitute *iron lung* for *tower*.
The Lady of Shalott was cursed in the same way—to
only see life through a mirror while she wove some
dumb tapestry. Then she dies when she leaves her
mirror prison and the loom and looks directly at life.
I couldn't believe that this was Phyllis's poem, or her
favorite poem. Phyllis turned her head toward me after
her mother had finished reading the poem. I could see
a rub mark just above the rubber-ringed collar that
sealed her into the iron lung. But our eyes only met in
the mirror. I dared not look at her.

"That's your favorite poem?" I asked softly.

"It's my poem," she whispered.

"Well, Alfred, Lord Tennyson wrote it, and Phyllis is a romantic. Loves the romantic poets just as I do. That's what I teach at Butler College: romantic poetry and Victorian literature. Look at this." She bustled over to a box and got out an embroidery hoop and brought it over to me. "Phyllis bought me this for my birthday. She had Sally order it from a catalog."

It was a needlepoint picture of the Lady of Shalott weaving in front of her mirror! This was absolutely sick! I didn't understand why Mrs. Keller didn't understand. I got it, and I was only eleven years old. Was she just being blind on purpose? Or was this some stupid way of not simply trying to make the best of a rotten situation but trying to lie about it? Turn it into something else. Something beautiful and romantic.

There was nothing romantic about "The Lady of Shalott"—poem or needlepoint. I looked at Phyllis again in the mirror. She was looking at her mother now. It was then that I knew that Phyllis had lied. I wondered what else she lied about. How much lying did Phyllis have to do? This was not only *not* her favorite poem; she hated it. But she would never tell her mother, just as she would never tell her father that it was not fine that the double-reading mirror with the patent pending would be named the Phyllis. I realized that the entire Keller family was caught up in some strange web of lies, and there was nothing magical about it. However, not only were the Kellers caught up, but maybe even Emmett. They all had their games going with Phyllis: poems, patented inventions, mechanical problem-solving. You name it. But I had no games.

Although I hated the poem, I was fascinated by it at the same time. I have to admit that I was sometimes drawn to things that would scare me, like horror movies. Emmett had a book of monsters. It really scared me when I was little, but sometimes I would go into his room and I would dare myself to look at it, look at the very scariest monster. It was as if I had to try to master my worst fears. It was the same with "The Lady of Shalott." I dared myself to read it. I asked if I could borrow the book with the poem in it. But maybe it was more than just daring myself or mastering a fear. Maybe I thought in an odd way it would be a key to understanding Phyllis. But in truth it made Phyllis even more mysterious than ever, and I sensed some sort of danger. I wasn't quite sure what the danger was, but it was there, and it seemed important that I try to understand it—for Phyllis's sake, for my sake, and for Emmett's sake. From all my reading about the polio virus, I knew that polio victims like Phyllis were not infectious. And yet I felt vulnerable. It was as if an even stealthier virus were lurking. Phyllis's small world had turned things upside down. She was supposed to be the victim, not us. After all, I was a builder of small worlds. I manipulated them. Not the reverse. I was determined to help Phyllis, but I would not be her fool. I was going to find out everything I could about people who had managed to live outside iron lungs, escaped the tyranny of the beast on which they were dependent for every breath.

It occurred to me that I more than anyone else was the perfect person to help Phyllis. Why? Because I believed in Phyllis in a way no one else did. She filled my imagination with images that were not reflections but what she really was. Her spirit, her beauty, her liveliness. In my dreams she was a cheerleader, a fashion model. This was her reality. She had created a little world in my head. But at the same time, I knew that there was something dangerous. Mirrors had to be shattered, and with the shards, this particular dragon might be slain.

✦ ✦ ✦

"Oh, you can take the book home, dear," Mrs. Keller was saying. "I always like to encourage young people to develop good reading habits. You couldn't do better than Tennyson."

Or maybe I couldn't do worse, if she knew my strangely morbid fascination. Even though it was ninety degrees outside and Mom wasn't home to drive me to the library, I was determined to go and find out everything I could about polio victims who had escaped the clutches of the iron lung.

Chapter Thirteeen

I went to the library and found precious little about
polio victims who had survived outside of iron lungs.
But it was a branch library, after all. Mrs. English,
the golf-socks-wearing librarian, told me that the
main library would have much more information.
They had something called microfiche files that you
could hunt through. Microfiche was basically photos
of newspaper and magazine articles that were projected on a small screen, and you could flip through
them really fast. I thought this would be the perfect
research expedition for me and Evelyn. She would be
back from the wedding in two days.

So it was the following day that I brought the poetry book back. When I got there, Mrs. Keller and Phyllis and Phyllis's tutor, who came three days a week, were having tea, Phyllis of course sipping hers through the gigantic straw. Mrs. Keller was working on the needlepoint of the Lady of Shalott, and the tutor, Miss Crenshaw, was admiring it. They were all nattering on about romantic poetry. Mrs. Keller turned to Miss Crenshaw and said, "You know, Georgia here is just a sixth-grader, but she has very sophisticated tastes and a real appreciation of poetry. She loves 'The Lady of Shalott.' Don't you, Georgia? And I gave her a copy of one of my Tennyson books. Do you have a favorite stanza, Georgia?"

"Mother!" Phyllis sighed.

"Well, I only thought maybe she'd like to recite it."

I felt something grip my stomach and my throat begin to lock. I didn't have a favorite stanza. I could hardly speak now. Words began to scatter in front of me like little birds struck by a big wind, winging off, tossed and tumbled by the currents. "I-I . . . I . . . c-c-c-can . . . c-can—"

"Mother," Phyllis said sharply. "I'll recite you my favorite stanza." And she began.

"But in her web she still delights
To weave the mirror's magic sights,
For often thro' the silent nights
A funeral, with plumes and lights
  And music, went to Camelot;
Or when the moon was overhead,
Came two young lovers lately wed;
'I am half sick of shadows,' said
  The Lady of Shalott."

My face was caught in the mirrors with Phyllis's. Hers, I could see, was deathly pale. Our reflected eyes exchanged glances, and for once there was truth in that mirror. I wasn't sure, but I think in that moment Phyllis might have been envisioning her own funeral. Her death.

Miss Crenshaw soon left, and Mrs. Keller went upstairs to grade term papers.

"Phyllis, I've got a question."

"What's that, Georgie?"

"Why do you do it?"

Phyllis's eyes in the mirror slid toward me, wary but comprehending. "You mean play their games? Play my parents' little games?"

I nodded slowly. "Like your mom said that you

found her that needlepoint thing of the Lady of Shalott, but you just pretend to like that poem, don't
you?" Phyllis's eyes were steady in the mirror. "And
all that stuff your father invents for the Creature and
puts your name on it. You don't give a hoot about
most of it, do you?"

"Look, Georgie, if there is one thing that sickness
does, it makes you old real fast. It makes you old in
good ways and bad ways. Grown-ups can be great
liars. Kids, well, we're just pikers compared to adults
when it comes to lying. Adults are so good at it that
they don't even know they're lying. Lying is all my
parents have now. Lying about me, lying about my
so-called life. It's very important that they think I'm
sort of, well, if not happy, content in a way. That is the
only way they can vaguely even approach not going
crazy. That is all we've got, Georgie—the pretense of
contentment. It keeps the devils away."

"The devils?" I said softly, but she didn't answer.

She just said, "I'm very grown-up now. Very
adult."

"What about Emmett? Do you lie to him?"

"No, Emmett lies to me."

"I know," I said in barely a whisper.

"I know you know, Georgie."

"You do." She blinked rapidly. It was her way of nodding. She could nod a little, but this was easier.

"I mean I really think he likes you but he's just scared."

"I know." There was another little storm of blinks. "And you don't lie to me, do you, Georgie?"

"Never!" I said.

"That's why I'm going to call you Saint Georgie." Her eyes danced now with delight.

"You are?"

"Yes, ma'am!" She paused. "See, when you brought over your small world, Saint George and the Dragon, I kind of knew right then when I saw that little knight with tinfoil armor and his little sword raised that you were going to help me."

Maybe I should have been complimented, but instead I sensed something dangerous again. *It's just a tinfoil sword,* I wanted to say. *Tinfoil. Not real. You're the one in the shining armor,* I wanted to say, *and I'm going to have to smash those mirrors before slaying any beast.*

"You're right about Emmett," she continued. "He's scared to show his feelings. He's hiding behind all that science he knows. It's easier for him to talk to my dad."

This was dangerous territory. I couldn't help but think about what Evelyn and I saw that night when we had spied.

She narrowed her eyes. They became kind of smoky. "I know guys."

Chapter Fourteen

The Trunk was what I called the Central Indianapolis Library. Everyone else called it the Central Branch. I thought it was absolutely stupid to call the main library a branch. Anyway, the Trunk down on East St. Clair Street was as different from any branch as could be, especially El Rancho. It was limestone, but a darker one, maybe dark from age, and inside there was lots of marble. Shadows and dark cool stone. It wasn't air-conditioned, either. Nevertheless it was tens of degrees cooler on the inside than any non-air-conditioned building you could imagine. Evelyn and I had settled at two microfiche machines, and the reference librarian, who reminded me of a dried twig, had shown us how to work them. She was nice enough, but she didn't offer lemonade like Golf Socks at El Rancho. She wore old-lady shoes that clacked on the marble floors.

You had to get the hang of moving the microfiche dial because stuff slid by so fast. Evelyn also had requested the *New England Journal of Medicine.* This was a publication for doctors that she said her mom and dad swore by. So after maybe a quarter of an hour of trying to get something off the microfiche, she started looking through the journals.

She sighed deeply. "What?" I asked.

"This is really depressing. It says here in this article by Dr. Samuel Gluckmeir that the longer people stay in an iron lung, the harder it is to wean them."

"Wean?"

"Yeah, take them out of it. Let them breathe on their own." *Wean* seemed like a really peculiar word to use. My grandfather talked about weaning farm animals from mother's milk all the time, but weaning from a machine's air . . .

"It's like," Evelyn continued, "their muscles have atrophied."

"Atrophied?"

"Grown useless. So how long has Phyllis been in an iron lung?"

This caught me by surprise because I wasn't even sure. "Gee, I don't really know for certain."

"Well, the patients who have the most success, it seems to say here, have been in it for a week or less."

Oh, God, I thought. This wasn't Phyllis. I had known her almost a month now. "I'm pretty sure she's been in there maybe a year or more."

I went back to the microfiche. A picture flashed by. "Whoa!"

"What is it?" Evelyn asked.

"Just a second, I have to back up." I moved the dial slowly in itty-bitty little turns. There was a grainy photograph of a man in a huge rocking chair. He was actually smiling. The caption read, "Rodger Mills in his rocking bed." It went on to explain the principle of the bed, which was that when a patient's head was up and his feet were down, the internal organs were pulled by gravity. When this happened, the diaphragm was pulled with them, and this sucked air into the patient's lungs. Then when the bed rocked back to the reverse position, air was forced out of the lungs.

"Does it say how long he was in an iron lung before they put him in the bed?" Evelyn asked.

"No, but it says that he spends 'extended periods of time' out of the iron lung." I read on a bit. "Oh, wow! Get this. It says here that since polio does not affect the sensory nerves, but only the nerves that control voluntary muscles, people like Rodger and his wife, Minerva—Minerva, what a name! Anyhow, Rodger and Minerva can have a healthy, but modified, physical relationship."

"That means sex!" Evelyn said.

"Duh, I know that!"

Chapter Fifteen

The rocking bed, I felt, offered some kind of hope. But I wasn't exactly sure how I was supposed to bring this up. Also there were some things I really wanted to know, since even the rocking bed didn't work all that well with people who had been in an iron lung a really long time. But how to ask Phyllis? And then there was the other problem. Phyllis had originally wanted me to help her, but in a much different way. Saint Georgie or not, after Evelyn and I witnessed Phyllis and Emmett on our spying expedition, I wasn't so sure that Phyllis had need of my Cupid services. However, I also sensed that she still wanted me to somehow back her up in the relationship. Or maybe it was to act as a go-between. Maybe I was just supposed to monitor Emmett's feelings and tell her. So if I wasn't Cupid and not Saint George, did monitoring Emmett's feelings make me a spy of some sort? Although I had spied on them that night, going from saint to spy was a hard transition. It wasn't quite the noble role I had imagined. I thought again of the shattered mirrors and the shards with which a dragon could be slain. Maybe there was a saint who smashed mirrors, the scourge of Shalott but nonetheless a savior?

For these very reasons I had kind of avoided going to Phyllis's for a couple of days because I knew that we both had different ideas of what my helping meant. But I finally went over one afternoon when I was completely bored. As I walked into the sunroom, the mirrors swiveled and brought my face in closer. There was one mirror that was perfect for holding a conversation between two people if that person sat at about a forty-five degree angle from where Phyllis's head came out of the cylinder. So I moved to a barstool and perched on it.

"So, Saint Georgie, how are you progressing?"

How am I progressing? Jeez, I thought. Did she mean in furthering the romance? This seemed a little false to me, knowing what I did, and now I was going to have to be equally false and pretend total innocence, pretend as if nothing had happened that night when Evelyn and I saw them. OK, so they didn't kiss, but almost, and Emmett had slid his hand into the port of the iron lung. I'd seen enough to know that Cupid could retire. I sensed that what she really wanted to know was had Emmett said anything to me about his feelings for her. *Dream on,* I felt like saying, because Emmett never talked about feelings. I was amazed that lying came so naturally to me—me an aspiring saint. "Well, it's been hard to catch him because pre-season practice is starting, and you know the basket-ball scouts will be snooping around."

"Even before school starts?"

"Yeah, they come early and try to catch the practices." This wasn't exactly the truth.

"Oh," Phyllis said quietly. "I see." Then something began to happen. Phyllis's face grew pale, and I saw the features begin to twist. She didn't look so pretty. Every single mirror now flashed with her face that was suddenly ugly, contorted. Her mouth dragged down in a terrible grimace.

"Get Sally."

"Sally!" I yelled.

Sally appeared in a split second.

"Spasm in the left leg again?" she asked.

"Yes," Phyllis said. Her voice was taut: the Creature was gasping for her. Nothing was hers, I thought. Nothing went untouched by the Creature—not her giggles, not her gasps.

Sally fetched a hypodermic needle from the small refrigerator in the room. She was on the other side of the iron lung from me, so I couldn't see everything she did. But I think first she must have slid her hand through one of the sealed ports on that side and swabbed down a patch of skin on Phyllis's leg with some alcohol. Then her hand came out again and she took the hypodermic needle.

"Maybe your little friend should go."

"Maybe not!" Phyllis said through her clenched teeth.

I was too scared to move an inch, but despite my fear, a sudden joy flooded through me. She wanted me to be there at this moment. Then Phyllis gave me a quick smile as her face began to relax. "Don't worry, Georgie. This happens sometimes." I felt as if the sun, a private little sun, was shining on me, pouring through me. I felt illuminated by her smile. Her eyes were growing heavy.

"She'll sleep for a little while," Sally said. She came over with a damp cloth and wiped Phyllis's forehead, which had broken out in beads of perspiration. Then she went and got a hairbrush. She began brushing Phyllis's hair back into a ponytail, a beautiful ponytail of blond curls. It didn't swing, though. It just sort of trembled with the vibrations of the machine. That's when I got up to leave.

"Bye, Phyllis," I whispered.

Later that day, I got out my diary. I got the key and opened it and started writing. But the only word I could write, and I wrote it over and over again, was *Why? Why, why, why?* And while I wrote, a voice beneath the silent cry of that word hissed at me. Finally after the twentieth *why,* I got up my nerve to actually write what I was thinking. I pressed hard with the pencil, grinding it into the paper. *I think God is a jerk if He let this happen to Phyllis. Maybe Jesus, too. He should know better 'cause He suffered.*

When I finished writing those lines, I slammed the diary shut and locked it. I was proud. Yes, really proud! And now I knew what I was going to do. It was going to be tricky because I knew, I was sure, they had kissed and other stuff, and yet he probably never really talked to her. I marched right over to Emmett's room. I knocked loudly on the door.

"Who the heck is it?" He opened the door. "Jeez, Georgie, what are you trying to do? Break down the door?"

"Emmett, you know and I know that she likes you a lot. A whole lot. You've got to grow up." He blinked at this. Yes, it was definitely laughable; me, barely five feet, looking up at all six-five of Emmett and telling him to grow up. "I'm talking about Phyllis. Whenever you go over there, you talk to Dr. Keller. You talk about that stupid machine."

"That's not true. I talk to Phyllis a lot. I bring my scope over and look at the stars with her."

"You're hiding behind your telescopes. You're hiding behind the stars. You're hiding in the night." I decided to go for broke at this point. "Do you ever tell her how you feel?"

Emmett grew very quiet. He didn't blush. He just looked down at his bare feet. "You really think she likes me?"

"I don't think. I know. She told me so."

"She told you?"

"Yes, Emmett." I hesitated. "Emmett, it's not just that she's in this horrible contraption. There's this other thing."

"What other thing?"

I wasn't sure how to exactly explain it. "Everyone lies to Phyllis—her mom, her dad. Everyone has this fake cheeriness, and now you."

"I'm not cheery."

"Jeez," I muttered, and rolled my eyes. "No, but you lie. You play that lying game along with the rest of them. And why don't you just tell her how you like her? Because that's the truth, isn't it?"

He dodged the question, dodged it as skillfully as if he were escaping the most incredible blocking move on a basketball court.

"And you don't lie, Georgie? You tell her some kind of truth?"

"Well, I just don't always agree that everything is hunky-dory like all those gadgets Dr. Keller puts on the machine. Emmett, you've probably said more to Dr. Keller, and when you do talk to her . . . it's . . . it's not like you're really talking to her." I kept plugging on. I was actually feeling almost saintly. "Emmett, I know. I am an expert at feeling left out. It's like being sidelined, Emmett!"

"Sidelined?"

"Yeah!" I said this slowly for emphasis. I almost managed to make *yeah* into a two-syllable word. "It's happened to you in basketball only a few times, and you got so awful, I heard Mom and Dad talking about taking you to a psychologist."

"They did?"

I nodded solemnly. This was not quite the truth. Mom said this kind of as a joke, but I know she was plenty worried.

"So what am I supposed to do?"

I wanted to say it's not just about doing whatever you were doing that night—like feeling up Ralph! But I couldn't, obviously. So I slipped back into the innocent again. Georgie Mason, master of disguises! "How am I supposed to know? I'm a sixth-grader. Just . . . just . . . just don't get all wrapped up with Dr. Keller and the machine. She doesn't have anybody." Then it just slipped out. "Not even God." I paused. "And that goes for me, too."

"What are you talking about, Georgie?"

"I mean, Emmett—and don't tell Mom and Dad

this and not Grandma and Grandpa—but I don't think I believe in God anymore. I mean, how can I believe in God when someone like Phyllis winds up in an iron lung? If there were really a God, I don't think there would be polio."

"Or the Black Death?" Emmett said.

"Exactly. Or the A-bomb," I said.

"It was Truman who dropped the atom bomb," Emmett said.

"Yeah, but if there were a God, he wouldn't have let President Truman do it, and he wouldn't have let those scientist guys invent it."

"Yeah. Well, this is all very interesting, Georgie, but I don't see how this exactly relates to me and Phyllis."

"Just talk to her. I mean, Emmett, you like her, don't you?"

Emmett turned a little bit away from me and began tucking in his T-shirt. "Oh, yeah. I really like her." There was a huskiness in his voice.

"What's that?" I asked, suddenly noticing a pile of wire on his desk. I hadn't noticed what Emmett had been doing. "The lights that your friend Evelyn brought you." I felt a twinge of guilt. Evelyn had offered to bring them on the night we went and spied. "I'm wiring them together for your Orion thingamajig."

"My diorama."

"Yes. You said you really couldn't get much further without the lights. I found some more for you, too. I can show you how to do this yourself if you're interested."

"Gee, yes, thanks, Emmett." Now of course I felt a little guilty about sticking it to him the way I just had.

I left his room, and just then the phone rang on the upstairs hallway extension. I picked it up. It was Phyllis.

"Saint Georgie?"

"Uh, speaking."

She giggled.

"Hey, this is the night of the meteor showers."

"The Perseids."

"Yes, that's it. And guess what?"

"What?"

"The stars are aligned, Georgie." There was silence. I wasn't sure what she meant by that. Astrology? Emmett said astrology was a fake science. "You get my meaning?"

"Not exactly."

"My parents are out. Only the nurses are here, and Emmett and I could have maybe a . . . should I say . . . real date?"

A date, I thought, *an honest-to-gosh date!* But it was the Perseids, and Emmett always watched them with me. "Put Emmett on the phone."

"Just a minute."

I ran to get Emmett. "She wants to talk to you, Emmett."

He didn't even have to ask who.

Chapter Sixteen

It was mid-August, and the Perseid meteor showers were in full swing. But tonight I would not be going to watch these starry showers. I was a casualty of my own success. Emmett was seeing her more than ever, and they were now talking on the phone a lot, too. Not as much as Evelyn and I talked, but Emmett rarely talked on the phone. Indeed, it appeared that I had managed to penetrate my brother's brain with the fact that Phyllis really liked him and that he should stop acting so dense. The long and the short of it was as soon as it got dark, dark enough for the stars to break out and start scrambling around up there, Emmett planned to set off with his telescope. He even said to me very plainly, "You can't come, Georgie. This is a date!"

It was the first time he had ever referred to visiting Phyllis as a date. So my hypothesis had been proven beyond a shadow of a doubt. All the date data was in, and where was I? Sidelined. Left out! Call it a corollary. We learned about corollaries in the beginning geometry unit we did the previous year in math. A corollary is a proposition that follows from one already proven: a direct or natural result. That's me—a walking, talking, living corollary.

To contemplate the universe on a star-pricked August night is a recipe for feeling small, insignificant, and alone. I felt especially alone, not looking at the Perseids with Emmett. But this was the price I had to pay for him having an actual date. A girlfriend!

When Emmett and I watched, we had our routine. We did it the same way every year. We got out the plastic lounge chairs and put our sleeping bags on them. We set up a table in between the chairs. Then we made two big thermoses of lemonade. Under the table we had an ice chest with Popsicles. Only orange and grape flavors. He liked grape. I liked orange. In a picnic basket, we had four packages of Hostess Twinkies, which according to Emmett are "the finest baked goods ever invented." But then we had our own invention, and this was pure genius. I actually had thought it up, even though Emmett liked to take credit. It was the potato-chip sandwich. Here's the recipe:

Take two pieces of very fresh Wonder bread. (It can't be stale or it won't be squishy enough. It's very important that it be squishy. We call it the squishiness quotient.)

Slather on mayonnaise—lots and lots.

Arrange a layer of potato chips on top of the bottom piece with the slathered mayonnaise. Slather a second layer of mayonnaise over the chips, then add one more layer of chips on top of this. Then put on the top of the sandwich.

It's not just scrumptious; it is *crumptious* (another invention of mine—that word). It is the best sandwich in the world. And we usually ate about three or four during a night of meteor showers.

I really did hope he and Phyllis were not eating Twinkies and Popsicles. I wanted things to work out, but there was no banishing the loneliness feeling for me, and I was already beginning to feel spectacularly insignificant when I suddenly was ambushed by the complete injustice of my life. It just seemed all wrong that here I was, the one who had no friends on this side of town. Well, I had one, but she was pretty odd, although I had grown used to Evelyn's oddness. I wondered what my old friends at my old school would make of Evelyn. And it seemed really unfair that I was the one who had to start at a new school. I was mentally whining to myself. I thought this was all happening just in my head, but somehow my mopiness might have oozed out because after dinner I was very quiet and suddenly Dad said, "What's bugging you, Georgie?" I immediately started leaking tears.

"Georgie, sweetie, what's wrong? Is it baton twirling? You don't have to go to the mother-daughter Hoosier Twirler thing if you don't want to." My mom gave my shoulders a squeeze. This of course made me cry harder.

"No, no. Mom and I were discussing that, sweetie." Dad was now patting my head. "I said just last night, 'Dottie, let's ease up on the twirling.'"

"It's not baton twirling," I sobbed.

"Well, what is it, honey?"

A tiny bubble of snot dripped from my nose. Things had escalated, or at least the mucus had.

"I have no friends. Emmett's going out tonight on a date. The night of the Perseids."

"A date!" both my parents blurted out. You would have thought I had said Emmett was running for president of the United States. Emmett had just come down the stairs with his telescope. "Emmett, a date?" Mom almost squealed. Poor Emmett was turning red. If blushing was fatal, he was about three seconds from death.

"Yes, it's true!" I said. "And this is the first time ever that I haven't watched the meteor showers with him."

"Not when you were a newborn baby," Emmett said feebly.

"That's not funny, Emmett."

"Well, I won't go. I don't mind," he replied.

"What? You've got to go!" I wanted to say, *After all the work I've done, you better go!*

"Well, maybe Georgie could go with you," Mom suggested. Whenever moms try to be helpful in situations like this, they always sound so unbelievably stupid. Emmett and I both looked at her.

"Noooo!" I said. "What's that supposed to be, when the little sister tags along? A date with training wheels?"

I could see Mom and Dad trying not to laugh.

"Tell you what, Georgie," my dad said. "How

about I take you out to play miniature golf this evening."

"But I want to see the meteor showers."

"We'll get you back in time."

"Would you take me to the movies?"

"Well, we already saw what was playing at the drive-in theater."

"What about the Ritz?"

"No, Georgie, we've been through this before. It's not safe. Besides, I just read in the paper today that the Vogue Theater is closing and the Ritz probably will be, too."

"I don't think there'll be one open in the city by next week," my mother said.

"But miniature golf, well," Dad continued, "no problem there. That's outdoors in the fresh air. Come on, we could have ourselves a nice little game. I bet we could get in a quick nine holes right after supper, and it won't be getting dark till late. I'll tell you what: I'll even take you to the drive-in for ice cream."

"I am not going to go to a drive-in restaurant with my dad, Dad! Teenagers go to drive-ins with dates and friends. And I have no friends."

"OK. But how about miniature golf?"

"Maybe," I said, and walked into the kitchen for a second dessert. Emmett followed me.

"Georgie, I can explain to Phyllis."

I glared at him. "Emmett Mason, if you back out of this, I'll kill you."

I took a piece of paper towel. I had to stop this crying. I had to get back into gear as Saint Georgie or Saint Whatever. "Just forget it, Emmett. I'll be fine."

I walked over to a kitchen counter, where the newspaper was, and began turning the pages. Mom was right. The Vogue Theater had closed. Then I went to the front page and looked in the corner at the bottom where they always had a report on the most recent polio cases. There had been four more in one day. That made twenty for this week. They never gave the people's names, but you kind of wondered who they were. Before polio, I used to only read the crime section of the paper. But now sometimes I read the obituaries. It was strange to look at the obituary page, because it wasn't just old people's pictures anymore.

I went back into the living room.

"OK, I'll go play miniature golf. But can we go to Round the World and NOT Old MacDonald's Farm?" Old MacDonald's Farm miniature golf course had a giant chicken that clucked very loudly if you sent the ball through its mouth. If we ran into people we knew there, they always made poultry jokes to Dad. Poultry jokes were not that funny, and I didn't need them in the mood I was in.

"Why don't you call one of your old friends, like Susie?" Mom said.

"She lives on Park. It's the other side of town," I said, trying to make it sound like Siberia, or rather that we were in Siberia and Susie was actually in the city of Indianapolis.

"Don't worry. We'll pick her up. She can spend the night. And if she can't, come ask one of your other old friends."

I went and dialed Susie's number. It rang and rang. No answer. I tried Jody, then Ellen. Nothing. Just as I imagined they were all having a slumber party at, say, Minnie's house, the phone rang. It was Evelyn. So I invited her to come play miniature golf and spend the night. She could do the miniature golf but couldn't spend the night.

At Round the World, you could shoot a ball through the sphinx in Egypt or the Eiffel Tower. Evelyn knew more about Egypt than she did about miniature golf, that was for sure. She had no hand-eye coordination, but she was a good sport. And I have to say that she looked even weirder than usual. Evelyn's clothes were odd, to put it mildly. They often looked too big for her and as if they had been made for someone else. This suspicion was confirmed that night. She was wearing a pair of madras plaid shorts (that was OK, very popular print), but they looked way too big. It turned out that they had once been her mom's madras skirt, and her mom had cut them up and turned them into shorts. With her mom being a doctor and all, I hoped she was better at cutting and sewing up people than clothes. Her mother, I felt, should give up on fashion and hair and just stick to being a doctor. For it was her mom who was responsible for Evelyn's disastrous hairstyle.

Evelyn had told me this about the second or third time we got together, when I said that her hair looked a lot shorter. She explained that she cut it every two weeks to get rid of the frizz from the home permanent her mother had given her and botched. Apparently her mom hadn't left the neutralizer on long enough, so Evelyn's hair sizzled off her head as if she had stuck her finger into an electrical socket. Again, one would think that a doctor would have known better. After all, it was chemistry and stuff.

We had fun playing mini golf. The hardest shot actually was the Great Wall of China. Evelyn knew about this, too—four thousand miles long, started around 200 BC by the first emperor of China, Qin Shi Huang—Evelyn was amazing! Dad won, but not by much. His score was fifty, mine was fifty-two, and Eveyln's was ninety-seven!

After the game, he took us to the Dairy Queen, and I got a vanilla swirl cone dipped in chocolate. Then we dropped off Evelyn. Her dad was a tall skinny man. When he came down the front walk, he reminded me of one of those stick-legged birds that wade in marshes. His head bobbed a bit, as if he were ready to poke in the mud for a tasty morsel. I noticed his shorts were too big. I wondered if his wife had made them out of a coat or something.

"She's a lovely girl," Dad said as we drove home.

"Yeah," I said.

"Just *yeah*? That's not very enthusiastic."

"No, I mean I like her a lot. She's real nice." But when your parents said someone was *lovely,* it seemed as if even they knew she was not very cool. It was a kind of tacit acknowledgment of that person's weirdness. I tried very hard not to think of my old friends having a slumber party that evening. The more I thought about it, the more certain I was that indeed there was a great party going on with my old friends on the other side of town and that if it weren't for the fact that the temperature was still in the high eighties, I might as well be in Siberia.

By the time we got home, it was just starting to get dark. Emmett had already left for Phyllis's. Mom had set up a reclining lawn lounger with my sleeping bag spread out and a small table that had a thermos of lemonade. I didn't make the potato-chip sandwiches. It didn't seem right without Emmett. He had left me, in addition to the Lancaster telescope, another smaller telescope that I could operate from a reclining position.

Through the trees, I could just catch the gasps of the great insect. I settled back, tipped my face up to the sky, and tried to see what might be happening or about to happen as we humans on our teensy-weensy planet Earth in its orbit around the sun passed through the trash of blown-up comets. See, that's what shooting stars really are—comet bits. Emmett explained it to me. The bits are vaporized by friction, and what we see as a streak of light is really heated up vapor that looks like a shooting star.

The truly good show wouldn't begin until close to midnight, because that was when Earth began to turn so that it was facing the stream of oncoming comet bits. But it was a clear night, and Mom and Dad had thoughtfully turned off all the lights on this side of the house so as not to spoil the darkness. One good thing about our new neighborhood was that there were no street lights. So this made it even better to see the sky. Emmett would always talk about people who abuse the night, and he didn't mean criminals. He meant families and towns and big cities that had so much electricity that they ruined the darkness, the black that allowed the stars to be seen. But nothing was being abused tonight. It was clear and the sky was powdered with stars. The Milky Way arched over me, and I knew that we, our solar system, were no more than a grain of salt in it. So why in this infinity of things did one beautiful teenage girl on the planet Earth have to be locked in that gleaming cylinder, her lungs useless, and life brought to her through a cable and tricks with mirrors?

There was a meteor in the poem, the awful poem

that I had read now with a kind of terrible fascination
at least four times. The meteor came with the knight
Lancelot, and the lady in the tower caught a glimpse
of both in her mirror.

> All in the blue unclouded weather
> Thick-jewell'd shone the saddle-leather,
> The helmet and the helmet-feather
> Burn'd like one burning flame together,
>   As he rode down to Camelot.
> As often thro' the purple night,
> Below the starry clusters bright,
> Some bearded meteor, trailing light,
>   Moves over still Shalott.

> His broad clear brow in sunlight glow'd;
> On burnish'd hooves his war-horse trode;
> From underneath his helmet flow'd
> His coal-black curls as on he rode,
>   As he rode down to Camelot.
> From the bank and from the river
> He flash'd into the crystal mirror,
> "Tirra lirra," by the river
>   Sang Sir Lancelot.

That was the beginning of the end for the Lady of Shalott. She left the web, she left the loom, and it was just when I was lost in the hypnotic rhythms of the poem that ran through my head that the first shooting star came by. "Oooh!" I rose up from the lounge chair and let the night swirl around me.

There were at least three more in the next quarter of an hour. I was waiting for another one and had set up the Lancaster to look at the dark regions, the "ditches" is what Emmett called them, in the Milky Way. The ditches intrigued Emmett. He thought there was stuff, cosmic stuff in them that we just didn't have the technology to discover yet. That's what he wanted to do— discover a hidden universe.

The moon had risen and was really full. It made it harder to see any shooting stars now. So I decided to go around to the driveway and try to shoot some baskets myself. I really wasn't that bad. Emmett had taught me a few things. I had pretty good aim if I just stood still and shot. But he had been teaching me layups, and maybe one out of twenty times I actually did get the ball through the hoop.

When I came around I could hear music coming from the house and a voice like a velvet ribbon sliding through the night. It was Frank Sinatra.

My parents were dancing! Their silhouettes glided across the drawn shades of our living room. They periodically did this. It was terminally embarrassing to me. But tonight I wasn't embarrassed. I was just once again engulfed in that feeling of loneliness and utter insignificance as I stood there in the middle of our driveway holding a basketball. It just seemed that of the four people in our family, I had to give up the most of anyone. I looked up at the hoop. The moon sailed right over it. What was I supposed to do— slam-dunk the moon?

Chapter Seventeen

It was the morning after THE DATE. I was in my room working on the diorama. The first level was almost complete. This was the undersea part, and if I do say so myself, it was beautiful. I had ripped out the old green-and-blue clay and put in this clear gel stuff that came in two colors, aquamarine and turquoise, that I found at a craft store. My mom had found me a teeny-weeny pink rubber baby that was used for decorating packages for baby showers. This was Baby O., as I called him, son of Poseidon, the sea god, and Euryale, the daughter of the king of Crete. I had whole boxes of miniature figurines that I had either made or found in the dollhouse sections of toy stores. So his childhood and youth took up one half of the bottom level of the diorama. I was planning on mounting the entire thing on a lazy Susan, one of those spinning trays for serving food. My mom had one and said I could use it. But Dad had cut me a bigger platform to put on the spinning base so I would have more room to develop the story. You turned the tray to see the scenes in his life, and this first level was his subterranean life, which would transition to a slightly higher level, that of his terrestrial life. The third level would be the stars. But he doesn't get there until he dies. I had the three levels all worked out. It was a kind of spiral from sea to sky.

Due to Orion's marine heritage, he had this knack of being able to walk on waves. He would do this to get to land, where he became the mighty hunter, followed by a big dog and a little dog, or, as they are known in astronomy, Canis Major and Canis Minor. I was right now building the waves that were really steps to land when the phone rang.

"It's for you, Georgie. It's Phyllis!" Mom shouted.

I had not seen Phyllis since the weird spasm thing in her leg had happened, but seeing as it was the morning just after THE DATE, I was certain that this was what she wanted to talk to me about. I was dying to know how things had gone but was afraid to pry. To my delight, she was eager to talk.

"Come over here, Georgie," she said as soon as I set foot in the sunroom. She rotated the mirrors so they all caught my reflection. I didn't even have to walk over. She had me. When Phyllis asked someone to come close, it was really just her way of being polite. They didn't have to move an inch to speak to her. She caught them in her web of mirrors. Sometimes I thought of Phyllis like a spider. She sat in the middle of this web of light reflected from all those mirrors and drew us in. The beams of light were like the silk threads of a spider's web.

"You got scared here the other day." It was not a question. Phyllis, unlike most people, never asked questions that she knew the answer to. Perhaps that's what happened when you were hooked to a mechanical creature that doled out one thousand breaths per hour and eight-and-a-half million per year. You didn't waste air. "Look, Georgie," she continued. "I've been lying in this machine for over a year. Things happen to your legs, your arms, everything, when you can't move them. My spine is a tangled mess. Probably looks like a cross between a fishhook and a corkscrew. When I got sick, I weighed one hundred and twenty pounds. I think I weigh about seventy-five now. My body has changed. No muscle mass."

I know this! I know so much! I wanted to say. I had read about it. The March of Dimes reports. The articles Evelyn and I found at the library. All of it.

"I can't move. My motor nerves are destroyed but not the sensory ones. So I can still feel things. Mostly pain, unfortunately." Her voice lowered. "The thing that I am supposed to say now is that I haven't changed. That my mind, my brain, is still the same. But that's just a lie, and don't let anyone tell you otherwise, or don't believe it if they do."

I had wanted to ask her what she was like before, before these awful things had happened to her and twisted up her body and crumpled her lungs. But I never did. I wasn't sure why she was telling me this now except that there were no lies between Phyllis and me, and she wanted me to know the truth about her and the disease. And I wanted to know. I wanted to know it all.

"What happened when you got sick? Were you just well one minute and then sick the next?"

"Not minutes, more like hours. But it was still

fast. It was in August, August fifth, 1951. I had gone to a party the night before with a bunch of kids and then me and Melinda and Betty had wound up at North-view, the drive-in restaurant. We were in Betty's new car—two-tone blue Chevrolet convertible with the top down." Phyllis gave a little hicuppy laugh. "We were actually following a really cute guy who we all had a crush on. He had just moved to town. . . . Well, not exactly following him, but you know."

I sat there, and in every mirror there was a reflection of my mouth hanging wide open listening to Phyllis. This story was an Archie comic book come true. Phyllis had been having the perfect Archie evening. Cute girls with ponytails swinging, one even named Betty, driving around town in nifty cars—a two-toned blue Chevy convertible, she had said—plotting how they were going to meet this new guy!

"Well, the next morning," Phyllis continued, "I was just exhausted. I had never felt so tired in my whole life. I thought it was just from staying up late, but still it seemed a little strange. At the breakfast table, I got sort of dizzy. I remember trying to hold on to the edge of the table, actually, and then I just excused myself and went upstairs to my room to lie down. That was the last time I ever walked. That was one year, eight days ago." She looked at the clock mounted on the ceiling over her head. "Seven hours, fourteen minutes ago. Within a half an hour of lying down, I couldn't move my legs. I called to my mother, and she called my dad at work. He got an ambulance. In the ambulance, I started to have trouble breathing. They called ahead on the radio phone and told the Saint Vincent's Emergency Room to prepare an iron lung. I nearly died that night. If it hadn't been for the iron lung, I would have." She bit her lip when she said this, and the color drained out of her face. "If it hadn't been for you!" There was a hiss that lashed the air, and it was not the taunting mechanical hiss of the machine. It was human and purely malevolent. And all the mirrors snarled with the reflection of Phyllis's twisted face. "If it hadn't been for the Creature."

Something inside of me began to cave in. She didn't look fragile anymore. Deep inside me, a sense of danger welled up. Except this time it was a little different. It wasn't just some vague danger. It was Phyllis who looked dangerous.

Chapter Eighteen

Emmett was going over there every night. They were officially dating—at least in my mind. One evening Phyllis asked that I come over, too. Emmett seemed sort of surprised and not entirely enthusiastic. But I suddenly realized that maybe she was including me because she had told me so much about the day she got sick, maybe even more than she had told Emmett. It was as if the barriers had come down. She knew that she could be truthful with me about everything now.

Emmett was already there, and when I came up on the patio, she was looking up at the sky. The mirrors did not even swing to catch me. "I want to know if something is real, or if I am just hallucinating. You know that they have me on all these drugs, and sometimes they have side effects."

"OK, what do you want to know?" Emmett said.

"Well, is that star in the beak of the swan sort of blue?"

Emmett froze for a couple of seconds. An expression washed over his face that I had never seen before. He was very still. For the first time he was not simply looking at Phyllis's reflection, but directly at her. "Goddamn, Phyllis are you really seeing blue?"

"Yeah, am I crazy or what?"

Emmett and I were both amazed, amazed almost beyond belief. There is a sort of trick to seeing colors, and the trick is to use contrast. So if you pick out a white star next to one rumored to have color and flick your eyes back and forth between the two you can sometimes pick up the color of one. It's a talent really, a gift. Phyllis had that gift. She saw both the blue and the gold of the stars in the beak of the swan Cygnus. It was a binary star, a double star.

"You're not crazy," Emmett said. "But there's a definite knack to it."

"Well, I must have it. 'Cause I think I see other colors, too."

"Where?" He came over and crouched down next to her. His eyes were following her eyes. Her blond curls shimmered, and I saw his left hand trembling slightly. It was as if it were in a fight with itself. He wanted to touch her head, but he was afraid to. I couldn't take my eyes off either of them. Binary stars! That's what Phyllis and Emmett looked like. With interlocking gravitational fields, the two binary stars orbit each other. It is like a slow dance in the night sky. They were whispering now. I could barely hear them.

"Over there. What's that constellation that's rising, I don't know, sort of to the right near the swan?" Phyllis asked

"Arcturus?" Emmett said. There was real excitement in his voice.

"Yeah, yeah, looks kind of purple—like neon grape," Phyllis said.

"Neon grape!" Emmett spoke in a hush, an awed hush.

It was so extraordinary that he wheeled the scope over and adjusted the eye cup to her eye so she could see the colors better. I watched his fingers lingering on her cheek and around her eyebrow. Their heads were so close together, one blond, one dark red, that their hair grazed. And once Phyllis began looking through the scope, she just went on and on naming colors. She wasn't a primary color type of person. She would never just settle for red, white, or blue, or yellow. No, it had to be a "creamy ruby," a "dusty emerald."

So that night, as the stars rose in the sky and sorted themselves into constellations, Phyllis became the namer of colors. And she named them, hues that no one had ever thought of but were in fact their true colors if you took the time to really look. I'll never forget Emmett's face that evening. When he wasn't looking at the sky, he was looking at Phyllis. She might as well have been a star, a star that had fallen straight down into this backyard in Indiana.

So together they wandered the constellations until morning when the black of the night faded to gray and the first of the morning stars began to rise and tremble in the dawn.

And where was I in all this? Not merely sidelined, but forgotten in a distant galaxy. Colorless, not even a pinpick of light. So much for my theory of being included. I had decided to go home. I didn't belong with them. They barely noticed when I left.

Chapter Nineteen

"Don't tell me you're going to a family wedding! Or you have to babysit your sister!" I said as soon as Evelyn picked up the phone.

"No, my great-aunt died. Have to go to the funeral. It's down in Bloomington."

"Polio?" My heart skipped a beat.

"No, myocardial infarction."

"Huh?"

"It happens when the blood supply to the heart is interrupted, usually by something called vulnerable plaque."

"Like teeth plaque?" *Good grief!* I thought. *How do you brush your heart?*

"Well, I suppose you could think of it that way. It usually occurs in the anterior wall of the heart—"

"OK, OK." I cut her off. "But guess what?"

"What?"

"They're going to try and wean Phyllis, this morning." I was whispering in the phone because I wasn't supposed to know this, but I had heard Emmett telling Mom about it.

"Are they going to do the rocking bed thing?"

"Yes, a van came last evening with it. And all these specialists are coming today."

"Are you going over?"

"I wasn't exactly invited."

"Is Emmett?"

"Yes. But if you came, I thought maybe I might get up the nerve to, you know . . ."

"Spy?"

"Yes, they've put in some more bushes over on that side of the house where we were. Right near the sun porch. That's where they'll be doing it."

"You should go anyhow."

"I don't know."

"Look, there's no sense in two of us missing this just because of my great-aunt's infarction."

Somehow an infarction didn't sound exactly like

death. Actually, it sounded more like a gas problem—
a little fart in the heart.

"OK, I'll think about it."

"You probably know more about that rocking bed
than your brother." Evelyn was right, of course, and
what I did know was that people who had been in an
iron lung as long as Phylllis had were not very success-
ful with the rocking bed. What they called *pulmonary
atrophy* had set in too long before.

"All right," I said. "Maybe."

Earlier that morning, I had been upstairs sitting
on the top step while my parents had been in the living room talking with Emmett. This was how I heard
about the experiment. I crept halfway down and listened to the whole conversation about how they had
tried once before, earlier in the spring, but it hadn't
worked. But this time they were going to try a new
way. There were drugs to make her relax and they
would immediately put her on a rocking bed that
would tilt her up and down and let gravity help force
air in and out of her lungs. The Kellers, especially
Phyllis, wanted Emmett to be there. Not me. But I
felt that I deserved to be there. But I knew there was
no way I could ask or push this. I even knew the drug

they would use to relax her. It was an antianxiety drug. Lex-something or other.

Emmett had already gone over by the time I got hold of Evelyn. The Kellers wanted him there before the team of doctors and specialists arrived.

I was eating a grape Popsicle and standing in our backyard with the hose, watering one of our stupid little trees, when I heard cars rolling into the Kellers' gravel driveway. I jammed the last bit of the Popsicle into my mouth and, using both hands, twisted the nozzle on the hose to stop the water. Right then I decided I was going. I knew that there was this huge new bush by the window of the sunroom. No one would see me if I just crouched down beneath the windowsill. Yes, it was sneaky. Yes, it was spying. But I was a good spy, I rationalized. After all, I was Saint Georgie. I remembered the sermon the minister at our church preached about being a witness. To witness was a Christian act of belief and faith. So I wasn't a spy at all. I wasn't a communist. I was a Christian witness, except, of course, for the small matter of my calling God a jerk.

There were four men. Two looked older and wore shirts and ties. But the other two were younger and more casually dressed. In addition to them, there were two nurses, Sally and another one I had never seen before. Dr. Keller was there, but not Mrs. Keller, and then there was Emmett. Dr. Keller had a pretty loud voice, so I heard him introducing Emmett to all of them. I couldn't catch all their names, but I did hear him say something about how so-and-so and so-and-so were "respiratory therapists." There was the rocking bed set up, and I saw Dr. Keller go over and show Emmett something about it. He tipped it so it rocked back and forth.

The thing that struck me is that no one was paying much attention to Phyllis. They had removed most of the mirror from the sides of the iron lung, but there was still one left on the ceiling so she could watch everything. And I had a pretty clear view of her face, but thank goodness she couldn't see me. She didn't look at all nervous. In fact, she looked completely calm and there was almost an expression of happy anticipation.

"OK," Dr. Keller said cheerfully. "I think we all know the drill. Places, everyone!" What was this, I thought, a play? I really did not like Dr. Keller at all.

Emmett was at the foot of the machine. He was turning some dials. He didn't even look at Phyllis. Didn't say a word!

"Sally, I believe you're first," Dr. Keller said.

Sally came up with a hypodermic needle and reached through one of the ports. I looked at Phyllis's face in the mirror. She didn't even flinch. One doctor stood by the rocking bed. The other doctor stood near Phyllis's head. He was at least speaking to her. One of the respiratory therapists was stationed near the midpoint of the iron lung. On a table was a box and I could see the words *cardio resuscitator* on its side. The other nurse was fiddling with it while Sally, finished with the shot, went over to another table where there was always this tall box with a panel of dials and displays that monitored Phyllis's vital signs.

I suddenly saw Phyllis's mouth move. I tried to hear what she was saying. Then Dr. Keller said in a loud voice, "Your heart is not going to stop, Phyllis, and you are not going to be brain-dead."

And Phyllis replied in a surprisingly strong voice, "But if I am, you know . . ." Then I couldn't hear the rest of what she said, but I saw Dr. Keller's face turn white. I felt something squirm inside me. Like maybe I really shouldn't be here, and what would Mom and

Dad say if they knew? Then I heard Dr. Keller say, "None of that nonsense, Phyllis. It's not going to stop." But Phyllis's eyes had closed. It looked as if she were sleeping.

"Ready for the intubation, Dr. Samuelson?" Dr. Keller said.

I noticed now that the doctor named Samuelson, who was standing at Phyllis's head, was wearing rubber gloves. With the help of one of the respiratory guys, he opened her mouth, and I saw them stick a long, thin tube in. The tube connected to an oxygen tank.

"All right, Emmett. You ready?"

It looked to me as if Emmett's hands were shaking as he turned a dial. Suddenly the whooshings decreased to barely a whisper. "Real slow," Dr. Samuelson was saying. "We'll let her get used to that for a couple of minutes, and then you can adjust the rate."

Sally, monitoring the vital signs panel, gave a report: "Pulse steady. Heart rate good."

"All right, Emmett, you can start decreasing the rate now," Dr. Samuelson said.

Now there was a real change in the sound of the beast. The horrible rhythm of the whooshings dissolved into a new beat. Very slow, very menacing.

"Pressure decrease, go down two-tenths," Dr.

Samuelson said. Another change in the beast: the breaths were shallower, the whooshing even quieter. Within another two minutes, a strange hush enveloped the room. The throbbing, panting machine was almost completely silent as it operated at a minimum level.

Now I watched as the two respiratory therapists began to unlock the hinges. For the first time, I would see all of Phyllis. They slid her out. I gasped. Her body was shriveled to the size of a tiny kid. The skin draped on her bones like a transparent fabric. Around her right thigh was a belt with a sensor. So this was how she moved the mirror! This was Ralph. The contact for the sensor had been disconnected.

When the therapist picked her up from the bed of the iron lung, she was completely limp. She didn't look unconscious exactly, nor did she look dead. Her weeny little legs flopped over his arms, and her body was plastered against the therapist's chest like a wet leaf. There was nothing human about her. It was deeply disturbing, but I could not look away. The therapist quickly moved her to the rocking bed. They had barely gotten her into the rocking bed when the first spasm came. I watched, horrified, as her legs began to jerk. Her back arched in a terrible contortion, and her face was pulled into a ghoulish mask. This was not television news. This was not a picture in a newspaper. Despite all my research, this was far worse than I could have ever imagined. The articles never told you about this kind of stuff. I wanted to stop looking. I really did. It was disgusting. But I was disgusted with myself for staying there and looking at this. I wanted someone to come and take me away. I felt ashamed. In the back of my throat, an icky sweetness surged, and then the overwhelming smell of grape. I vomited and then stared in disbelief. There were purple-colored scrambled eggs on my sneakers. The odor was so strong, I was sure they smelled it inside, but I didn't wait to find out.

When Emmett came home, I was still in the backyard hosing down my sneakers. His shoulders were hunched and his hands jammed in his pockets. His face was absolutely white. I thought he would just rush right by me. But he didn't. I kept looking down. I prayed that he would not be able to tell from any look on my face that I had seen it all. *Maybe I didn't see it all,* I thought with sudden alarm. Maybe Phyllis had died. He stopped right in front of me, then grabbed me tight and hugged me. And all he said was, "Goddamn, goddamn, goddamn."

I was really scared, but I looked up. "Did she die?"

"No, that would have been too easy."

He let me go, went upstairs to his bedroom, and slammed the door. I was scared. Scared for everyone—for Phyllis, for Emmett, for me. But really I think I felt most scared, in a funny way, for Emmett. I had never seen Emmett like this, ever.

Chapter Twenty

To me it was sort of eerie the way "life" seemed to continue. I mean life for Phyllis and for Emmett. He kept going over there. Not quite as much since the preseason basketball practice schedule had been stepped up. It always did in the few weeks before school began. I had preseason nothing. So there was no excuse for me not to go over to Phyllis's, but I just couldn't, not after what I had seen. Nobody had found out about my spying, which I supposed was good, but I felt somehow different. I didn't feel as if I were quite the same person anymore and felt that somehow people might sense this. It was as if telltale shreds of those awful minutes clung to me, maybe even a smell of grape vomit. I knew for one thing that I would never ever again eat a grape Popsicle. The worst part of all was that I had actually gone over there thinking that I was doing some dumb Christian thing. I wasn't spying; I was witnessing! I thought witnessing it would make me more compassionate, not nauseous. I thought that through my compassion, I could understand Phyllis better, therefore help her more. But this just didn't happen. I only felt shame, disgust, and fear.

It was as if during those few minutes crouching under the windowsill, all my illusions had vanished. I felt old—terribly, freakishly old. Yes, I'd become a freak.

"Georgie! Georgie! Earth to Georgie!" I looked up. Mom had been standing practically in front of me, and I hadn't even noticed her, I was so lost in my thoughts. I looked up at her. Mom sighed. "Are you reading about polio again, Georgie? You've got to stop."

"No, no." I had the newspaper in front of me but was not really reading it. Just staring at it. She turned her head a fraction to one side and looked at me out of the corner of her eye. This was her suspicious look. "So," she said with a kind of chirpiness that signaled she wasn't going to question me too closely, "you want to go get some new clothes for school?"

"Uh." I hesitated and looked at her, wondering if she noticed a difference in me. Did I still look like the same Georgie to her? Or was that old person inside me who had replaced the kid that was Georgie peeking out? Did she catch a glimpse of that old person? Or maybe she saw only the empty space where the child had been. I felt this deep anguish inside of me, this grieving for some part of me that I knew was gone.

Going school shopping didn't help. Usually I loved buying new clothes for school. I couldn't wait for the weather to turn cold so I could wear my new fall outfits. But all afternoon in the department stores, I stood in front of mirrors in plaid skirts and denim jumpers and felt as if I were looking at a ghost of myself. "Honestly, Georgie," Mom finally said, "you've been so quiet all afternoon. Are you feeling all right?"

"Not exactly," I said slowly.

"What's wrong?"

"I don't know. I guess I'm not quite feeling myself." The truth of this seemingly casual answer nearly knocked me over. That icky grape smell rose up inside me again. "Mom, I think I might throw up."

"Oh, dear! Oh, dear!"

She rushed me off to the ladies' room. I went into the stall by myself. I retched, but nothing came out. I started crying, not loudly, but certainly wetly.

"You all right, honey?" Mom called into the stall.

"Yeah! Yeah! I'll be fine. Just a minute."

When I came out, she clapped her hand on my forehead. "You don't feel feverish," she whispered with a trace of relief, then added, "No stiff neck?"

"No, Mom. I don't have polio!"

"Must have been something you ate. You'll feel a lot better if you can bring it up."

This was my parents' standard response to vomiting. I hated throwing up more than anything in the world. Usually I would rather not feel better than to have to go through the hideousness of having that tsunami of vomit rush out of my mouth. But this time I thought that my mother had a point. Now I wished I could have thrown up that whole experience. I wished that I could throw up that creepy older person who had invaded me when I watched Phyllis being weaned. But nothing came up. Nothing at all.

"Feel better?" Mom asked.

"Sort of."

When we got home, I carefully unpacked all my new clothes from the tissue paper and hung them in my closet. The plaid skirt had a cardigan sweater that went with it that was trimmed in the same plaid. It was really a cute outfit. A perfect first-day-of-school outfit, if the darned temperature would go below ninety.

Chapter Twenty-one

I hadn't been over to Phyllis's for a week. Not since the weaning attempt. Supposedly nothing had changed. She was back in the iron lung, for good, I guess. But I felt I had changed, and for me, Phyllis had changed as well. It scared me. It's not exactly accurate to say until that horrible day I had only thought of Phyllis as a head sticking out of a machine because I hadn't seen her whole body. I suppose I had just imagined that the rest of her body was normal-looking even though she had told me that time that her spine was all tangled. I still thought of the polio as most damaging to her ability to breathe. I could never have imagined that her body would look so weird. I kept thinking that if I went over there, all I would think about was this beautiful head attached to a deformed body. So in a sense on that day we had both become freaks of sorts. But Phyllis had called and asked me to come over that afternoon with another small world after Emmett left for basketball practice. I told her about the Orion one and how it wasn't done. She didn't mind. She just said how great it would be to see a work in progress. It was still pretty movable. I would just bring the first level, the sea one. I hadn't attached the waves Orion would walk on to the land.

On my way over, Emmett came jogging out of the grove, almost bumping into me, with the weirdest look on his face. He was sort of laughing to himself and looked quite pleased, but his face was the usual bright red it got when he was embarrassed. Needless to say, I was very curious, but he was in too much of a hurry. As I was about to come into the sunroom, where Phyllis was, I heard Sally talking.

"That's what you call flirting? Whatcha trying to do with that boy, gal?"

I stopped to listen, thinking that might explain why he was blushing like crazy. I once said that there should be a lipstick color called Emmett's Embarrassment Red, or maybe Emmett's Shame. He didn't think blushing was funny, and Dad tried not to laugh when I said this, but Mom and I were howling. So when I heard Sally say this thing about flirting, it didn't take me long to put two and two together. The romance must have made some progress. Maybe a little beyond first base, like an inch. But I, of course, pretended I hadn't heard them and just set down my diorama.

"Just having fun," Phyllis replied to Sally. I was standing in a hallway off the sunroom, and though she couldn't see me, I could see Phyllis's face in a big wall mirror. She looked deadly serious. In fact, she looked so serious it almost scared me. She had narrowed her eyes until they were just these little blue slits. I couldn't help but wonder what Sally had seen Phyllis and Emmett doing.

"Did you have him wear the rubber gloves in the port?" Sally asked.

"Sure," Phyllis said.

"I didn't see any when he left, and he sure did skedaddle out of here."

"Maybe he wore them home." Phyllis laughed harshly. "A souvenir of good times."

"Don't go talking slutty now."

I coughed slightly to announce my arrival.

"Well, Saint Georgie." Phyllis sounded sweet as pie now, and her eyes were no longer those little blue slits. "What do you have there? Another diorama?"

"Yep. It's a myth."

"Which one?"

"Orion, but it's just the first level."

"You mean it's going to be on different floors or stories?"

"Yeah, because his life was kind of made up of three different parts." I explained quickly the Orion myth and held up the seascape so it reflected in the mirrors.

"Oh, my goodness, such detail," Phyllis said. "Look at this, Sally."

Sally came over, and Phyllis kept exclaiming about the detail. "You've even got the little baby and his mother's crown and the father's trident . . . so when does he get to the sky?"

"When he dies."

"And what is it that kills him?"

"A scorpion. But first he goes blind."

"How does he go blind?"

"Oh, he falls in love with this girl. That's in the next part I have to build. He walks across islands to one called Chios. And he falls in love with the king's daughter, Merope. And the king makes a deal with him that he would let her marry him if first Orion would rid the island of animals, 'cause, you know, Orion was this mighty hunter. But the king reneged on the deal. Orion got mad and went to get the girl, and the king blinded him."

"End of story, eh?"

"Not exactly. He stumbled around blind for a while, then regained his sight and even found another true love."

"You don't say!" Phyllis exclaimed.

"And then finally a scorpion stung him in the heel and then he died."

"Life's tragic!" she said almost gaily. There was something very weird in the way she said it that made Sally and me look at each other. "Are you going to put Scorpio in your diorama?"

"Not in the sky part. Orion and Scorpio never appear in the sky at the same time, same season."

"You need anything else, Phyllis?" Sally asked, shifting her attention.

"Nope," Phyllis replied quickly. She slid her eyes toward me and gave a slightly impatient look as if she were anxious for Sally to leave. I felt a little tremor of excitement. Was she going to tell me something about why Emmett was blushing? Had there been some action with Ralph? Second base? Phyllis after all had told me herself that although her motor nerves were destroyed, her sensory nerves were all right. So that patch where Ralph resided in her thigh was one of the few motor nerves that worked—and how far was it from Ralph to . . . ? I cut off the thought. In another two seconds, I would be blushing as hard as Emmett.

Phyllis watched in her mirrors as Sally went through the doors of the sunroom to the kitchen.

She breathed a sigh of relief, or rather, the machine breathed it for her. "Phew! I thought she'd never leave."

"She's so nice," I said.

"Yeah, but there's always some nurse around. I do need my privacy, now and then."

"You want me to go?" I asked.

"Oh, no. Don't get me wrong. I like my privacy with my friends." Then she paused. "Especially with Emmett."

I took a deep breath. "Are you like, uh, sort of . . . uh, liking each other?"

Phyllis's eyes crinkled up, and she made a little giggle noise. "Well." She gave me that crafty look she often had. "I'm trying to figure some things out, Georgie, and maybe you can help."

"Sure. What?" This was what I had hoped. But ever since that one day, I had the feeling that Phyllis really felt I understood her better than a lot of people, like her parents for instance. I sensed that unlike her parents, Phyllis knew somehow that I had made a separation in my mind between her and the machine. I saw her as a person in her own right. I wasn't quite expecting her first question, however.

"Has Emmett ever done more than kiss a girl before?"

What was I supposed to say? I was sure he hadn't, but I felt as if I shouldn't exactly be talking about my brother's love life or nonexistent love life. Still I had to try my best to answer her. This was Phyllis, not the machine. She was seeming whole to me now. More whole than ever before. This was the Phyllis that I had vowed to protect. And I had honestly begun to forget about those scrawny little legs, or Phyllis the wet leaf, or Phyllis the freak. "If he has, I wouldn't know. I mean I'd be the last to know. But to tell you the truth, I really doubt it."

"Well," she said with a new light dancing in her eyes, "how would you like to be the first to know?"

There was something definitely weird about this conversation. I started to get a little bit scared. And I thought briefly that maybe I shouldn't be the first to know. But I told myself that this was part of my mission. "Well, I don't know. I mean, I guess if you want to tell me—yeah, OK."

"Well, I won't tell you everything, but it was a little more than just kissing!"

I really did not want to hear about any of this, and I didn't know what to say. I wasn't sure really why she was telling me, except that she trusted me and that she knew I believed in her, not simply the machine that ran her. It did seem funny to me when I thought about all the time I had spent worrying about Emmett's social life and now here I was in a front-row seat having it served up on a platter with all the trimmings. Still, I was at a complete loss. "So?" Phyllis pressed.

"Uh, so, I guess that's nice. I mean, you didn't mind?"

"No, not at all. As a matter of fact—how should I put this—I encouraged him."

"You did?" I don't know why I sounded so surprised. It was almost impossible to think of Emmett making the first move.

"I did, and I'm really worried that maybe he doesn't like me as much as I like him, and you know

I'm not such a great date, after all. And all this basketball stuff."

"Oh, that is a big deal for Emmett."

"So I gather." There was an indifference in her voice. I felt I had to somehow defend Emmett.

"You see, it's not just basketball. A lot depends on it for college. I mean, this is the time the scouts come around and if he can get a basketball scholarship, well, that's really, really good."

"Why?"

Her reply caught me by surprise. "Why?" I repeated. "Well, it's just like, you know . . . we don't have that much money. For two of us to go to college, it will cost Mom and Dad so much."

"Oh," said Phyllis, as if she suddenly had the whole picture on us Masons. I was left wondering if I should have said that stuff about money. Mom always said it wasn't very polite to discuss money in public. But Phyllis seemed so clueless, I guess because her family had so much money, it was hard for her to imagine people who didn't have enough, or quite enough.

"Well, I suppose basketball is as tough to compete against as another girl or a prettier girl." Phyllis sighed. The beast made her sighs sound hollow, not really like sighs at all.

I felt a panic well up in me. "Oh, but Phyllis there's no one at Westridge High School half as pretty as you. I mean you're so pretty."

"As pretty as Betty?" She slid her eyes slyly in my direction. "Or wait—who was that girl who Orion loved—the princess?"

"Merope?"

"Yeah, Merope. Greek goddess. As pretty as her?"

"I'm not sure what she looked like, but you're definitely prettier than Betty."

"Well, there's a problem," she said.

"What's the problem?"

"Promise not to tell anybody."

"Cross my heart and . . ." I could have bitten off my tongue for starting to say that stupid thing.

"Hope to die?" She smiled, a hard glittery smile. "Hoping is easy."

A dread began to swim up in me. I shrugged to try and cover it. "I-I don't know wh-wh-wh-what you mean." I had started stuttering again. This was not at all how my mission was supposed to go. Was she really talking about dying? A few seconds before, it had been about kissing—or a little more than kissing— Emmett, for God's sake.

"What's wrong?" she asked. I hesitated. "Come

on, Georgie," she coaxed in a sweet sympathetic voice. "Is what's going on here too much for you?"

"No! What do you mean, what's too much?"

"I mean that I'm sick—that I could die."

"Did you almost die when they tried weaning you?"

"I'm not sure. I never know. No one tells me much. I just know it didn't work." She paused. "And Georgie." She flashed a mirror that she seldom used. It had some slight magnification in it and both our faces seemed huge and crowded together on its surface. Her eyes had turned a sharp, brittle blue. "Georgie, it didn't hurt. That's one thing I can tell you."

"It didn't hurt—not breathing?"

"No. In fact, it felt good in a way. Even though it was scary and even though I have so little feeling, you know the weird thing is I can feel air—I mean real air. Not this pumped stuff that swirls around me. It's sort of a beautiful place that I get to live in for a while."

"A beautiful place?" I said. "You mean like my small world of *The Martian Chronicles*."

"Yes, sort of. Maybe it's like Martians—the stars could shine through them. Yes, the stars shine through me, and I am folded into the wind." She closed her eyes as she talked now. "It's like I am dying, but I feel so connected to life. Isn't that odd? I mean the iron lung is supposed to be the thing that connects me to life, to breathing, but when I'm almost not breathing, just on the edge of dying . . ." She paused a moment.

I didn't know what to say. This was a huge idea. How can someone feel so alive when they are almost dying? Usually big ideas excited me, but this one scared me.

"You know, maybe my life is like Orion's—three levels. This is my second level, here in the Creature, floating somewhere between earth and sky on this manufactured air."

I scratched my head and tried to think about these bizarre things Phyllis had just said.

"I'm not sure of any of this. Uh . . . you're not really like Orion."

Phyllis laughed at this, then began speaking again. "OK, then think of it this way. A person falls into the sea and cannot swim and knows that she is drowning. Do you think that at some point that person just opens her mouth and lets the ocean rush in, falls in love with the very thing that is killing her?

Like if you would fall off a cliff, would you fall in love with the falling?"

I started to feel that she shouldn't be talking to me like this. Phyllis must have sensed that I was thinking this was all very creepy.

"Oh, never mind," she said brightly. "Listen, I have a great idea for a diorama for you to make."

"What's that?" I asked, relieved that we were talking about something else.

"How about Snow White?"

"Snow White?" I asked.

"Yeah, you know, 'Mirror mirror on the wall, who's the fairest of them all?'"

All the mirrors began pivoting madly, rotating and sparkling with Phyllis's face. She was flashing smiles, winking one eye; even her dimples were twinkling. It was like an ambush—an ambush of Phyllises. And yeah, I did feel panic. Oddly enough, this panic was not for me, not for Phyllis, but for Emmett. I was scared for Emmett. This little-more-than-kissing did not seem at all romantic but dreadful in some way. How could everything change so quickly?

Nonetheless, I felt I had to be committed to my mission and charge ahead. My mission had been to be truthful. Never to lie to Phyllis. That was still my mission. After all, I'd given up God for Phyllis. But I wasn't sure if this was enough. It seemed that there was more at stake here than I had thought. More risk, more danger. But I wasn't sure what it was.

In the last days before school started, there was a beautiful stretch of cool, clear evenings. Emmett and Phyllis were together constantly, and I was rarely included in their star watching. It happened to be an exceptional time for watching, especially if you were like Phyllis with this weird talent of hers for seeing color.

One night just before school started, I decided to go over uninvited. Cygnus was absolutely blazing up there. I had even made potato-chip sandwiches because Phyllis had once asked about them. So with my snacks packed in my school lunch box, I made my way through the grove. When I came up on the patio, they didn't even notice me. Their heads were very close together as Emmett was adjusting the scope to Phyllis's eye. He had even built a little extension piece onto it so it could dip right down and fit close to her eye.

"You see," he was whispering, "if you get it out of focus a little bit, sometimes it actually helps bring the colors out more." Phyllis said something I couldn't hear, and they both giggled and Emmett ran his fingers through her hair.

"Oh, Saint Georgie!"

"I . . . I . . . I brought you some potato-chip sandwiches." I was sorry I had come. It was so embarrassing to barge in on them like this.

"Oh, how sweet. I've been dying to try one ever since you told me about them. Oh, Emmett, you'll help me, won't you?"

"Sure thing."

I opened the lunch box and handed him one. He crouched by Phyllis and began to break off little pieces. He was feeding her! I felt I shouldn't be watching. It was so . . . so private.

"Mmmm good!" Phyllis said. She was still looking through the eyepiece. "Oh, Emmett, I'm starting to see the colors."

Please, please, I thought, *don't say neon grape. I'll throw up.*

"Rumpelstiltskin gold!" she sighed. "Yes, someone is spinning gold up there in that beautiful place."

"That beautiful place," Emmett echoed.

I almost gave a start when I heard those two words. It was bad enough the first time she had said it when she was talking about the weaning. But now it was worse. It was as if she and Emmett had stolen them from me for their own private reasons. *Beautiful place* were my words for the ancient city Ray Bradbury had written about.

And then Emmett got this dreamy look on his face. The two of them seemed to have a special knowledge of the beautiful place, but I was the one who had named it. It was my small world, not theirs. Why had I shared it with Phyllis, and why had I brought over the Orion one? I suddenly felt a fierce sense of possession about my small worlds. It was almost as if they had been invaded. In my head I seethed, *Get out of my small worlds! Get your own damn worlds.*

Emmett and Phyllis whispered some more. Sometimes the words were intelligible, but they had no meaning for me. It was as if they were speaking a private language and we were in two different worlds. They were nestled in this little cocoon of light and stars and colors. I knew I didn't belong on the patio. I picked up my lunch box and left. No one said good night. They weren't being rude or anything. They just didn't notice.

✦ ✦ ✦

When I got back, I went right to work on the second level for Orion. I completed the staircase of waves and was now at the fun part of landscaping the earth. I used some more moss from the grove, which I could keep alive if I spritzed it every other day or so, and then I had these tiny model trees that are used in architectural models. By the time I went to bed, I had built half the forest. The next thing I would have to do was make Orion the hunter. I had a patch of fake fur that I would sling over his shoulder, like an animal pelt of something he killed, and I would string a belt with itty-bitty sparkly beads. It would be beautiful. But I was too tired now. So I went to bed.

That feels squishy, but nice, *I thought, looking down at my toes. They were slightly submerged in the green blue gel.* It hasn't set yet, but I'll try it. *I took a tentative step on the waves staircase.* Like Orion, *I thought,* I'll become a wave-walker! *I was determined to get to land and help Orion. I carried a piece of fur for him. The small trees that had somehow grown huge shook as the ground on which I stood began to reverberate with a thunderous thumping. The trees shook, and many of them crashed.* "They're only little fake ones!" *I cried out.* "Model trees for architects! Not real life. What is happening?" *A figure streaked by half-naked. Orion! And then from deep in the tremulous woods, the very woods I had anchored in the clay base, came an immense boar, followed by a lion.* This is all wrong! *I wanted to shout.* All wrong. You are the hunter, not the hunted! *Not yet.* "NO!"

The sound of my own voice woke me up. I sat straight up in bed. A cool breeze was blowing through the window, the coldest of the entire summer. I was shivering, but my arms and face were slick with sweat. I got up and, as if still in a dream, walked across my bedroom to the window by my desk where the diorama sat, but I didn't look at it. Maybe I was frightened. I reached up to pull down the window sash. Outside, the Milky Way undulated like a ribbon in the sky, but I caught the red glow of that heart, Antares, rearing high in the night. Scorpio had risen to his highest point in the summer sky. I shivered and closed the window as if to shut out the deadly venom that dripped from his claws.

Chapter Twenty-two

Five days later, I was off to Crooked Creek School, and Emmett to Westridge High with all his old friends. Except for Evelyn I didn't know a soul at Crooked Creek. It was good that I was one of the first kids on the bus. It would have been terrible getting on toward the end of the bus route and having to face all those new kids in one big clump. I did not go straight to the back, because I knew that those were the seats the kids really liked the best. It was where they could cut up and flirt and tell dirty jokes without the bus driver hearing. There was no chance of Evelyn being on this bus, as her house wasn't on this route. So I sat right down in the seat directly behind the bus driver and scrunched myself as close to the side as possible. I had one goal: not to be noticed.

It wasn't long before lots of kids began to get on. At one stop, about six girls came onboard chattering away, their ponytails bouncing. They headed right toward the rear of the bus, clomping down the aisle in their new saddle shoes. I could see in the driver's rearview mirror other kids scattering from the coveted rear seat as these girls approached. In addition to the saddle shoes, they were dressed almost identically. Every single one of them wore a short-sleeved Ship'n' Shore blouse either with a skirt or jumper. They were dressed in the latest cool styles. I was sort of glad that Evelyn wasn't on this bus. I didn't even want to imagine what her first-day-of-school outfit would look like. They also were all fiddling with the little glass spheres that hung on gold chains from their necks. These were mustard seeds that were enclosed in glass balls, and they were the latest rage, but mostly among high-school girls. All of them were huddled together whispering now.

"Hey, sit down, back there!" the bus driver yelled. One girl had stood up to join the huddle.

We got to school way too quickly. All the girls

rushed forward before I could even get out of my seat. I knew as soon as I got to school that I would hate it. I didn't like the school building, which was dark and old-looking, and all the Mustard Seeds were in my class.

Evelyn was in my class, too, however. Her bus had arrived before ours, and there she was in Room 22 standing by her desk in the same laundry-bag dress she had worn the first day I met her at the library. It had these huge patch pockets on the front that she claimed she liked because she could put stuff in them. She could have gone camping and had a week's worth of provisions in those pockets. And as if the dress wasn't bad enough, she had added a beret! I guess to cover up the perm that still had several inches to go before the last frizzy traces would be history. "Wanna sit next to me?" she asked. "I saved you a place. Teacher said we could sit wherever we want."

"Sure," I said. I knew right then that my fate had been sealed. My destiny fixed. I would remain on the fringes, if that, of the popular kids. But I felt a certain defiant pleasure at the same time. I didn't want to be with those Mustard Seed girls. They weren't nearly as neat as my old friends anyhow.

We each had to stand up and say our names and

one thing about ourselves that no one would know just by looking at us. For instance you couldn't stand up and say, 'My name is Carole and I have straight blond hair.' The teacher, who had a face like a prune—dried, not canned—began with the Mustard Seeds.

"My name is Amy Moncton, and I like fashion."

"My name is Patty Werthheimer, and"—giggle, giggle—"I like fashion, too." By the time it came to the fourth Mustard Seed, the Prune said, "No more fashion. Think of something original."

"My name is Linda Dorf."

"Dwarf?" one of the boys said. There was a roar of laughter. This did not faze Linda. She spun around and glared at him. "No, the name is Dorf, *D-o-r-f.*" If that had been me, I would have vaporized on the spot. But these Mustard Seeds were something else. Then she cocked her head almost flirtatiously and said, "In addition to liking fashion, I think Grace Kelly is the most beautiful woman in the world." I dreaded when my turn would come. I frantically tried to think of something I could say about myself. Evelyn was next, then me. She stood up, engulfed by her dress. She had taken off the beret because you were not permitted to wear hats in class. Her hair, though somewhat improved, still looked pretty bad. It was as if the electrified frizzle was hooked up to a lower voltage. "My name is . . ." But she spoke so low that even though I was sitting next to her, I could hardly hear a word. I suddenly felt terribly sorry for her. I realized that Evelyn, who was so confident about a lot of things, was absolutely terrified now. This was a new school for her as well.

"Speak up, dear," the Prune said. As soon as a teacher calls you "dear," you know you're in trouble. You become an instant object of pity in the eyes of everyone else in the classroom. "My name is Evelyn Winkler, and I like reading books." She sat down very quickly. I couldn't help but look at her now. Everything was wrong with Evelyn Winkler. She wore glasses that belonged on the face of a grandmother, not even a mother. Her name was an old-lady name. Who named a baby Evelyn? And her dress looked like it had belonged to some very dowdy grown-up woman. The kind of woman that maybe works in a city office inspecting records. I once had to go to the department of motor vehicles with my mother, and there was the grayest bunch of little old ladies with gray hair and bad permanents behind the high counters shoving forms through little slotted windows. I mean, even my grandmother dressed more fashionably than Evelyn.

But now it was my turn. "My name is Georgia Louise Mason. But people call me Georgie." I began to sit down.

"One minute, Georgie," the Prune said. "Don't you want to tell us something about yourself that we wouldn't otherwise know?"

"I just did."

The Prune blinked. "What did you tell us?"

I was halfway between standing and sitting. "I told you that people call me Georgie. You didn't know that before." There were some giggles from the back of the class.

Then I heard someone whisper, "Her name, is that all there is to her? Wow!"

"No, triple wow. She has three names!"

There was a ripple of giggles from the back of the room. I felt something begin to wither inside me. Then to add insult to injury, the Prune sank me with the *d* word. "That's true, dear, but could you tell us something more?"

So I blurted out the first thing that came to my mind. "My next-door neighbor is in an iron lung and she's very beautiful and fashionable!" I plopped down in my seat. There was a collective gasp that swept through the room like a rogue wind and then giggling shrieks.

"Quiet! Quiet! Class!" The Prune slammed her palm on the desk. "There is nothing funny about being in an iron lung. Nothing at all."

Oh, Lord, what had I done? Why had I ever said that? I just closed my eyes. I wanted to dissolve. I wanted to vanish.

Arithmetic was our first class. The Prune was trying to figure out what we knew. So she put some fractions up on the board and then wrote them as decimal points and wanted to know if we knew how to do that. So she put up another fraction. No one raised a hand. I knew, but I wasn't going to raise my hand. I looked over at Evelyn. She knew too. I could see her writing it on a piece of paper, but she wasn't going to raise her hand either. Safety in silence.

Things did not improve at recess. The Mustard Seeds had brought jump ropes. They were very good. They knew all the jump-rope rhymes.

"Cinderella, dressed in yellow,
went upstairs to kiss a fellow,
made a mistake
and kissed a snake.

How many doctors
did it take?"

Then they all started counting. Amy Moncton
was jumping as her mustard seed glinted in the sun
and flopped rhythmically against her chest. Evelyn
and I just watched.

"Aren't you broiling in that outfit of yours?" a
Mustard Seed asked me as we lined up to go back into
school.

"I'm fine."

She turned to the other girls clustered around her
and began giggling.

The second day of school was just as awful. A girl
named Charlene pointed at my feet and said, "Oh,
look, she's wearing those socks again—anklets!" All
of them had thick socks that rolled over, making a
nice cuff at the top of their brand-new saddle shoes.
I did not have saddle shoes. I wore sneakers because
they were more comfortable, and thin socks. I was
simply mortified. When I got home that day no one
was there because Mom had an after-school meeting.

I decided to call Phyllis. "Phyllis?" I felt this huge lump swelling in my throat."

"What's wrong, Georgie?"

"Everything. Can I come over?"

"Sure."

She was in the sunroom. The tears were leaking down my face.

"What is it, Georgie?"

"Phyllis, school is so awful. I tried, I really did. I know it's only been two days, but these girls are mean and horrible. They think they are so great. They all dress a certain way and they think I'm weird. And they all wear mustard seeds and saddle shoes with thick socks and I . . . I . . . d-d-d-don't even own saddle shoes." Then I felt so terrible. I mean, here was poor Phyllis who two weeks before had had some sort of seizure when they tried to wean her. Imagine crying to a young beautiful teenage girl in an iron lung about not having a mustard seed and saddle shoes and thick socks.

"Oh, Georgie." There was the hollow sound she made when she sighed.

At that moment, Emmett came in.

"Emmett, take this girl out and buy her some saddle shoes, thick socks, and a mustard-seed pendant."

"Huh?" Emmett said. He looked at me

Sally had come in and said that she knew there was a sale going on at L.S. Ayres department store.

"You mean, all the way downtown?" Emmett said.

"Yes!" Phyllis said. "Come on, Emmett. This is important."

I was still snuffling wetly, hiccuping and stuttering out rags of sentences. It was fairly ridiculous to think that a mustard seed and saddle shoes could have enhanced my appearance that much, or my dignity in the eyes of my Crooked Creek peers.

"OK," Emmett said. So we were off.

"Oh, yes," the saleslady was saying. "All the girls want to wear mustard seeds. How they ever get that little tiny seed into the glass ball, I'll never know." Emmett and I were standing at the jewelry counter in the department store, looking at the display of the mustard seeds trapped in what appeared to be solid spheres of glass. "I've sold over fifty of these in the last week alone. They are the rage."

"So which one do you want, Georgie?"

"There's quite a price range," the lady offered. "It depends on the quality of the glass and the size of the seed, and of course if you want a gold or silver-plated chain."

"We better go for one of the less expensive ones," Emmett said. I stood staring at them. I certainly couldn't tell the difference. But suddenly I didn't even care. "I'm not sure," I said.

"Come on, decide," Emmett urged.

"I can't."

"Look, this is not an earthshaking decision." The saleslady walked away.

"Yeah, that's just the point," I muttered.

"What do you mean?"

"Just that I don't think that me buying this is going to change anything."

"Whoever said it was?" Emmett asked. He looked confused.

"Look, never mind. I don't want it. The saddle shoes you got me are fine. Enough."

I didn't want to explain it all to Emmett, but all of a sudden I wasn't so sure I wanted to be included with the mustard-seed girls. As a matter of fact, coming home in the car, I thought I might wait a day or two to wear my new saddle shoes. I could just start with the socks tomorrow and my old sneakers.

✦ ✦ ✦

By the end of the second week of school, one good thing had happened. They changed the bus route a little bit. So now Evelyn was on my bus. At least I had someone to talk to. We avoided the Mustard Seeds as much as possible. During recess we discovered this big anthill at the edge of the playground, and this was where we had our longest talks, just looking at this anthill. It sounds dumb, I know, but Evelyn made it all very interesting. She knew a lot about ants, it turned out, because her grandfather was an ant specialist and taught at Indiana University in the ant department or something like that. There was a big word for what he did. One of those "ology" words. But it was just easier to think of it as ants. So we would sit there and poke *T* sticks into the holes, just to disturb them a little bit, not to wreck their houses or whatever it was under there, but just to stir them up a bit. Then a few would come trailing out. Evelyn started saying things like—"That's a minor worker," or "That's a major worker," or "Those over there are soldiers."

"They all look the same to me."

"Nope—all different castes."

"What do you mean by castes?"

"Just different groups in the one big group. They

all do different things in the anthill. Some work; some fight. Some just sit around and make babies. Well, really only one—the queen. She's got the biggest ovaries. So that's why she's the queen."

"Ovaries?"

Evelyn looked at me. "You surely know what ovaries are?"

"Sort of, but not exactly."

"Women have them. They have the eggs. Do you get your period yet?"

"The curse?"

"Yes."

"No, do you?"

"No."

I was so relieved! Evelyn continued talking. "You start to get it when your ovaries start sending out those eggs."

"Oh, yeah, I guess I knew that. But how come this ant is the queen? Aren't there other girl ants with ovaries?"

"Not as big as hers. Anatomy is destiny."

"Huh?"

"Just a saying. I don't really believe it. At least not with people. Probably it's true with ants."

"I don't know what you're talking about." This, of course, was what I liked about Evelyn. I could be completely honest with her.

"What don't you understand?"

"That thing you just said anatomy is."

"Destiny. It just means that some people think that if you are born with a penis"—I tried not to look surprised but I had never in my life heard this word spoken out loud—"that you can do certain things, get paid more, be a soldier. Do what is thought of as man kind of things, and if you are born with a vagina"— holy smoke! I could not believe this—"that you stay home, have kids, and cook. But it's not true, of course, because my mother is a doctor and she has a—" At that moment, the whistle blew for the end of recess. But as we got up to leave, Evelyn took the stick and bent over so that one or two of the ants crawled on to it. "See what I mean?" I prayed she wouldn't say the *v* or the *p* word again, because once a day was enough for me. "See this ant. He's a soldier. It's because he has huge jaws—sharp, too. They call them mandibles."

Mandibles, I thought. That's such a nice, decent-sounding word, unlike you-know-what and you-know-what.

Chapter Twenty-three

"Would you have taken Evelyn and me to the drive-in if Phyllis hadn't pressured you, Emmett?"

"What are you talking about?" We had just dropped Evelyn off at her house. It was a Friday afternoon, and Emmett had agreed to take us after school to a drive-in restaurant for a hamburger and a Coke.

"Well, would you have taken us if Phyllis hadn't asked you to?"

"That's not fair, Georgie. Phyllis doesn't pressure me to do anything."

"Hmmm." That was all I said, but he looked at me real funny.

There was a pretty long silence, and then Emmett said, "Look, Georgie, I think you should butt out of Phyllis's and my business."

"What business?" I said.

"Georgie! I just told you to butt out, for Christ's sake."

"You shouldn't use swears. Especially Jesus ones. Grandma would be very mad at you."

"Grandma is not here. Besides, I thought you didn't believe in God."

"Does Phyllis believe in God?" I suddenly asked.

"That's a non sequitur," Emmett said.

"What's a non seckyturd?" I giggled.

"The word is *non sequitur*. And it's Latin for 'does not follow logically,' and it's not nice for little girls to talk about turds."

This ticked me off. "I don't know Latin. Remember I'm just in the sixth grade, Mr. Smarty-Big-Guy-Center. And I wasn't talking about turds, and besides, in my opinion, talking about turds is less evil than saying Jesus-swears."

"Are you finished?"

"Yep."

"Is this any way to treat your brother who has just

so kindly agreed to take you and your very strange friend Evelyn Sinkler to a drive-in for a hamburger?"

"Winkler. The name is Winkler."

"Whatever. As I was saying—who so kindly agreed to take you to the drive-in on a Friday afternoon."

"I know you're embarrassed to be seen in our company. We're little twerps, and everybody there is a big-deal teenager—cheerleaders, basketball players, football players."

"I didn't say you were twerps. Yes, you are shorter than high-school kids. But I didn't say you were twerps."

"You said Evelyn was weird."

"Well, she is."

"Not when you get to know her."

"I guess I could say the same thing about Phyllis," he replied.

"What, she's not weird once you get to know her?" I asked.

"Not exactly. But she doesn't pressure me at all, and if you really knew her, you would understand that."

I just shut up.

Chapter Twenty-four

"Do stars make noise, Emmett?" Phyllis asked one evening. I was sitting not more than five feet away, but I might as well have been five hundred feet away for all the notice they took of me.

"No, not in space."

"Not even when they're born and when they die, like you were explaining about all that fire and explosion, the popping and the sizzling?"

"It's a vacuum out there," I piped up. But no one paid any attention to me.

"Sound needs air to transmit it."

"That's what I just said! It's a vacuum. No air, no sound." Still no response.

Phyllis waited awhile before she said anything. Then she smiled. "Well, you know how easy it is for me to see colors; I think I can hear stars—music."

"Star music?" Emmett asked. Both he and I were completely bewildered.

"Yeah, think of it like whales singing."

"Whales singing? I don't get it," Emmett said.

"They say whales sing, you know," Phyllis replied.

"Well, water transmits."

"But no one ever thought they did until someone listened with whatever they use to listen with underwater."

"Hmmm," Emmett said. "It's the old tree falling in the forest with no one to hear it."

"Not exactly." The mirrors flashed now, and the only reflections were those of Phyllis and my brother. "I am there to hear it in my place. Our beautiful place."

A strange conversation. One that made me feel not simply excluded but a little scared. Why did she have to say *our*. But this actually was the way it had been for a while now, ever since an evening a few days before school started when they were looking at the colors in Cygnus—the Rumpelstiltskin gold—and started talking about the Beautiful Place. I sensed that Emmett and Phyllis had crossed some invisible line.

They were someplace else. If I asked him a question about Phyllis, he'd just snap sometimes as if it were not just a simple question but more like an invasion. I was invading that precious space, crossing into some forbidden zone.

With Phyllis it was a little different. She never snapped at me, and she never seemed to mind me being there. In fact, she seemed hardly aware of my presence. So when I was there, I began to watch Phyllis very closely.

More and more I had that feeling that they were speaking in some kind of code. What started out as a simple conversation that I thought I understood on one particular night in late September turned into one of their coded ones. I felt left out, but this didn't really bother me as much as it usually would have. What really bothered me was that Emmett seemed to be completely drawn into the Beautiful Place and that it was part of their code. Phyllis, Emmett, and I were still like night pilgrims as we followed the trails of the constellations across the sky, but Phyllis and Emmett were wandering into a different night, and I wasn't really sure if I wanted to follow them.

✦ ✦ ✦

One day when I came over, Phyllis and Emmett stopped talking as soon as I came into the room. They looked guilty, as if I had caught them up to something. But I knew they hadn't been doing anything except talking—talking about their Beautiful Place. I just knew it. It was in that moment that I knew for certain that the Beautiful Place was a very dangerous place. It had been over a month since I had that dream, the terrible one when the hunter was the hunted one, where Orion, not yet blind, was being chased through the forests. But I thought of it now. I slid my eyes toward Emmett. His eyes were so still, so . . . so unseeing, I thought, and panic seized me. *He is as paralyzed as she is!* He suddenly looked completely helpless, and yet he didn't even know it. It seemed impossible. This was like watching a collision about to happen in slow motion, and there was nothing I could do to stop it.

That same night I took out my diary again.

How do you ask about something you don't want to know? I wrote. *What do you do when you find out what it is? Can I love P. but be scared of her at the same time? Why is P. so scary and E. so fragile? She is the sick one. He is the big strong one. Why do I have these questions that I*

can never ask? I don't simply feel left out now. I
just feel incredibly lonely and scared. Scared for
Emmett. What is she doing to him?

I stopped writing for a moment. I remembered that
the night I had that very bad dream, I had left Emmett
and Phyllis in a huff, mad that they had somehow
invaded my small world, the Ray Bradbury one of the
ancient city in *The Martian Chronicles,* the Beautiful
Place. I had felt that something had been trespassed,
abused. They had hijacked my small world and
turned it on its end. Turned it into something it was
never supposed to have been and in the process made
a sham of it. Now I felt a sense of violation again. This
time it was different. This time I felt that Emmett had
in some way been violated as well.

It would be several days before I saw Phyllis again.
The last time I had been there, I had been so afraid
that I hadn't wanted to go back. But I kept reading
over and over again what I had written in my diary,
and it was like when you say a name or a word over
and over. It begins to lose its meaning and just becomes

a jumble of nonsense sounds. The same thing had happened with the words in my diary. They became a little less believable each time I read them. So by the end of almost two weeks, I was thinking, *There's something wrong with me. Phyllis isn't dangerous. This beautiful world doesn't exist in real life. It's just some sort of joke between Phyllis and Emmett.* So I went over to visit her to prove this to myself. I honestly thought that it would be like waking up after a bad dream and turning the lights on. Everything would be all comfy and make sense.

"Hi, Georgie. Where've you been?" She was reading a book in "the Phyllis."

"Oh, just around."

"Busy with school, huh?"

I caught a glimpse of the cover. It looked like *The Martian Chronicles.* My whole gut lurched. The Beautiful Place again! I felt ambushed. All of the old terrors, the ones I had talked myself out of the last two weeks stormed in. I wanted to run. But I didn't. It was like being in a bad dream where your feet won't move. You just stand there, frozen.

"Yeah, busy with school," I lied. I hated myself for lying. Phyllis was trying to catch me in the mirrors, but I just couldn't look into them. So I looked toward Sally, who was massaging Phyllis's leg through the sealed port. It was then that I caught sight of the ribbon, a velvet ribbon, the kind old-fashioned girls sometimes wore around their necks with a locket on it. Except Phyllis didn't wear it around her neck. She wore it around Ralph, the muscle in her thigh. There were little windows beside the portholes, and when I first saw the bright blue velvet ribbon, I thought it was on Phyllis's arm. It was the first time I had seen her legs since the weaning, and now that one leg seemed even more shocking with the bright blue ribbon tied to her so-called thigh.

"Toothpicks, huh?" She laughed as she saw the shock on my face.

"Oh, I think they've beefed up a bit, Phyllis," Sally said. Phyllis just rolled her eyes.

"What's that thing around your leg?" The consonants were slipping away from me, the words left dangling.

"Your brother gave it to me—locket on a velvet ribbon. Isn't it pretty?"

I had been standing by the side of the iron lung, and it was almost as if *my* legs had turned to toothpicks. Or maybe noodles, I thought as they began to feel limp. How could I have ever thought that Phyllis was anything but fragile, that she could have any kind of power over Emmett? How could I have written those things in my diary?

Chapter Twenty-five

I began to feel as if pieces of my world were slipping away, were being inhaled one by one in the thousand breaths per hour of the iron lung. The velvet ribbon continued to lace its way through my dreams. And now I kept thinking about it against the backdrop of Phyllis on her last night as a healthy, walking American teenager, driving a sporty convertible through a drive-in restaurant in the wake of a handsome guy. A guy she could have gone to a prom with. He would have worn a tuxedo, or maybe a white dinner jacket if it had been May, with a carnation in his lapel. And she would have worn a prom dress with layers of tulle, a crushed bodice, maybe even strapless—who knows?—

with a corsage, a gardenia corsage pinned to her waist and a small beaded clutch bag. In the clutch would be a five-dollar bill, mad money, that she would never have to use because her date would be perfect, so no need to escape, call a cab, or whatever. There would be a pocket-size comb, a small atomizer of perfume, a scent that would go with the gardenia and not clash, a tube of lipstick with a fabulous name like Hot Pink Cha-Cha-Cha or Mango Evenings, and two breath mints.

I had to try and stop thinking about stuff like this. I had to stop worrying about Emmett. September slipped into October, and I spent more time with Evelyn. I didn't much like going to her house. Her mother was a lousy housekeeper. Maybe that was because she was a doctor. But you would have thought that with two doctors in the family, their house would have been more sanitary. There were dust bunnies all over the place, and the kitchen counters were greasy. Often when we went to get a snack from the fridge, we'd find some disgusting moldy thing. Her parents were hardly ever there. But two days a week we had to be there for Edith, Evelyn's seven-year-old sister, who was about twice as weird as Evelyn. Edith was even paler than Evelyn. Mercifully, their mother had not given Edith a permanent. She had some natural curl in her hair, and it fuzzed in a soft, dark fog around her face. She wore very thick glasses and sometimes had to wear a patch on one eye.

"Strabismus," Edith explained, pointing to her eye patch the first time I met her.

"Huh?" I said.

"Wandering eye," Evelyn offered.

"It's not so bad," Edith said. "They caught it in time. I just have to do these boring eye exercises, and the worst is that I can't read for more than fifteen minutes without taking a break and doing three sets of them." She held up a timer. Edith read very fat chapter books way beyond her grade level. She was reading *Little Women,* for Lord's sake, and I had only read it this past summer when I was bored out of my mind. I didn't think that Louisa May Alcott could hold a candle, as Dad would say, to Ray Bradbury.

That particular afternoon I had come over to see the ant colony project that Evelyn had done for the science fair the year before. She had pictures of it, not the whole thing anymore, because it took up too much room. Her grandfather had transported the colony in its aquarium down to Indiana University, but I had a feeling a few of the ants had hung around. I was always finding ants in their kitchen when we went to make snacks.

"You can stay for dinner," Evelyn said as we were going down the stairs. "Mom is coming home early."

"All right, I'll call my mom. I'm sure she won't mind."

Evelyn led me to a wall near the washer and dryer. There was a huge pile of clothes in a basket on top of the dryer with a note pinned on it with the word CLEAN. "Oh, finally!" Evelyn said. "I desperately need clean underpants. Down to my last pair." She burrowed into the mountain of laundry and pulled out several pairs of underpants that had daisies on them, along with some socks.

"How come the clean laundry is down here and not up in your bedrooms?" I asked.

"Sorting laundry—borrring," Evelyn said. "We just come down and grab a few things at a time as we need them."

My mother would have had kittens if we ever decided to live with unsorted laundry.

"But what do you put in your drawers?" I asked.

Evelyn shrugged. "Well, I try to take an armload

back up with me each time I come down to the basement. Come on, I want to show you the ant project."

Propped against one wall were large sheets of white cardboard. She turned them around.

"Wow!" I exclaimed.

"This is a cross-section drawing of the architecture of the colony—the tunnels, all that stuff."

"But how did you see it? I mean, it was all sand in the aquarium, wasn't it?"

"Nope. I got clear plastic tubes and I built some little ramps and stuff like that, but then I let them have plenty of space to build their own stuff, too. I put out some sugar lures so they would build near the glass walls. They made walkways, subterranean tunnels, secret chambers. My grandfather gave me my starter set of ants—a few males and a queen."

"The one with the big ovaries?"

"Yep. Soon as I put the males in, she went to town. Babies all over the place. Some were minor workers, some major workers, some soldiers."

"But who tells them what to do?"

"Nobody. It's weird; they just know it. There's no real boss."

"Not even the queen."

"No, she's just an egg-laying machine. They are

very well organized. They all work for the good of the whole." Evelyn dropped her voice. "It's a lot like communism. Except my grandfather warned me not to say anything about that in my science project."

I opened my eyes wide with alarm. "Gads, Evelyn! Senator McCarthy might get you."

"It's not that bad. Don't be ridiculous. These are ants, not atomic bomb secrets. You're paranoid."

"What's *paranoid*?"

"Crazy scared. Crazy with fear. That's what my mom and dad say Joe McCarthy is—paranoid."

Just at that moment Evelyn's mother called downstairs. "Hi, Evelyn, I'm home. Early dinner. Is Georgie staying?"

"Yes."

"What do I call your mom, Evelyn—Mrs. Winkler? Dr. Winkler?"

"Marge."

"Marge? Why Marge?"

"That's her name. That's what I call her."

"You call your mom by her first name?"

"Sure, why not?"

This had to be the strangest family ever.

✦ ✦ ✦

Marge, even though her hair looked fried, was very pretty, and this gave me hope for Evelyn. They actually resembled each other quite a bit. So maybe Evelyn would eventually grow into her looks. I had heard my mom use that phrase—that some people grow into their looks. Some grow out of them, too. There were some Hoosiers Twirlers who mom said had been real beauties in their day, and they looked like absolute dogs now.

Dinner, however, was an unqualified disaster. I sincerely hoped that Marge delivered babies better than she did dinner. It seemed that Marge had forgotten to take the casserole out to thaw. So she tried immersing it, wrapped in foil, in hot water, and some water seeped into it and it got kind of mushy. So then Marge decided to stick it all back together again by putting American cheese on top and popping it in the oven. The top got scorched. But the worst was yet to come. When it was time for dessert, she set down unmatched bowls of—oh, good Lord, I could hardly believe it—prunes! And if that wasn't bad enough, she said they did this because Edith had been constipated. She actually used that word at the dinner table. If my mother ever announced anything about my poo at the dinner table in front of guests, in fact in any place other than the bathroom, I would disown her. But this didn't faze Edith. Not in the least. Edith, seven years old, started talking about fiber, and how she had this fiber and that fiber today. "Cheerios are fiber, Marge. I took them for snacks to school in a plastic bag."

I tried to mush my prunes up so it might look as if I had eaten some. But it didn't work. Marge turned to me. "You don't like prunes, Georgie?"

"Uh . . . I . . . I . . . I don't have that problem."

"Oh, I'm sure we have a cookie someplace around here."

She jumped up and went to a cupboard. A package flew out from a crowded shelf. "Mallomars!" she exclaimed.

I loved Mallomars. These were a little stale.

"I have got to straighten out these shelves one of these days," Marge muttered.

It was all so strange: bureaus empty of clean laundry, kitchen shelves stuffed to the breaking point. If I had gone to Alaska and had dinner with Eskimos in an igloo and eaten fried seal and whale blubber parfaits, it couldn't have been more foreign.

But Marge was very sweet. I liked her despite her lousy housekeeping. We played Scrabble and then we watched this new series that had just started called *Ozzie and Harriet*. Edith curled up on her mother's lap with a book and hardly looked at the television, but Evelyn and I thought Ozzie and Harriet's sons, Ricky and David, were so cute. David was too old for us. But Ricky was just our age. Marge wasn't interested in the boys. She just kept saying how Harriet always looked so "nice and put together." She liked Harriet's hair. "Maybe I should get a permanent like that."

"Marge, get it done professionally. Don't do it at home," Evelyn said.

"Suppose you're right," Marge replied, and drew a strand of hair in front of her eyes to examine it.

"You don't like women to have babies at home. You like them to get to the hospital. Same thing. Go get a professional to do your hair *and* mine!"

I giggled. I liked the way Evelyn and her mom got on. They were fun even though they were kind of sloppy. And I realized that for the first time in a long time, I had not thought for one second about Emmett and Phyllis. I wasn't sure if this was good or bad.

Chapter Twenty-six

I still went over when Emmett and Phyllis were star watching, or if it was too cold outside, I'd sit on the sun porch with them, but mostly it was when Emmett had to babysit me because Mom and Dad were out. I can't exactly say they invited me; however, I would definitely show up. Because by no means had I given up on anything. My mission had just changed. Ever since I had come to the conclusion that Phyllis had in some way hijacked the Beautiful Place, that it had become dangerous, I felt that it was more important than ever for me to figure out why it was so dangerous. It wasn't simply a question of reclaiming my lost small world. There was something much greater at stake. You see, I was beginning to suspect that Phyllis did not have dibs on being the victim. Emmett might be every bit as much of a victim himself.

Once when I came over in the evening, I think that Emmett had been holding Phyllis's hand through the port because I heard a little popping sound just as I came up on the patio. I had heard this sound before when Sally or Marie, the other nurse, had been washing Phyllis. The pop was the sound of the airtight seal shutting.

"Hi, Saint Georgie," Phyllis said. I heard that popping noise, and Emmett stood up a little too quickly.

"Hi, Georgie. Guess what we're waiting for?"

"Pizza?" I asked, and Phyllis laughed.

"No, Pegasus, not pizza. We should have a fair shot at it. No clouds."

How was I supposed to know it was Pegasus and not pizza? Lots of times they ordered in a pizza, and Emmett would hold it up while Phyllis took small bites. She had to eat in small bites because she was flat on her back. She was pretty good at eating, though, unlike some polio people. She didn't have choking problems, but in case of an emergency, they did have something called an aspirator hooked onto the iron lung that could suck anything out of her if it went down the wrong way. Emmett knew how to work this, too. Phyllis looked very pretty tonight. It was chilly and she had a fuzzy knit cap on her head and her cheeks were nice and rosy. Emmett was busy moving the telescope up to her eye and fiddling with the focus. "OK, first star you're going to see—well, I can actually see it now with my naked eye."

Naked—the word flared in the night. Would Emmett and Phyllis ever see each other naked? What would he think when he saw her twisted spine? When they took her out of the iron lung and tried to wean her, she had had clothes on. But naked! Suddenly there didn't seem to be enough air, or maybe I was intruding on it. I knew I didn't belong there. The night was simply not big enough for the three of us.

Chapter Twenty-seven

"Why don't you two girls go as the parts of a cell for Halloween?" Marge suggested. I was over at Evelyn's working on our project for the school science fair. My small-world building skills had come in handy. We were constructing basically a diorama that was a cell and all of its parts—the cell membrane, the cytoplasm, the nucleus. Instead of a cardboard box, we were doing it in a clear bowl. We made the cytoplasm out of two quarts of lime Jell-O. Then in the middle of it, we suspended a clear plastic ball that had been a Christmas tree ornament that you could put glitter in. The two halves of the ball came apart. So we separated them and put in more Jell-O, this time orange, and in the middle we suspended a green grape—that was the nucleolus. The best were the chromosomes. We floated little pieces of black thread around the grape. Mom said it was the most complicated Jell-O mold she'd ever seen. It was all very realistic. But the last thing I wanted to go as for Halloween was a human cell.

"No, I always go as a witch," I replied politely.

"Oh, why's that?" Marge asked. She always wanted to know the why's and the how's behind everything.

"Because I have a fantastic fake wart and a great rubber nose and I just like wearing 'em, I guess."

"You don't get tired of wearing the same costume every year?"

"No."

"Well, Evelyn, what are you thinking about going as?"

"Not sure."

I knew what Evelyn should go as: either a ghost— she had the whitest, almost see-through skin I had ever seen—or an owl. I had a sudden inspiration.

"A ghost owl!" I blurted out.

"What?" both Evelyn and her mother said at once.

"A ghost owl. That's what they call barn owls, because they have white faces."

"Well, I never knew that, Georgie." Marge said this very seriously, as if I had just revealed a deep scientific truth. "Let's look it up in our *World Book Encyclopedia.*" This was a very Winkler-ish thing to do. They loved looking things up in books. She went to their sagging bookshelves. In a few minutes she was back.

"What a beautiful bird!" she was exclaiming.

We looked at the page in the encyclopedia. The owl's face was white and heart-shaped. The rest of the owl's head was covered with tawny speckled feathers. Everything about the owl except for its eyes, which were coal black, reminded me of Evelyn. I'm not sure if Evelyn and her mother saw the resemblance, but they both agreed that this was a fine idea for a Halloween costume. "My mom's really good at making wings," I offered.

"Really, now, how's that?" Marge asked.

"Well, before I got set on being a witch, every year I was a bat."

"Oh." Marge blinked her own pale gray eyes just the way Evelyn did when she was confronted with a curious fact.

I was, I admit, a creature of habit. For three years, the only sandwich my mother could make for me to take to school was cream cheese and jelly. I switched to peanut butter in the fourth grade and was by this time, now in the sixth grade, considering salami. But only considering.

"Look at this, Edith," Marge was saying. "It's a picture of a barn owl, and Evelyn is going as one for Halloween."

"*Tyto alba,* member of the Tytonidae family," Edith said in a small, whispery voice.

"What's that she's talking about?" I asked.

"The Latin nomenclature for the class of owls to which a barn owl belongs," Marge offered. "Now, Edith, wouldn't you like to go as a baby one? You and Evelyn and Georgia could go together."

My heart sank. I did not want to go trick-or-treating with a seven-year-old, even if she could read Latin. "Together, Marge?" Evelyn moaned.

"Now, Evelyn, you only have to take her in this neighborhood for a little while. Dad and I are both on call, but we'll be back early. Then you can go off with Georgie."

"I don't want to go as a barn owl," Edith said quietly.

"No, dear?"

"I want to go as a gherkin."

I nearly gasped. "A sweet pickle?"

"A gherkin. There's a difference," Edith said, and blinked at me through the thick lenses of her glasses.

Making the owl costume was easy. But it was also left to my mom to make the gherkin costume, which was not so easy. She did it somehow using green felt, onto which she sewed tufts of lighter green fuzzy stuff. Marge was very grateful. The Winklers were nice and all and very, very smart, but they didn't know all that much about kids and how to do for them—like making costumes, or even really feeding them. The stuff that Evelyn came to school with for lunch was just awful. This led me to the conclusion that it was much better to have a kindergarten teacher for a mother than a gynecologist. I made it real clear to Evelyn, and it didn't take much convincing, that we should eat Halloween dinner at my house. We could feed Edith whatever disgusting thing Marge had left thawing in the refrigerator and take her little sister out trick-or-treating. Then when her parents came back, we would go to my house and have my absolute favorite dinner, the one mom always made on Halloween—macaroni and cheese (not from a box), an orange-and-black-cherry Jell-O mold that looked like a jack-o'-lantern face, carrot sticks, black olives, and orange soda-pop. You see, when your mother is a kindergarten teacher she thinks about things like that—not just what tastes good, but she color coordinates it for the particular holiday. I'd much rather have a mom who could do that than deliver a baby. I was not planning on having a baby anytime soon, and when I did, I didn't want my mom delivering it.

So we took Edith out in her costume. She looked pretty cute, considering she had to wear her glasses and the patch over her eye that night. An intelligent pickle—pardon me, gherkin. When we got back, both the Winklers were there.

"You hardly touched the tuna casserole," Marge said.

Edith's eye, the one that didn't wander, slid over with an almost devilish look. We had actually dumped a portion of the tuna casserole down the toilet, but apparently not enough. Instead Edith had said she wanted to eat canned Vienna sausages and gherkins. What else? Evelyn pointed out that this was like being a cannibal—a gherkin eating a gherkin. I thought that was pretty funny. Then we started discussing cannibalism, which was kind of fun because if there had been parents around, they would have never let you get away with this kind of talk at the dinner table—even on Halloween.

There was just one strange thing that happened when the Winklers came back. Evelyn's father, Fred, had turned on the television. It was the evening news, and it showed a man in a white coat in a laboratory holding a cute little monkey. "Come here, Marge," Mr. Winkler called to his wife. The newsman was saying something about encouraging results in the testing of a vaccine against polio. Both the Winklers were standing up, still as statues, looking at the television. Then the picture cut to people in the iron lung ward of a hospital. There was a close-up of a young boy, maybe Evelyn's and my age, in an iron lung.

"It's a damn crime," Evelyn's mother said.

"What's a crime?" Edith asked.

"That!" Marge pointed an accusing finger at the television screen. "To allow someone, a youngster, to live out his life like that."

"They should have never put him in it," Evelyn's father said, and sat down in his easy chair.

I felt every hair on the back of my neck stand

straight up. I couldn't believe they could talk so casually right in front of their children about death. But deep down inside me someplace, I think I suspected that they might be right, that putting someone in an iron lung was a kind of murder. I had never thought of this before. I had preferred to think—well, not preferred, but discovered through my research, especially when I looked up all the stuff about the rocking bed and the failures—that people like Phyllis were suffering a very slow death in the name of trying to make them live and breathe. But wasn't it really another kind of murder—a slow one? Then, like an electric shock, a terrible question sizzled through me: Was it possible that Phyllis wanted a fast one, a quick murder? But for a murder, one needed a murderer!

I felt in one brief instant I had seen too much, learned too much. I didn't want to think about it. The pieces of a diabolical puzzle were coming together a little too quickly, and what in the world was I supposed to do? What I knew weighed on me. I didn't want to tell anyone, not even Evelyn, but I suddenly felt years too old. If I had looked in a mirror, I wouldn't have been surprised to see a bent over, ancient, gray-haired lady, her shoulders stooped with decades, her back crooked. And I wasn't even in my witch costume yet.

I was really glad when Evelyn said that we had to get on over to my house. We got on our costumes, and her father drove us. When we pulled into our drive, he turned around to us, in the backseat. "Now, you two go out and do some good spooking. See you later, kiddo." He gave Evelyn a kiss just like a normal dad would.

But I was in such a hurry to get out of the car that I knocked off my wart and didn't notice it until I got in the house. Luckily I had a spare wart. Mom had bought one for me at the place she got Halloween stuff. Still another good thing about having a kindergarten teacher for a mom. She thought of stuff like that. Backups. Dad used to say that he could send at least one of us to college on what Mom had given to kids who had forgotten their lunch money. And she even kept a couple of spare Halloween costumes at school for children whose parents were so darned stupid they forgot to dress their kids up for the school Halloween parade.

The dinner was as good as I promised. You would have thought Evelyn had never had a decent meal in her life, the way she tucked into the macaroni and cheese.

"For Lord's sake, leave some room for candy, Evelyn," I said.

"Georgia Louise!" Dad drawled out my name.

"Sorry, Dad."

My dad didn't like it when we used the Lord's name in vain. It really bugged him, even though he wasn't a real churchy sort of fellow.

"Phyllis said that you two should be sure to come over. She wants to see your costumes," Mom said.

We set out into the crisp October night. I could feel the light breeze curl around my witch's hat. I was really pretty excited. This was a new neighborhood for me, and with rich people around like the Kellers, there was no telling what good loot you could rake in.

"I hope no one gives out raisins or apples."

"Agreed." Evelyn nodded.

"In my personal opinion, I feel that anyone who gives out healthy treats should get a trick. They deserve to a) have their windows soaped, b) have their head examined, c) be arrested."

"It's a crime," Evelyn said. "Not the soaping, the raisins and apples."

I wished Evelyn hadn't said that word *crime*. I remembered what her mother had said standing there in front of the television pointing her finger at the people in the iron lungs, saying it was a crime.

We finally wound our way back to our street and went over to the Kellers'. Mrs. Keller had made the best treats of all—caramel-and-chocolate-dipped marshmallows, and they were tied up in pretty cellophane wrappers. "Now, go out onto the patio, girls, and show Phyllis your costumes."

The first thing that caught my eye was not the creature but a filmy wisp floating out from the machine itself. Then I saw that it was attached to a pointy hat, like my witch's hat, only it wasn't black; it was pink with silvery glitter. It was one of those hats like medieval princesses wore. But Phyllis was wearing it with earmuffs!

"Welcome, Saint Georgie, welcome to my court. Come to slay the dragons?"

"I'm a witch, not a saint," I said.

She rotated all the mirrors until they caught our reflections. "Oh, you both look great. Great owl costume!" Multiple owls and witches now appeared in the mirrors, and occasionally the wisp from Phyllis's veil floated across our faces. We made an odd assortment out there on the patio. Of course, Emmett wasn't wearing anything special, just his jeans and a heavy jacket. He was fiddling with the telescope that he had finally finished building.

"OK, I got Pegasus. Want to see it, Evelyn?" This was very polite of him to include Evelyn. "See?" he said to her as she pressed her eye to the scope. "It's an almost perfect-shaped square formed by four stars." The square was the reason Emmett built this new telescope. Other astronomers, he said, used the Square of Pegasus just like a signpost or way point in the grid they had placed on the sky, and it guided them. But for Emmett it was much more. For Emmett the Square of Pegasus was a treasure chest, and he just had to pry it open with his scope. The square, Emmett said, was more like a window to the very edge of the Milky Way galaxy. Through the window and beyond the edge, Emmett thought there were not just stars but maybe new undiscovered galaxies and other things I didn't half understand. It was very hard to imagine all this. I never knew how he did it.

Now Emmett looked through the telescope.

"What are you seeing out there, Em?" That's what Phyllis sometimes called Emmett, and he called her Phyll. Em and Phyll. Sounded like an old married couple to me, kind of fat, sitting in lounge chairs watching television or doing crosswords. "Grand and mysterious wonders?" she asked.

"Nothing is too wonderful to be true." Emmett

took his eye away from the telescope and winked at Phyllis. "I'm quoting—not original at all. The physicist Michael Faraday's words, not mine."

"Say them again, Em," Phyllis whispered.

"Nothing is too wonderful to be true."

"Like death," Phyllis whispered.

"Huh?" I said.

"Like breath," she said.

But I had heard the word *death*. I was sure. I looked over at Emmett. He had heard only what he wanted to hear; his face was tipped up toward the starlight, seeing everything and yet nothing.

That night after Evelyn went home, I got out the diorama. I had almost finished the second level, the earth level. I had made the islands that Orion walked across to the island of Chios out of small rocks that I had found in the grove. He was on Chios now and looking pretty angry because all the dead animals were lying around, and guess what?—no Merope! I rotated the lazy Susan to start the next scene, where he would try and abduct her and the king would put out his eyes. I worked carefully. Mom had some little toothpicks that were like mini swords. She used them for hors d'oeuvres. So I carefully put one in the king's hand and one in Orion's. But there is no way to really show fight-scene action in a diorama. So I laid Orion down on the ground as if he were dead, or rather gravely wounded. I placed one of his hunting dogs near him and the other staring at the eyes that had been plucked out by the king's sword and lay on the ground. I had de-eyed an old doll of mine that I never played with anymore. The scale wasn't exactly right, but it sure did get the point across, and it looked very eerie. I was just looking at the eyes in a little patch of moss that I had brought from the grove, and I started crying. I wasn't sure what I was crying about, but everything suddenly seemed so sad. It wasn't about a new school or old friends or our stupid new house. "I can't believe it," I murmured. "I'm crying on Halloween! Halloween, my favorite holiday!"

Chapter Twenty-eight

"So why does Phyllis call you Saint Georgie?" Evelyn asked.

It was when she asked me this question at recess the next day that I suddenly knew why I had been crying the night before. I wasn't Saint Georgie. I didn't even want to be Saint Georgie. The whole thing was a stupid idea. I couldn't save anybody, and I didn't know what I was trying to save anybody from. But I knew that Emmett needed help.

We were out on the playground, and it had begun to snow. A mean snow. Flurries whipped by the wind like tiny slivers of glass that pricked your face. The

Mustard Seeds were still jumping away, and Evelyn and I wandered over to the anthill. I hadn't told Evelyn about my fears, about how Phyllis had this strange hold on Emmett, but I decided right then to begin to tell her a little. Her question had sort of opened things up. "Uh . . . uh, I'm not sure why she calls me that. Just, you know, my name being Georgie and all." But since she had brought this up, I decided to ask her the question.

"Listen, last night when we were there and Emmett said that thing about 'nothing is too wonderful to be true' and Phyllis answered him, did you hear her say 'death' or 'breath'?"

Evelyn shut her eyes in a long owlish blink. "I'm not sure. Why?"

"I think I heard her say 'death.'" I just blurted it out. It seemed like such a relief.

"Really? You think she wants to die?"

"What?" I had heard her, but I really wanted Evelyn to say it again. This was the first time I had really gotten close to telling anyone my fears.

"I said, do you think she wants to die?"

"I'm not sure. But Evelyn, I've got to tell you something."

"What?" She seemed to sense my fear.

"I'm really scared. Scared for Emmett." I hesitated a moment before asking the next question. "Would you want to die if you were in one of those things?"

Evelyn took a long time answering. "I think so."

Just at that moment, Amy Moncton walked up to us. "What are you two always doing over here?"

Evelyn and I looked at each other. Playing with an anthill? What would the Mustard Seeds think of that? "Just talking," Evelyn replied.

"Just talking . . . hmmm."

"You have a problem with that?" It was not the nicest thing to say, and I really don't know why I came back at her like that.

"No, just wondering," Amy said. Another Mustard Seed came up. "They're just talking." Amy's voice was seared with contempt.

"What about?" Patty Wertheimer asked. Evelyn and I called her the Heimer.

"Death," Evelyn said flatly, and continued poking at the anthill.

"Ewww!" Their faces curdled in disgust.

"You guys are so weird!" Amy said, and both girls began giggling and raced off hand in hand.

Chapter Twenty-nine

The very next evening, I went over to Phyllis's to ask Emmett for help with my math homework. But I was still haunted by the two words *breath* or *death*.

"You know more about the machine, Emmett, than my dad does," Phyllis was saying as I came in. "Hi, Georgie. I was just saying that Emmett knows more about the iron lung than my dad. I think it's good that you know all this stuff about the machine," she continued.

"But I don't want your dad to, you know, feel . . . uh . . . uh . . ." Emmett replied.

"Topped?" Phyllis said. "Topped by a high-school senior."

"Naw, I didn't mean that exactly."

"Listen, I'm the one who told Dad to show you."

"You told your dad to show me?" Emmett asked.

"Yes, right after the second time you came over. I said, 'Dad, show him how it all works, the alarm and all.'"

I must have looked weird or something, because Emmett all of a sudden asked me what was wrong.

"Nothing," I said, then turned in the mirror to Phyllis's reflection. "Why did you ask your dad to show Emmett all that stuff?"

"You've got to know what to do if there's a short circuit. He's way smarter than any of the nurses around here. I just knew he was the one the minute he walked in here."

He was the one! *One what?* I almost screamed. "Listen, I've got to go." I forgot all about my homework question.

"What are you rushing off for?" Phyllis asked.

"Nothing," I said, and hurried down the steps. I knew Phyllis was trying to catch me in the mirrors. "You're rushing off to nothing! That seems kind of dumb."

She just knew he was the one! Dammit. What did

she mean by that? The one what? Was I going crazy? Crazy scared? I didn't want to think this way. Not about Phyllis.

That night in my sleep, I saw a face. It wasn't exactly Phyllis. The face was furry, and across the forehead there were eight shiny beads, so shiny that they reflected Emmett's face and mine, too.

"Come closer." It was a low, hoarse voice, but I knew it was Phyllis's. Emmett started to move, crawling up the trembling silver threads of a web. They jiggled, and he nearly lost his balance. "You won't fall. Come on, Georgie, you too." She was calling to me now. "Remember, the threads are sticky. Come closer." And I began to creep forward on the threads. With each dreadful step, I drew closer to this thing that I knew was Phyllis but not Phyllis.

"Why have the mirrors turned all black and shiny?" I asked.

"Those aren't mirrors, silly girl. They are my eyes. The mirrors are shattered."

I looked down at that moment and saw the razor-sharp shards beneath me, like a carpet of daggers, and then I felt myself falling and Emmett falling, too.

"You're ruining everything, Georgie! Saint Georgie!"

But the voice was not recognizable. It was a long sizzling hiss, and as I was falling, I saw legs—eight of them, but it was not a spider at all. It was a scorpion.

And in my sleep I felt a sting, a sting in my heel.

"Wake up! Wake up, Emmett!"

I went running into his room.

"What are you doing here?" He yawned. "Georgie, it's two thirty in the morning!"

"Emmett, there's something not right about Phyllis."

"What are you talking about? Of course there isn't something right about her. She's got polio. She's in an iron lung. She can't breathe."

"But she didn't say 'breath,' Emmett. I think she said 'death.'"

Emmett narrowed his eyes. "What are you talking about—breath, death? Are you going crazy?"

I looked at him, searching his face. Had he forgotten about that thing he said, and then that she said? Nothing is too wonderful to be true? Or *was* I going crazy?

"I don't know. I—I—I j-j-j-just." Emmett put his hand on top of mine. The jittering letter sounds stilled inside me. "I had a bad dream, that's all."

"Do you want to tell me about it? Sometimes that helps." I could see Emmett looking really concerned about me.

"It was about a spider and its eyes were like mirrors and somehow it reminded me of Phyllis and I was thinking maybe, maybe she was w-w-w . . . w-w-w-w . . ." Emmett patted my hand softly. "Wanting . . . to . . . die . . . or something like that."

"She doesn't want to die, Georgie. If anything, she wants to live more than ever."

"Really?"

"Really."

"But why?"

"She loves me, Georgie." He didn't blush when he said this. "And someday in the near future I think they are going to figure out how a person like Phyllis can come out of an iron lung and live. There's medical technology out there. It can be done. I know it. This is a problem, a technological problem, and it can be solved."

"Really?"

"Absolutely. They're really closing in on it. And after that it will be a man in space and after that a man on the moon. It's going to happen by the 1960s."

Getting a girl out of an iron lung didn't sound

as hard as getting a man on the moon. "But still, Emmett, it's just 1952. It could take maybe ten years. You'll be so old."

"Not that old, and I'll wait. I'll do anything for Phyllis."

"Really?" But I said the word so softly that Emmett didn't even hear it.

"What?" He leaned forward.

"Nothing, just nothing."

I went back to my room. When I saw the little poodle lipstick holder she had given me, I took it, went downstairs, and put it in the trash can in the garage—the one with all the disgusting garbage so I wouldn't be tempted to go get it again. Then I came upstairs and took out my diary. I unlocked it, and pressing so hard with my pencil that the tip broke, I scrawled, *Even though I might be crazy, I STILL DON'T BELIEVE IN GOD.*

And then probably because I was halfway to being certifiably insane, I went downstairs and got the poodle lipstick holder from the disgusting garbage. I guess you could say I was hedging my bets. If I kept the lipstick holder, maybe nothing bad would happen to Phyllis, to Emmett, or, I guess, to me.

Chapter Thirty

Emmett started talking a lot about new medical technology that could help people like Phyllis. "But she has to build up her lungs so she'll be ready," he said one night at dinner.

"How does she do that?" Dad asked.

"By weaning—longer and longer periods of time."

"But didn't you say she had a seizure the last time?" Mom asked.

"You know, this is the funny thing," Emmett said almost casually. Funny? What could be funny about having a seizure? "She doesn't even know she has them." I was shocked. I remembered Emmett coming back through the yard terrified after the weaning. But I also remember Phyllis saying that it didn't hurt, that it felt good in a way. A beautiful place!

Mom set down her water glass. She looked shocked, too. I was glad. Maybe I wasn't as crazy as I thought. "I don't think this is a case where ignorance is bliss. Couldn't she really do worse damage to herself?" Emmett got all huffy and told us it was none of our business.

He was probably right; it wasn't. But it didn't seem right that I, the youngest person at the table, was the only one to sense something wrong here, very wrong. Was Emmett putting too much faith in science? That would have been so like him. Was I the only person thinking this? Was I the only person really fearful for Emmett? I mean, I was younger and I was not nearly as smart as Emmett, but it was almost as if I were the single person in possession of a dangerous piece of information, even if I did not know precisely what that information was. I was eleven years old. What could I do? What was I supposed to do? I had tried to talk to Emmett once on the night when I had the bad dream. *Death? Breath?* The two words continued to haunt me. I couldn't stop thinking about it.

I could hardly think of those two words without going to pieces. So I had vowed never to go back. But now I didn't have a choice. I had to go back because my parents didn't want me home alone. Still I fought it.

"Georgie, you have to go over there. I don't care if you don't want to." My mom said this in her most firm, no-arguing-with-her voice.

"Mom, I still don't understand why I can't stay here by myself," I argued.

"Because there have been two robberies in this neighborhood and I don't want you staying alone when Dad and I go out."

"See? That's what we get for moving into a fancy neighborhood."

"I'm not following this," my dad said.

"In our old neighborhood, no one had anything worth stealing. People have fancy jewelry in this neighborhood."

"Now, how do you know that?" my mom said.

"I do. Mrs. Keller has a diamond necklace and matching diamond earrings. She lets Phyllis wear them sometimes—the earrings. Not the necklace." Actually I thought it was kind of sick the way Mrs. Keller did that.

"Can't Emmett come back over here?" I whined.

"Be reasonable, Georgie. Emmett is all that poor girl has."

That's just the problem, I wanted to scream, and boy did Phyllis have him. *He's the one!* The words crashed in my brain.

"Look, if I stay right here in the living room with my hand on the phone and all the lights on . . ."

"Put a button on it, Georgie. Get your homework and get over to Phyllis's." My dad spoke very sharply, which he rarely did. I knew I had hit the wall when he spoke this way.

So I went over. It was chilly, but not that chilly for early December, and when I came up those steps, I felt as if I were getting caught in a small world not made by me but by Phyllis. Those flashes of light as the mirrors moved around were like the silk threads of the spider's web spinning out into the night, capturing my reflection so quickly. But I saw it this time. I saw Emmett's hand pop out of the port by Phyllis's leg.

"Welcome, Saint Georgie," Phyllis said. It had kind of started to make my skin crawl when she called me this.

"Hi, Georgie," Emmett said. He was blushing.

"Guess what we're waiting for?" Phyllis asked.

"Pizza, I hope."

"Epsilon. We should have a fair shot at it, your brother says. No clouds."

Emmett had started fiddling with the scope. He looked up and pointed west of the Dipper to Epsilon. I could see it now without the scope.

"Flame rose," Phyllis said softly into the darkness.

They began talking, the two of them. It seemed like code again to me, but laced with all these flirty remarks of Phyllis's, and Emmett was all moony-faced and googly-eyed. He was hardly looking at the sky, just at Phyllis again, the namer of colors. Had he given up on the secrets of the Square of Pegasus? Did he really not want to know anything anymore? Was ignorance really bliss for Emmett? Finally I couldn't stand it a minute longer. "I'm cold. I'm going inside," I announced.

"Mom's made some hot chocolate," Phyllis said. "That'll warm you up."

When I went inside, Mrs. Keller was sitting in a rocking chair doing needlepoint and watching *I Love Lucy*. "Georgie, my goodness, I think you've shot up two inches in the past week."

"Uh, Phyllis said there was some hot chocolate."

"Yes, in the kitchen, and if you want to join me in here and watch television, I'd love it. This is a very funny Lucy show."

It was the commercial break when I came back. "My mom loves Lucille Ball, too," I said.

"She is simply hysterical. Look at that wonderful face." She nodded toward the television as the show came back on. Lucy was up to her old tricks. She was trying to get into Desi's nightclub act. She and her best friend, Ethel, were dressed in disguise. Lucy was even wearing a mustache. She was dancing around on the stage, trying to sound Spanish and doing her best to hog the stage from Desi, who had not yet recognized her.

When the show was over, Mrs. Keller said something about how she had seen Lucille Ball in person one time and that she had the reddest hair imaginable. "You'll see when we get color TV."

"Are you getting it soon?"

"Well, Don thinks certainly within the year."

This was an eerie echo of the time when I was trying on lipstick and Phyllis had made that weird joke about not holding her breath for color television.

Mrs. Keller looked over at me. I felt I had to say something quick. I might have been looking a little strange or something.

"What are you making?" I said, getting up and walking over to look at the needlepoint.

"A throw-pillow cover. Know what it is?"

I looked down at the square in the frame. There was a beautiful girl with what would be long hair when it was stitched in, and she was sitting at a loom. In front of her was a mirror. I swallowed as a queasiness welled up in the back of my throat. "It's that poem lady."

"Yes, dear, the Lady of Shalott." She looked up at me.

"The same one she gave you for your birthday?"

"No, I finished that one. This is a new one she gave me. She never stops thinking of sweet things, such a dear girl." *That is not the point,* I wanted to scream. *Why would Phyllis get you this picture all the time? The same one? Why this one? Is this some sort of bad joke?*

"Dr. Keller," she continued, "is actually working right now on a new device that would allow Phyllis to do needlepoint, too. A kind of special needle that could be held in her mouth."

"Does she like to needlepoint?" I asked.

Mrs. Keller turned around and cocked her head and looked at me as if I had said the most curious thing imaginable. "Well, my goodness, who's to know, except it would be such a nice way to pass the time."

Pass the time to what?

I snuck back to our house without telling Emmett.

He seemed kind of annoyed when he got home. "How come you're acting so weird these days, Georgie?"

"I don't know. I'll be OK."

"Phyllis noticed it, too."

"She did?"

"Yes, she sent a note for you."

"She typed it with that tongue thing?"

"Yes." He handed me a piece of powder-blue paper. It was Phyllis's stationery and it had her name inscribed in white at the top.

> Dear Georgie,
>   I've been worried about you. Are the Mustard Seeds making your life miserable? Come visit and we can have some girl talk.
>   Love, Phyllis.

I tucked the note into my pocket. It was strange. A few months ago, I would have been thrilled at the prospect of visiting Phyllis for girl talk. But nothing had been quite the same for a while. Since the spider dream, I had to admit I had grown fearful of Phyllis. I had to keep reminding myself how completely empty her life was, and when I did this, it was almost like a free fall through space for me. I was overwhelmed and, yes, ashamed that I had given in to my fears.

Still I had a feeling, no more than a feeling—I knew that she was manipulating Emmett to do something really bad, like maybe help her die. And when I thought of that, I have to admit that I came close to actually hating Phyllis. But I just wasn't really sure about how she would get Emmett to do it. Hating would not solve that mystery. It was kind of a relief not to even think about hating anymore. My job was to save not Phyllis, but Emmett. I had told him of my fears that night, and he had blown them off as if they were nothing. I somehow had to figure out when Phyllis planned to do this terrible thing and then I would some way, somehow stop it. I just had to figure out when this might happen. I wasn't Saint Georgie anymore. I wasn't the knight in the Lady of Shalott, ready to smash mirrors. The only person I really wanted to release into the real world was my own brother, Emmett.

Chapter Thirty-one

"I think a French twist, and then put the clip to the side that way," Sally was saying as Mrs. Keller arranged a sparkling flower-shaped clip in Phyllis's hair. On a small table beside her was a pile of jewels, the very ones I had mentioned to my mother, the diamond earrings, and now a diamond hair clip. She and Sally the nurse were fussing with Phyllis's hair.

"I'm not sure," Roslyn Keller said. "You know, I saw a picture of Grace Kelly, who I think looks so much like Phyllis—"

"Just like her exactly." Phyllis laughed and then flicked the mirrors. A fleeting expression of worry crossed her mother's face.

"Hi, Georgie," Phyllis said.

"Oh, hi, Georgie." Mrs. Keller nodded to me, then continued fussing with Phyllis's hair.

"Yes, definitely the hair down with the clip in the side. I'll look just like her. And the earrings, Mom, don't forget the earrings." I was getting a queasy feeling in my stomach. Was this the girl talk I had been invited over for? Her mother clamped an earring to each ear. Sally cooed. It was as if they were playing with a doll. It was revolting. The diamonds sparkled almost fiendishly above the high, tight rubber collar that gripped Phyllis's neck. Mrs. Keller stepped back to admire her handiwork. "There, pretty as a picture. Should I take one?"

"Oh, of course, by all means!" Phyllis said. Her mother looked confused.

But I suddenly had another picture in my mind. That of Phyllis when they tried to wean her. I imagined teeny little diamond bracelets on those withered legs, a necklace draping over her arched back. The face contorted into a horrendous agony, and her ears sparkling with the diamond earrings.

"Look how pretty you are, Phyllis!"

Phyllis just smiled and let them play with her. But I could hardly stand it. I made an excuse and went to the bathroom. I prayed that by the time I came out, they would be finished with their doll play. Was I the only adult here? The only one who had outgrown dolls?

When I came out of the bathroom, Mrs. Keller was in the kitchen. So I went in.

"Yes, Georgie?" she said. My heart was thumping. I had never in my life really questioned an adult in this way. This wasn't like begging for something from my parents that I wanted and they didn't want me to have. It wasn't arguing with a teacher over a grade, which I had also been known to do. This was different. My bottom lip had begun to tremble.

"My goodness, Georgie, you look as if you are about to cry." *Some Saint Georgie!* I thought. It took all my willpower not to cry. "Come sit down, dear, here at the table. Can I get you something?"

"Mrs. Keller." My voice cracked. She looked at me suspiciously. "Why do you do this?"

"Do what, Georgie?"

"Do this to Phyllis."

"I'm sure I don't know what you are talking about."

I don't think she did. "Why do you dress her up like she's some sort of doll?"

A shocked look swept through Roslyn Keller's eyes. "Why, Georgie!"

"Why do you want Dr. Keller to invent some contraption so she can needlepoint? Why do you just see her as only part of this horrible machine?"

I expected her to be mad at me. But she just shut her eyes tight for several seconds as if summoning up the strength to answer me. "But that is what she is, Georgie. She is just that—part of this machine. This marvelous machine. She must be able to live as fully as possible with her limitations, but the machine offers her—" She paused.

"What?" I said.

"Why, life, Georgie. Life." Then it seemed as if her jaw became unhinged. Her lower lip began to tremble, and her mouth moved as if trying to shape a word. "It's so hard."

I didn't say anything. I just got up to go back into the other room. Mrs. Keller grabbed my hand. "I know it's hard for you to understand."

I shook my head. *No,* I wanted to say. *I understand perfectly. But we just have a different idea about life and so-called life.* But of course I didn't say any of this.

Chapter Thirty-two

"That guy's gigantic."

"Seven feet," Dad said.

We were in the Westridge field house. The opposing team had just come onto the court. It was this new player, Cyril James, who had moved to Indianapolis from Kentucky. "How are they ever going to get around him?" I wondered aloud.

"They've got Emmett," Dad said. "And Emmett's fast. And they've got Buzzy Philby and Skeeter. They'll do fine."

Emmett just sauntered across the court as if he didn't have a care in the world. He passed the ball to some of the other guys. Stumbled once. Missed a few shots. All this was typical Emmett in a warm-up. It was almost as if he had to get all the mistakes out of his system before the real playing began.

But he didn't quite get all the mistakes out. Well, they were not exactly mistakes. He just seemed to be moving differently. His timing seemed off. He wasn't as fast. By halftime, Buzz Philby had had a bad landing after a layup shot and had to be helped off the court limping. Brian McPhee had fouled out, and Emmett had not once taken command in rebound situations. And Skeeter, according to Dad, was sleepwalking.

Dad was having a fit. "Emmett's not reading the defense at all. He's not making the fast breaks. I don't know what's wrong with him. The whole point of being a center is to be a little arrogant, snotty."

Dad was right. Even though Emmett was quiet off the court and shy, almost mousy despite his size, he had a completely different personality on court. But that personality was not there this evening. "He's lost his focus," Dad said.

These four words sent a chill through me. Phyllis! The question became suddenly so clear. How much was Emmett willing to lose for Phyllis?

The Westridge Wildcats' defeat was humiliating,

64 to 22. The only consolation was that it was a pre-season game. So it didn't count toward the sectionals, which was the World Series of high-school basketball in Indiana.

Christmas had come and gone. And a cold hard spell had settled in. There were days on end when the thermometer outside our kitchen window never got out of the teens. And there wasn't any snow, either. No sledding. So I concluded that this winter was about as boring as last summer, with its brutal heat and no swimming. New polio cases did drop off in the winter. I guess that was the only good thing to be said.

Basketball season was in full swing. Emmett hadn't improved much. He was faster, but as Dad said, he was not playing with authority. I heard Mom and Dad talking about this one night in the kitchen. They shut up almost as soon as I came in. They looked like they were kids with their hands caught in the cookie jar.

"You're talking about Emmett and basketball, aren't you?"

They both hesitated, and then Mom said, "Yes, we are concerned." And from the way she said *concerned,*

I knew it was not about scouts, agents, or getting a basketball scholarship.

"It's Phyllis." I didn't blurt it out. I just said it. Mom and Dad looked surprised.

"What do you mean, Georgie?" Dad asked.

"I mean that . . . that . . ." I wasn't sure how to say it—that he thinks about her all the time? No, that wasn't quite it. "She's very powerful," I said softly. The color drained from Mom and Dad's faces.

"What do you mean?" Mom asked again.

Good Lord, I certainly hadn't meant to scare them like this, but in an odd way it felt good. It felt like a relief to be saying this, telling Mom and Dad this. "I just mean she's, you know, kind of bossy, and it's hard to have authority if there's someone more powerful around."

Dad rubbed his chin and looked at the floor. "What's there to do?"

"You're asking me?" I said as I opened the refrigerator door for some milk.

"No, no, you're just a kid." Dad reached out and tousled my hair. I never thought I would feel good about being called a kid. But I did.

Chapter Thirty-three

Teachers' convention came at the end of January. Although it was a great vacation for kids, teachers had to go to workshops or something. So I was shipped off to Grandma and Grandpa's for three days on the farm. Emmett got to stay home because of basketball. I didn't mind going to Grandma and Grandpa's during teachers' convention. There was always stuff to do. In the evening I went over the Dairyman's Breeder's catalog with Grandpa. All dairy cows were artificially inseminated. I don't think they even allowed them ever to do it the regular way. Dairy cow farmers just ordered up the sperm of the stud they wanted and it was shipped to them packed in dry ice. Then they put it in the cows. "Think this studly fellow looks like a good bet, Georgie?" Grandpa asked.

"Bases Loaded? That's his name?"

"Yeah, sometimes these breeders try to get a little too cute."

The catalogs always had these weird descriptions of the animals. So here were the wonders of Bases Loaded. He was described as being a winner from "calving ease"—*Yeah, easy for him,* I thought. But I knew they were talking about the cows that would be delivering his offspring—to his lovely legs. And his daughters were described as "extremely wide-rumped with beautifully attached udders," big milk yielders. All this is good in a cow. "I guess he seems good," I said about Bases Loaded, "but I don't like his eyes."

"She's never going to see those eyes, darlin'," Grandpa said, referring to the cow intended to receive the sperm.

"I know, but his kids might get them. But I guess he's pretty good." I flipped the page. "Look at this, Breeder's Bonus and Breeder's Delight, Grandpa."

"I'm always suspicious of those economy packs. They're just for people starting out. Starter kits basically. Vernon's coming out tomorrow. I'll ask his advice too."

Vernon Albert was the veterinarian Grandpa used. "I'm sure he knows more than I do," I said.

The next day, Dr. Albert came out to treat a sick cow and give some sort of injection to the piglets born last spring. They weren't exactly piglet size anymore, but they weren't quite hogs yet, either. So I sometimes called them poglets. Seemed a reasonable name for a piglet on its way to becoming a hog. Vernon Albert was very nice, and he always let me follow him around. I got to help him check all the goats for hoof rot. One goat had pinkeye, and he let me help put the ointment on.

I liked Dr. Albert because he always treated me in a very grown-up way, never talking down to me but asking my opinion about stuff even though I hadn't gone to veterinary school. He would grab a goat, for instance, and hold its jaws, then fold back its lips and tell me to look at the gums, and then do the same with another goat and ask me which one's gums looked healthier and why. I might say something, just a guess; then he'd ask me another question and kind of teach me how to look for the first signs of something he called blue gum, which wasn't good, and before you knew it, I really had learned something.

I said, "Dr. Albert, I think they should send you off to that teachers' convention, because you could teach those teachers a thing or two about teaching."

"Oh, you do, do you, Georgie?" He cut off a plug of chewing tobacco and jammed it in his teeth.

"That stuff taste any good?" I had always wondered. Grandpa chewed it sometimes, and all the baseball players on the Indianapolis Indians did. They could spit like nobody's business. Dad said they could spit a heck of a lot better than they played ball. Anyhow, Dr. Albert just looked at me and said, "Wanna try a plug?"

"You gotta be kidding."

"No, try it."

He cut me off a little plug—a pluglet, I suppose you could say—and I put it in my mouth. I don't think I did more than half a chew. Good Lord, that plug came flying out of my mouth and hit a haystack. "You spit better than a ballplayer." He laughed.

"Worst-tasting stuff ever!" I was almost gagging.

Luckily I had a Tootsie Roll in my pocket. So Dr. Albert and I sat there in the barn, he on his examining stool probing a milk cow for a carbuncle in its groin area and me watching him, both of us just chewing away. When I polished off the Tootsie Roll, I thought of something. "Dr. Albert, you ever treat a monkey?"

"Naw, I'm a large animal vet. It'd have to be a gorilla." He laughed.

"I saw this thing on television where they are using monkeys to test some new polio medicine."

"Oh, that they are. Yes, indeed. That's a little out of my bailiwick, as they say."

"Well, I still got a question." I took another Tootsie Roll out of my pocket.

"Shoot," he said.

"What do you think about iron lungs?"

"What about them, Georgie?" He looked away from the cow's carbuncle.

"What do you think about people being kept in them, like forever and ever?"

"I think I'd rather be dead. You know what they call them? The iron lungs, I mean."

"No." It was so quiet in the barn, and in the dim light I could still see little bits of dust circling slowly. It was as if the whole world had slowed down and everything suddenly stood out sharp and with a hard, bright edge, despite the dimness.

"Coffins with legs—that's what some people call them."

"I think you're right, Dr. Albert." I felt a really bad, deep sadness begin to fill me up, but it was different from when I had stood in the Winklers' television room and Evelyn's mother had pointed her finger at the TV. I can't explain it, but I just felt it was different. I didn't feel that there was anything dangerous here. I felt real comfortable, very safe just sitting there in the barn with Dr. Albert chewing, the both of us, just chewing silently in the cold barn air on this winter afternoon.

"You got old Missy here with a carbuncle in her groin, Ed," Dr. Albert said to my grandfather when he came in. "I'm going to drain it with the help of my able assistant here. Then I'm going to have to put the cow on a course of antibiotics, so you'll have to take her off the milk wagon for a while."

"It wouldn't be January if I didn't have a cow off the milk wagon," Grandpa said. Being off the milk wagon meant that a farmer couldn't sell that cow's milk for a time.

Draining the carbuncle was kind of neat, even though it was terrifically disgusting. I had to go wash my hands with some solution that Dr. Albert carried with him, then put on rubber gloves. First he shaved the area with a battery razor he carried. He let me swab on the antiseptic to the spot with a giant Q-tip that looked more like a baseball bat. Then he rubbed on some stuff to numb the area. Missy was very patient through all of this. After the numbing stuff set in, he took out a hypodermic needle and put in another anesthetic that would go deeper. Next he pulled out a thin rubber tube and put a needle on the end. My job was to hold an enamel bowl and make sure the other end of the tube was in it. He inserted the needle, and in about thirty seconds the most disgusting greenish glop started to drop into the bowl. When he had finished "the procedure," as he called it, he let me swab down the hole where the needle had gone in. Then he put a kind of large Band-Aid over it. "Tell your grandpa to take that off tomorrow evening. Missy'll be fine by then."

That night Evelyn was coming out to spend the night. I was pretty excited. I had told her to bring her skates because Grandpa and Grandma had a pond right near the house that was perfect for skating. The ice was so thick, and Grandpa had had some of his "boys," as he called the men who helped him on the farm, clear it off for us and give it a good scraping. So it was really smooth.

After dinner Evelyn and I bundled up and went out to skate. There was an immense full moon. And between the full moon and the snow on the ground, it was as if God, or maybe so-called God, or somebody had just bleached the night. You couldn't see that many great stars. We still skated around with our heads flung back, looking for constellations. But I knew there was one that we would catch, always could no matter how white the night—Orion rising in the East.

"I see his belt!" I cried. I felt a great relief: Orion was back in the sky. This was the first clear sighting I had of him. His belt was sparkling.

"Look there's his foot, his left foot." I spun to a stop in the middle of the pond.

"Where?"

"Look, see the top of that tree over there?"

"Yeah."

"Now see the edge of the barn's roof?"

"Yeah."

"OK, right between the tree and the barn—there's a really bright star. That's his foot star, Rigel.

Now let's see if I can find his armpit." I skated off a few yards. "Yeah, I got it. That's Betelgeuse, and if you follow it out, you can find the stars of his club. Muscle boy: he bulges with stars."

Evelyn laughed. "That's good, since he's blind. He should have something going for him. Look, it does seem as if he's sort of stumbling, doesn't it?"

Evelyn was trying to do one of those spins where you draw your arms in and go faster and faster.

I had stopped skating. I looked at Orion's legs. He really did look as if he were falling down. I didn't like thinking of Orion stumbling blindly across the sky, his club raised in vengeance as if he were doomed. It seemed almost pitiful.

"I'm cold. Let's go in," I said.

I skated off, my shadow lengthening in the glare of the moon-bleached pond. I vowed that when I made the sky part of the Orion diorama, he would not look as if he were stumbling. He would run straight no matter what.

Chapter Thirty-four

When I got home from Grandma and Grandpa's, I knew right away that something was beginning to change in our house. I walked in the door with Dad, and I saw Mom's back as she stared out the window toward the Kellers'. It was just something in the way she held her back, so tight and rigid, her shoulders hunched forward a little. There was a new tension in our house. I was wondering if they had said something to him after that night in the kitchen. "Where's Emmett?" I asked.

"Over there." She turned around, and her eyes looked a little too bright and she had a kind of funny smile. Her smile looked as if it had been drawn on, not well, by one of her kindergarten students.

The next few nights were warmer. So Emmett could roll the Creature out onto the patio, and he and Phyllis watched Orion in the waning of the February moon. I didn't go because these were school nights. Then by the weekend the weather turned cold again and the moon was completely gone. This had been such a cold winter.

Valentine's Day was coming up. I was wondering if Emmett might give Phyllis a present. I was really hoping that he would not ask my assistance. He didn't, thankfully, but he did seem quieter than usual, not that he ever was a really chatty guy.

The weather right after Valentine's Day became a lot warmer, almost unseasonably warm, as it sometimes could. So there was lots of star watching. It was a Friday night, and Phyllis and Emmett had ordered in pizza and I was invited. It had been a while since I had been there. I was wondering if I could figure out what gift Emmett had given Phyllis for Valentine's Day. Would I see anything? A bouquet of flowers? Another velvet ribbon, or something for Ralph?

"Hi, Georgie—Saint Georgie," Phyllis said with her eye to the telescope. They had been out on the patio for a while when I came. "Long time no see," she said cheerfully. I always liked seeing Phyllis look through the scope. The mirrors in the scope brought the stars closer, and for some reason I thought of them as more honest than the reflections in the Creature's mirrors.

"What's happening?" I asked.

"We're going to the dogs tonight," she said with a laugh. But it made me shiver. Did her laugh sound sort of phony? I couldn't help but think that behind the dogs, in a few months, Scorpio would be rising. I hadn't forgotten the naked terror of that dream of the spider's web and how that spider had become a scorpion.

I looked up. I could see them scampering, all right. Little Dog and Big Dog, Canis Minor and Canis Major. Big Dog chasing at the heels of Orion, Little Dog at his shoulder. There would only be one more month that was good for seeing Orion in all his glory. By the end of March he would begin to slip out of the sky. By May he would be gone entirely, and the first glimmer of Scorpio would show on the southern horizon. Often just a slight stain of red from Antares. It was as if a time bomb had started to tick. Soon Scorpio would dominate the summer skies. I didn't have much time to figure out how Phyllis would reel Emmett in on her own silken threads.

There were a lot of quiet little laughs between the two of them. Code time again. Although I have to admit, Emmett didn't seem quite as relaxed as Phyllis.

It was getting on toward nine thirty, and Mom had said I had to be home by then. I started to leave, then remembered to ask Emmett for something I needed for school.

"Do you have a protractor, Emmett?" I asked him. "I left mine at school."

"I got at least a half dozen of them up in my room in the right-hand drawer of my desk."

I said good night and set off across the Kellers' lawn and through the grove. The whooshing sound seemed to follow close at my heels and breathe right up around my shoulder blades, as if the star dogs were following me home. It gave me a strange feeling.

I went up to Emmett's room, which was a mess as usual. Mom made him set his basketball sneakers out on his windowsill to air every night because she said nothing stank like a teenage boy's basketball shoes. I went to his desk and found the protractor. But in the drawer beneath, I saw the tip of something red sticking out. I don't know if I really thought twice about opening that drawer until after I did it, and then it was too late.

It was a big red envelope with *Emmett* scrawled on it. It was Phyllis's handwriting, or rather, mouth-writing. She could write short messages by holding a special pen in her mouth (another invention of Dr. Keller's). I opened it up.

It was the perfect Valentine for Emmett. I don't know how she found it. She must have had Sally pick it up for her, or maybe she ordered it from a catalog. There was a constellation of stars that was in the shape of a heart, and when you opened up the card, there was a quote that said:

> *Take him and cut him out in little stars,*
> *And they will make the face of heaven so fine*
> *That all the world will be in love with night*
> *And pay no worship to the garish sun.*
> —William Shakespeare

And then again in Phyllis's scrawl there were the words *I'll love you forever and a day. P.*

I slipped it back into the drawer and felt something grow hot behind my cheeks, behind my eyes, like the way you start to feel before you cry. What did *forever* mean here? Phyllis's forever and Emmett's were different. But did he know that? He was truly in love with her. And she in her twisted way with him. But this couldn't mean forever. I had to somehow stop forever—now. I'd been such a fool with all my dreams about romance, teenagers. Archie comic books. I had wanted all that for Emmett. Now I just wanted him to live here on Earth and not in the stars.

Chapter Thirty-five

Carbuncles are not life-threatening in dairy cows. They can, however, invade the ductal system of the milk glands, which then could cause permanent damage to the udder by weakening the suspensory ligaments. And in this case a farmer might be forced to put down the cow rather than to go to the expense of feeding and pasturing it. These are what my grandfather calls "the harsh realities" of life on a farm for an animal: produce or die. So you could say that carbuncles can be fatal. It was my privilege to assist Dr.

Vernon Albert, doctor of veterinary medicine, specializing in large animals, in the draining of the carbuncle of a dairy cow named Missy on my grandfather's farm in Carmel, Indiana. This was a real experience that I think maybe changed my life, as we are supposed to write about in this composition. . . .

Of course that was a lie. It didn't change my life at all. I didn't dare write about what was happening that was changing my life, but the Heimer—as in Patty Wertheimer—had just read her composition about how she had helped her sister pick out a prom dress last year and was looking forward to being her "fashion consultant" again when spring came, and how that had changed her life.

Everybody lied in these stupid compositions all the time. We're sixth-graders, for Lord's sake! How many life-changing experiences can an eleven-year-old have had? Not ones that they want to stand up in front of a whole class and talk about. I actually got an *A* on the composition, and the Prune wrote at the bottom of the paper, *Georgia, I hope you follow your dreams of becoming a doctor of veterinary medicine. I shall bring Sweetie Pie to you if she is ever sick.* Sweetie Pie was the

Prune's poodle. Miniature poodle! Even though it was a lie, the Prune had missed the point that I had been talking about becoming a *large* animal vet.

I had to go over to Phyllis's that day after school because Mom had a faculty meeting.

"I really wouldn't discount it, Phyllis." Mrs. Keller was knitting, and her mouth was pursed up as if she had just dropped a stitch. "I mean, Tudor Hall is willing to accommodate us so beautifully."

I wasn't sure what they were talking about. Was Phyllis maybe going to go back to school or something? "I'm sure Emmett would enjoy it," Mrs. Keller continued.

Oh, my God, I thought. *This cannot be happening.*

"All your friends want you to come. The theme is April in Paris."

"But the prom is in May," Phyllis said.

"Oh, you're such a stickler!" Mrs. Keller laughed and stuffed her knitting into the bag. "You talk to her, Georgie," she said, and gave me a pat as she got up to leave.

"Maybe you should talk to you-know-who!" The mirrors started to flash madly, cutting the soft spring light in the room. "And see how he feels about it?" Phyllis almost hissed.

"Now, now!" Mrs. Keller said softly. She tapped on the iron lung as one might pat a child's shoulder to calm it.

"Don't now-now me, Mother!" I had never seen Phyllis so openly angry. But what Mrs. Keller was suggesting was absolutely unbelievable.

Roslyn Keller's eyes filled up with tears, and she rushed out of the room. The mirrors stilled and now were filled with only my and Phyllis's faces. "As you might have gathered, Mom and Dad have set their hearts on me going to the Tudor Hall prom with Emmett. Real freak show that would be. They already hired a medical van to transport me and the Creature and Emmett. A merry threesome! Oh, God, and now Mom's all upset. Georgie, run and get her. I have to apologize."

Mrs. Keller was in the kitchen, crying softly.

"What am I going to do, Georgie?" she said when she looked up.

All of a sudden I realized that recently several adults had started asking me what they were going to do. First Mom and Dad when they were worried about Emmett, and now Mrs. Keller. I didn't think that they were really counting on me, but it made me sense how out of control this whole situation was. And then I had the worst thought of all. Nothing was ever going to be in control until Phyllis died. "Uh, Phyllis feels really bad. She asked me to come and get you. She wants to say she's sorry."

"She never has to say she's sorry to me." Mrs. Keller pressed a dish towel against her mouth as if she were stuffing a sob back inside. She must have had an ocean of unsobbed sobs in her.

"I'm sorry, Mom. I'm really sorry," Phyllis said when her mother bent down to give her a kiss.

"It's all right, dear. Your dad I and just thought it would be a nice way for you to be with your friends in a festive setting."

I wished Mrs. Keller had not said the word *festive*. I caught a look in Phyllis's eye that I had never seen before. It was soft and longing. I knew that in that moment Phyllis would have given anything to touch her mother's face. When her mom left the room, the look did not linger in Phyllis's eyes. "So, Georgie, tell me this."

"What?" I asked.

"Do you believe in God?" It was the non sequitur thing again. *Why,* I wondered, *did God always come up as a non sequitur?*

"I don't know. I used to."

"I never did, I am proud to say. I take solace in that. There's no letdown if you don't believe in God. Even though I went to church, I used to cross my fingers when I said the Creed."

"The Creed?"

"The Nicene Creed. It's an Episcopal thing, I guess, and Catholic."

"We're Presbyterians."

"Oh, see, we go to Trinity Church. Very 'high Episcopalian,' as they say. Mom loves the church. She likes its rituals. Smells and bells but not really Catholic. She likes the fact that Henry the Eighth started the whole thing. Natch, this would appeal to the English literature side of her."

"What's a king got to do with religion?"

"Yeah, my sentiments exactly, and what a king! He chopped off his own wife's head."

"He what!" I was stunned.

"He surely did, and I told my mom once, before I got sick, that I would never go to a church founded by a man who cut off his wife's head."

I didn't quite know what to say to this. But then Phyllis suddenly caught me in the mirrors again. "Now, come on, tell me truthfully. Do you or don't you believe in God, Georgie?"

Her eyes bore into me. I knew in that moment what I was supposed to say: *No. How can I believe in God if he lets something like this happen to you?* But I didn't want to say that. I didn't want to be forced into saying anything about what I believed or didn't believe. And that was what Phyllis was trying to do—force me to say something. It was a kind of loyalty test: if I believed in one—God, that is—then I couldn't believe in the other, Phyllis.

But I was quiet. I said nothing. Just at that moment a blast of sunshine poured through the windows and reflected off the mirrors like lightning. I was caught again in this snare of light, and at its center I knew was the dazzling spider-girl weaving a tangled web of death, her death. That was what Phyllis was talking about. She was absolutely masterful at talking about dying without talking about dying. As a matter of fact, I began to think that maybe she really did or had believed in God, and that her death was not solely an act of escape but of vengeance against that God.

"You're mad at God, aren't you?" I said quietly.

I saw a pulse tick in Phyllis's temple. When she laughed there was a hard glitter in her eyes. "How can I be mad at God if I don't believe in him?"

"I don't know."

"I'm sorry, Georgie. I shouldn't have asked you these questions. They're personal, I know."

But you did ask them, I thought. The minutes seemed to drag until four thirty, when I could leave. I'm not sure what we talked about.

"Well, I better be going now. Mom's home."

"All right." I started for the door. "Hey, Georgie, I'm really sorry about all that. It was very intrusive of me. I should mind my own business, eh?"

"Yeah, sure," I said. Her business was death. But as I walked back through the grove, my fear set like cold lead in my gut. And though I was filled with thoughts of death, I began to search for signs of life. It was early March, and I went around our yard looking for the little green points of the daffodils and tulips pushing up through the winter-locked ground. I had helped Mom plant the bulbs last fall.

When I got back to the house, Mom was beaming. "Emmett got a full scholarship to Purdue," she said, waving an envelope.

"Mom, did you open his mail?"

"I didn't open it exactly."

"Well, what exactly did you do?" I asked.

"It's a fat envelope—see? If they get rejected, it's always a skinny one, and this was sort of open and I just took a little peek inside."

"Mom!"

"Don't tell him I looked—please, Georgie."

"I won't. But really, Mom, don't do that with me. Besides, I'll probably get a skinny envelope."

Mom batted me on the shoulder with the envelope. "Nonsense, Georgie. You're every bit as smart as Emmett."

It wasn't true, but I wasn't going to argue with her. I just wished that Emmett could go off to college right now, today.

Chapter Thirty-six

By mid-April, all the Mustard Seeds who had either older brothers or sisters were all talking about prom season and going downtown with their mothers and sisters to look for prom dresses. I had gained some stature among the Mustard Seeds because they knew of Emmett being a basketball star at Westridge. One day on the playground, Amy Moncton said, "So who's Emmett taking to the prom?"

"I don't know." Ever since that afternoon at Phyllis's, the word *prom* had a terrible meaning for me. When I got home that day, I buried my Archie comic book about the prom at the very bottom of the stack.

"My sister says he's cute."

I didn't know what to say. For a girl, let alone a Mustard Seed who had snubbed me all year, to say something like this was truly daring. You just didn't go around blabbing stuff like this. It wasn't cool. There must have been desperation in the Moncton family. My first instinct was to say he's not the prom type, which of course was the truth, seeing as he never had gone to a prom. I certainly couldn't say that his girlfriend is in an iron lung. I thought briefly about lying and saying he had a girlfriend but she lived out of town. But that would be so disloyal to Phyllis. I was at a loss. So I just mumbled, "I don't know."

Please, please don't ask Evelyn about her outfit, I thought as Mom, Grandma, Evelyn, and I sat down in Block's tearoom for lunch. I was staring straight across at the froth of pink frills that gushed from the neckline of the fitted jacket Evelyn was wearing. Her mother had bought her a new outfit. From the top up, she looked kind of like a birthday cake. From the waist down, she looked like an old lady, a chopped-off sixty-five-year-old without wrinkles. Marge, how could you!

I, on the other hand, looked pretty good. I was wearing a gray princess-line dress with a soft cream-colored velvet collar and matching velvet cuffs. Mom and Grandma were both wearing hats, and as I looked at Grandma across the table in what she called her spring-green suit, I knew that underneath, harnessing her in, was the pink flamingo that I had seen flapping on the clothesline last summer. The big thing was that Evelyn and I were both wearing nylon stockings for the first time. And we both had Capezio flats on. She and I had each talked our moms into getting us the shoes and the stockings, and we were very excited about wearing them. There was not much that could go wrong in selecting a pair of flats and nylons. Marge had at least done that part right.

It was always a custom for Grandma and Mom and me to have a Saturday spring lunch downtown at the big department store, the William H. Block Company. They had a tearoom where they served what Dad described as fussy ladies' food. Drinks came with little parasols in them. And if you ordered chicken that wasn't à la kinged (meaning, I think, off the bone and stewed in cream sauce), but on the bone, the drumsticks came with little frilly paper pants on them so you wouldn't get your fingers greasy when you picked them up.

There were fashion models who drifted through and would stop and twirl in front of your table in pretty pastel-colored suits. Mom said that I could bring Evelyn along. It was unbelievable to me that this would be the first time Evelyn had ever been to Block's tearoom. Every mom took her daughter there. It was like taking a little bitty kid to see Santa Claus. You just did it. Not the Winklers, I guess.

"So it's getting near the end of school, girls," Grandma said. "Any plans for summer?"

Not getting polio, I thought, but didn't say it. We both shrugged.

"Not really," Evelyn answered.

"Mom," I said, "I had this neat idea. If we could build a swimming pool in our backyard, a private swimming pool, would you let me go swimming?"

"Georgie, there is no way we are building a swimming pool. They cost too much money, and I don't want the responsibility of other people's kids sneaking into a pool."

"They wouldn't sneak in. I'd invite only a couple. Like just one—Evelyn."

"Kids sneak into people's pools all the time, and then someone drowns or something and you're liable. So forget it."

"Why don't you rent a cottage up north on a lake? Lake swimming is safe," Grandma suggested.

"That's an idea," Mom said.

I wondered whether Emmett would even go if we got a cottage.

Then Grandma turned to Evelyn. "I understand that you and Georgie entered the science fair together and got third prize."

"Yep," Evelyn said.

"Now, what was your experiment?"

"It wasn't an experiment, Grandma. We built a model of a cell with the nucleus and all that stuff."

"Oh, that's interesting. If you are learning all about cells and genes and hereditary things, that's what interests Grandpa and me in building our herd."

"Nobody knows what the structure of a chromosome looks like," Evelyn offered. "It's a mystery, but my dad says whoever figures it out will get a Nobel Prize."

"Hmmm," Grandma said. "You know, we've been building our Holstein herd from this one bloodline, and I'm beginning to suspect that some of those prize bulls they advertise, well, they aren't sending us the good stuff." I could see that my mother was getting a little nervous over the direction of the conversation. She was twirling the little paper umbrella in her iced tea. It wasn't the kind of conversation that one usually had in Block's tearoom. Just as the waitress was setting down our plates, Evelyn's and my chicken with the frilly pants, Grandma said, "It's not truth in advertising. I think they've been slipping in some puny sperm." It was one of those unfortunate moments in a restaurant when there is a sudden lull in the conversational din, and that word *sperm* just sailed right out into the void. The waitress turned bright red. Mom cleared her throat and I think wished for a coughing fit or some sort of camouflage, but the word was out there. It took Grandma a second to realize what she had said—well not *what* she had said but *where* she had said it. She just laughed and twirled the paper umbrella in her iced tea. "Well, well, Dot." She turned to Mom, who looked as if she had been sucker-punched. "You can take the girl out of the country, but you can't take the country out of the girl." Then she turned to Evelyn and me. "Sorry, girls." Evelyn, of course, just blinked in that way she had. The Winklers probably talked about sperm and stuff like that at the dinner table all the time.

After lunch we rode the elevator down from the sixth floor, where the tearoom was, to the fifth floor, where the ladies and what they called the Young Deb department was. Evelyn and I were not quite big enough for the department yet, but we wanted to browse. I soon enough realized that I would rather be anywhere but in the Young Deb department. It seemed as if the entire floor was in full prom bloom. Evelyn and Mom and Grandma were oohing and aahing over rainbows of tulle confections. The dresses had layers upon layers of the pastel netty material, some sprinkled with rhinestones and some with confetti-like dots of color. Others had seed pearls embroidered on. There were two mannequins, a girl in a beautiful pale-green tiered dress with a thin silvery thread running through the edge of each tier, and a boy mannequin in a white dinner jacket with a pink carnation pinned to the lapel. They were perched in a dancing position on a rotating platform.

"Georgie!" someone squealed. It was Amy Moncton, accompanied by the Heimer and their mothers and older sisters. They were indeed helping to pick out prom dresses and shoes to go with the Heimer's sister's dress. The first thing they did after taking in Evelyn's odd outfit was to look at our feet. Then Amy said in a low whisper, "Isn't wearing a garter belt hard? Those little metal garters really dig into you when you sit down."

She might have just been trying to be friendly, trying to say we are almost teenage girls. Isn't it great? Isn't it exciting? Here is something we have in common; you might someday be a Mustard Seed, too. She probably was, but I felt this terrible anger welling up in me. I wasn't the one who had nothing in common with all the pretty girls in the Young Deb department who were flitting around holding up shoes to dresses and jabbering about would they have to get them dyed or not; it was Phyllis. I think I might have closed my eyes for a second, wishing that it would all simply go away. When I opened them, nothing had gone away, but good old Evelyn had taken up the conversational ball and was talking about garters and then before you knew it, being led over to a dress that Amy's sister was considering.

"You OK, Georgie?" my mom asked. I was not OK at all. I felt my anger collapse inside of me. I turned to my mother. "She's not ever going to get to do any of this, is she?" I was half sick with myself for even giving in to this kind of soppy sentimental stuff. There was still a part of me separate from my deep apprehensions about Phyllis and her devious designs on my brother that wanted to see her as a tragic figure. The Lady of Shalott watching the prom as reflections in her mirror!

Mom knew exactly who I was talking about. She put her arm around my shoulders and gave me a squeeze.

Chapter Thirty-seven

I think it was one night shortly after I went downtown with Mom and Evelyn and Grandma that I realized our dinnertimes had grown kind of quiet. It might have started that day when Emmett got his acceptance and scholarship letter from Purdue. Mom and Dad were ecstatic, but Emmett didn't seem excited at all, not even relieved. It wasn't like he had just assumed he would get the scholarship. It seemed to me that he should have been happy just for Mom and Dad's sake, for saving them so much money. I could tell that Mom and Dad were disappointed that he wasn't more enthusiastic or excited. But they didn't say anything.

I knew Mom and Dad had the usual worries of parents as summer approached because summer was polio season. But I also knew that other families just didn't go quiet at the dinner table the way ours had in recent weeks. It was as if our dining room swirled with unspoken thoughts, unasked questions. There was this terrible tension as if we were all waiting for something to happen. Maybe this was in fact malaise. But we hadn't a clue how to figure it out, or what to do if something did happen. Maybe, I thought, there was nothing we could do. It was like if the Russians dropped the A-bomb on us. It was useless to build a bomb shelter, because all that stuff was in the air. It would get you in the end. But what was it that would get us now, soon? We were all of us, I knew, feeling helpless.

Later one night, I was working on the diorama. I was finally doing the dome of the sky. I had learned from Emmett how to wire all the little lightbulbs. I had borrowed an embroidery needle from my mom to poke tiny holes in the curved dome that made the sky. I would then thread the wires through, following a pattern that I had traced with chalk and would later erase. I had been very careful to make the outline of Orion not look as if he were stumbling. He thrust his legs out like he was a track star. It was coming along nicely, but I decided to go down to the basement to do a bit more soldering with one more length of the lights. When I went out into the hallway, I heard Mom and Dad talking. I stopped to listen. Their bedroom door was open, and they didn't know I was out there. All I really heard was my mother say, "I don't know, Don. Maybe it was a mistake to move here."

It was enough. I knew then exactly what they were talking about. It was not about polio season. They were worried about Emmett and Phyllis.

"Do you think he'll go next fall?"

This shocked me. Would Emmett actually consider not going to college because of Phyllis? This was unthinkable.

The night I heard them talking was the night the spider dreams started coming back. Only this time they were a little different. It was even more cruel than before. You see, I thought I heard the *thwup* of a basketball outside my window. Emmett's back! He's back. He's shooting baskets. It was so real-sounding. And in my dream I was out in the drive watching him. He was playing the way he used to play, fast and bossy. Oscar Robertson was there, too. They were inventing shots together. I was so happy. I was spilling with joy.

But then Oscar started to walk away and Emmett was left alone staring up at the hoop. I came up beside him and looked up at the hoop. It started to rearrange itself. The strings of the net dissolved into the night, and instead a furry face with the eight shiny beads across the forehead appeared in the darkness as it had before. But this time on each of the spider's eight legs a corsage hung, a dead corsage just like the faded ones in the lamp in Phyllis's old bedroom.

Then the spider itself began to elongate and become a scorpion suspended by its long, curving tail. It spoke in the same unvarying rhythms of Phyllis. "Emmett, did you bring me flowers for the prom? How sweet." Emmett suddenly was no longer bossy but meek as could be. He began to move forward. He was wearing a white dinner jacket now and holding out a corsage of rosebuds and baby's breath.

"Don't, Emmett. Don't!"

I sat up in bed. The prom! The night of the prom! She was going to get him to help her die on the night of the prom. I knew this as sure as I had ever known anything. And maybe in a funny way this was the thing we had all felt coming. Not even Emmett could name it. But I had named it. In my dream I had named it!

Phyllis had probably talked him into some experiment where he would try to wean her from the machine. It would all look like an accident but most definitely be on purpose. It all made sense because Emmett knew everything there was to know about that machine. She had trained him, groomed him for this job. Maybe that was the worst realization I had to face. Phyllis had never loved my brother. She was only using him. And then it really hit me. I was the one who had caused all this. Wasn't I the one who had thought how great it would be if Emmett started to like Phyllis just a little bit? "She could be sort of like your starter kit," I had said! It had all been a game to me, and now look what was happening! How stupid I had been.

What could I do to stop it? I had to stop it because I had been the one who started it. If you break it, fix it—that's what my dad always said.

Chapter Thirty-eight

"Euthanasia." Evelyn whispered the word even though there was no one in her house at the time.

"What Youth in Asia? What does Asia have to do with it?"

"No, not Asia!" Evelyn's pale eyes flashed behind her glasses. "It's *e-u-t-h-a-n-a-s-i-a*."

"Well, what does it say?" I asked. We were standing in the room that the Winklers' called the library. Evelyn was reading from a dictionary. "'Euthanasia,'" she began. "'Also called mercy killing, the act of putting to death painlessly a person suffering from an incurable and painful disease or condition.'"

Every word dropped into my mind with crystal-line clarity. It all made perfect sense now.

"What can I do, Evelyn?"

Evelyn stood very still with the dictionary pressed to her chest.

"We could look in my parents' medical ethics book."

"What's that?"

"It's a book about what doctors should and shouldn't do in situations like this."

"Like what's legal and what's illegal?"

"Yeah, and kind of what's right morally and not."

"But Evelyn, I heard your parents say right in this room that it was a crime to put someone into an iron lung—'a damn crime'—those were your mother's exact words."

"I know. I've heard her say that at least a hundred times."

"So it's not illegal, right?" I asked.

"I think it's illegal. As a doctor, you take an oath to try and save people's lives, no matter what."

"Then why were they talking that way?"

Evelyn shrugged. "Maybe they wished they could change the law."

"What if it were you or Edith in the iron lung, would they do it?"

"I don't know. I don't think they know. It's easy to say that to let someone live is a crime when you see them on television in an iron lung."

"But they're both doctors. They must see people in hospitals like this every day."

"Yeah, but Georgie, until it happens to someone you love, your own family, you don't know what you'd do—even people as smart as my mom and dad." There was a long silence. Then Evelyn spoke again. "What are you going to do?"

"I don't know. That's the trouble. My parents are totally clueless except for just being worried about Emmett. I don't think Emmett himself realizes how Phyllis is jerking him around for her own purposes. I think I'm the only one who sees it. If I tell anybody, they'll think I'm crazy."

"You're not crazy," Evelyn said. I should have been relieved by this pronouncement, but it made me feel worse than ever.

"What do you think I should do?"

"You mean like to stop it?"

"Stop it? I'm not even sure what I would be stopping, 'cause I'm not sure how Phyllis is planning this out."

"Yeah," said Evelyn. "I . . . I don't know."

Chapter Thirty-nine

The daffodils were almost gone by, and the tulips were up. Our one-year-old yard showed promise, Mom said. Emmett was now finished with exams and spending most of his time at Phyllis's. I didn't even bother to ask anymore where Emmett was. One night I was setting the table for dinner and Mom called in from the kitchen, "Don't set a place for Emmett."

"What?"

"I said, don't set a place for Emmett." She came through the door from the kitchen and leaned against the frame. She looked tired. "He's eating over at Phyllis's tonight."

I looked away. I didn't say anything at first, but I felt a terror swimming up inside me. "What do you mean?" I asked.

Mom snapped at me. "Just what I said. He's eating at Phyllis's. That's all." She turned and went back into the kitchen.

Mom and Dad had always been very strict about us all eating together on weekday evenings. Eating together was like a religion with them. Mom even quoted statistics about how kids who don't eat with their parents had lower reading scores or something. Did this mean they were giving up on Emmett?

Dinner was just awful. Everything seemed out of whack. The table seemed unbalanced.

"Nice weather," Dad said. "Bet Grandpa's happy he'll have a good haying."

"Yes, it's nice when that first haying can come in all dry," Mom replied.

"Hope it's good for the 500."

For crying out loud, I thought, *it was at least three weeks until the Indianapolis 500-Mile Race. Why are we talking about it now?* Weather. You always know that things have deteriorated if you start talking about weather. There is nothing you can do about it. Weather is just there. You have to live with it, so why talk about it? "Can I go this year to the race if there's an extra ticket?" I said this just to make conversation.

Dad started talking about a new television set he saw downtown. "You should see it, Georgie. Best reception I ever saw. I'm tempted to get it."

"I don't think we need another television set," Mom said. I knew a reading readiness statistic was coming up.

From television sets we moved on to freezers. "I think we could use a bigger freezer. I could only take half a lamb from Dad this year because we didn't have the room. Oh, and by the way, Georgie, I had to throw out those old Popsicles. They were getting gummy. There were grape ones. You never leave the grape ones. It's usually the green." I simply shrugged.

This conversation was unbelievable to me. Half-frozen lambs, TV sets, gummy Popsicles. I wanted to scream, *Something terrible is happening. Please STOP IT!*

Right after dinner, I went upstairs and got the Orion small world. I had almost completed it. With its three levels, I would have to transport it in parts. It would take at least two trips back and forth, but I had decided that I was going next door, invited or not. In the grove between our house and the Kellers' I saw some wildflowers pushing up—a jack-in-the-pulpit, some lilies of the valley, a trillium, still pink, not yet turned to white. There was no breeze that night in mid-May when I made my way through the grove, but I noticed that the wildflowers did tremble as if there were one, and then I realized that they were actually moving to the vibrations of the Creature's whooshing sounds. This seemed so wrong to me.

"Saint Georgie!" Phyllis said as I climbed up the steps of the patio. "What did you bring? A small world?"

"Uh, yeah, sort of a big small world. I have to set it up. It has three parts. I have to run back and get the rest of it." It was actually a perfect way to stall for time. I would drag it out into three trips, although I could have easily done it in two. But I had no more come to show her this small world than to hang upside down naked in a tree. I wanted to stop what was happening or going to happen. I wanted to shout at Phyllis to leave us alone, get out of our lives. I wanted to scream at Emmett that he was a fool.

Finally I got it all set up. Then with the little needle-nose pliers that Emmett let me use, I attached the wires to the battery terminal.

"Behold! The winter sky," I said, trying to sound cheerful, and spun the lazy Susan around.

"It's the Orion small world, the one you showed me months ago!" Phyllis's breathy exclamation rippled the night. "My, my, you are an excellent builder of small worlds, Georgia Mason, an excellent builder." She paused and then said, "And just imagine: you said that Orion and Scorpio were never together in the sky. But tonight they are." The mirrors flashed, and suddenly there was a red spark in them. She had caught Antares perfectly. I felt my heart begin to pound thunderously in my chest. It seemed to actually drown out the gasping noise of the Creature.

"Can I keep it for tonight?"

"You can keep it forever." I saw Emmett and Phyllis exchange glances in the mirror, and then something went still inside me. "I mean for as long as you want. It's a present."

"Thanks, Georgie."

"No!" I nearly barked the word. "No, don't thank me." They both looked at me with alarm. Or, I should say, our three faces floated into the mirror. Three sets of eyes darting back and forth.

"Something the matter, Georgie?" Emmett asked.

"Yes, Emmett! Everything is wrong. You weren't

home for dinner," I yelled, and then ran down the patio steps and tore through the grove.

I couldn't sleep. I got one of Emmett's scopes and brought it to my bedroom window. It was close to midnight. He was still over there. So we were all three looking at the same thing. Scorpio was burning higher in the southeast sky.

Ursa Major had risen very high now. She is the home of many galaxies. There were no clouds, and I found one of these galaxies, M81, right away. It was a perfect spiral galaxy about seven million light-years away, which is, according to Emmett, a very short distance on an astronomical scale, relatively speaking, like from our house to downtown Indianapolis. With the naked eye, it just looks like a fuzzy little patch up there below the head stars of the Big Bear. But through the scope, it's like a lazy swirling pool of stars, a slow commotion of billions upon billions of suns that have flattened out into a spiraling disk. I looked at it for a long time. The night was warm, but I was suddenly cold. How far would Emmett go to be with Phyllis forever? I began shaking. I went and stood in front of Mom and Dad's door for a long time. I knew that every second that slipped by was a second lost. I had to stop whatever it was. I had to go back.

Our yard, newly seeded, had just begun to sprout, and the grass was more like a green mist than actual grass. It seemed to hover rather than grow, and it was as fine as babies' hair. I wound my way through the grove of trees for the second time that night. I did not rush. I paused to look at things. It was strange, but everything seemed to loom out at me with extraordinary clarity. I saw the lovely patterns of the veins in unfurling leaves. I took note of the jack quivering in its pulpit, the lilies of the valley nodding their heads, the snowdrops like little earthborn galaxies lighting the mossy floor. This was life. This was for Emmett. So it was astonishing to me that I, who months before had thought of myself as Phyllis's knight in shining armor, was not coming to slay her beast. I was coming to slay a dream and save Emmett. Saint Georgie the dreamslayer.

And to do this I had had to slay my own dreams. But there was no turning back. I was nearly there.

Chapter Forty

"What are you doing here?" Emmett's voice was taut as he saw me. He had put on Dad's white dinner jacket. In the lapel was a carnation.

"Georgie, go home," Phyllis barked. She had a corsage pinned in her hair.

"No," I answered simply. And sat down on a bench.

"What are you doing here?" Emmett was almost pleading.

"Why are you all dressed up? Prom night?" I cut my eyes to Phyllis.

"This has nothing to do with you, Georgie," she snapped.

"Yes, it does, Phyllis." The defiance in my voice surprised me.

"It's our prom," she replied. I decided I wasn't having any more conversations with mirrors. I walked right up to her, leaned over her face, and looked directly into her eyes. I whispered to her in a low voice. So low that Emmett couldn't hear.

"It's not your prom, Phyllis. Remember? We talked about the prom. You have a funny way of turning the meaning of things inside out. We talked about the prom and then we talked about God, Phyllis." A look of panic swept through her eyes.

"It's none of your business!" Phyllis said in a cold voice.

I walked right up to Emmett. "You're not going to do it. She's never loved you. She's used you. Used you from the start."

Emmett looked stricken. "That's not true. That's simply not true, Georgie. You have it all wrong."

"No, you have it all wrong, Emmett. She craves death."

"Georgie, I wasn't going to kill her. It's like I am training her to make her stronger. She has to be strong in order to wean from the lung. If it didn't work, I'd put her right back in."

"And I would tell you not to," Phyllis said in barely a whisper.

"What?" Emmett said. "You wouldn't want me to put you back in?"

"No," she replied quietly. There was a long pause. "Go home, the two of you, and don't come back—ever!"

Emmett's face turned ashen. I took his hand and led him down the patio steps. He stumbled slightly when we first came into the grove, and I gripped his hand tighter. Yes, like blind Orion I led him. Every little wildflower shivered as we walked. I heard a bird land on a branch, and I felt the sighs of the moss beneath my feet.

"It's going to be all right, Emmett."

I looked up at him. His face was wet. I had never seen my brother cry.

Chapter Forty-one

I called Evelyn first thing in the morning.

"I tried to stop it," I whispered into the phone.

"By stop it, you mean . . ." She hesitated.

"Yeah, that's what I mean, killing Phyllis."

"Did it work?"

"Well, Emmett came home. I'll explain more when I see you in school."

And when I came home from school, Emmett was still asleep in bed. His door was open a crack. Mom must have checked on him. I peeked in. He was sleeping on his side, and I could see the rise and fall of his shoulders. At dinner that night, there were four places set, but Emmett didn't come down.

"He's not feeling very well," Mom said. "I'll take him up some soup after dinner." I was glad that she didn't ask me to take it up.

But later that night I got up my nerve to tap on his door.

"Yeah?"

"It's me. Can I come in?"

"Yeah."

He was propped up in bed reading a comic book.

"You mad at me?"

"No."

"Really?"

"Yeah, really. You were only trying to help."

"I was trying to stop it, Emmett."

He put down the comic and wiped his hand across his face as if trying to get rid of his weariness, his thoughts. "Do you think she ever loved me at all?"

I didn't really know what to say. Love? Did Phyllis really know what love was? Did I know what it was? "I think in her own way she did. It was just sort of different."

"Sort of different," Emmett repeated. "Yeah, I

guess you could say that about Phyllis—sort of different."

Here is what happens when a star dies: For its entire life, it has burned and cast off its skin of fiery embers and gases and dust, dust made from the atoms of carbon, nickel, gold, and, yes, iron. From their first breath, stars are burning and giving back to space what they had once sucked in. But now they are weak, fragile shells of starry matter. And in their fragility, they begin to burn faster and hotter at an insane rate. So soon, in a quarter billion years or so, gravity begins to crush the star's thin, brittle bones. In reaction, its core puffs, bloats, and then explodes, and so a star dies and gives up its last to the swirling streams of space.

We had not seen Phyllis since that night three weeks before. My parents only asked once why we no longer visited her, and Emmett told them honestly that she didn't want to see us anymore. Then one night the phone rang. It was Dr. Keller for Emmett. We all watched as he nodded and said, "Really? Yes, yes, I understand. I'm not sure." He hung up the phone and left his hand on the receiver for a long time. Finally he turned to us. "That was Dr. Keller. He says that Phyllis got a cold a few days ago and that she's really"—he hesitated—"failing. She won't speak to anyone, not her parents, not the nurses, and now she's not eating. They're having to feed her intravenously." My mother shuddered and gripped her arms as if to stay herself against a cold wind. "He wants me to come over and visit her. He thinks it might start her eating again."

"Are you going to?" Mom asked.

"I . . . I don't know. I think maybe this is the way it should be." He started up the stairs to his bedroom. None of us were sure what Emmett meant exactly. But he never did go, as far as any of us knew.

It was a beautiful Sunday morning when Mom came into my room. She touched me lightly on the shoulder.

"Honey," she said. I opened my eyes. She swallowed and tried to speak. "Georgie, Phyllis is gone."

"You mean dead," I said. Mom looked stunned when I said this. With her finger she began to trace a line down my cheek, her eyes searching my face as if she were looking for someone, the shadow of someone, the old Georgie that she thought she knew so well.

But I knew that Phyllis had not "gone" to a "beautiful place." She had not gone anywhere. She was dead. I felt sorry for the life she had led, but I also felt great relief.

"How's Emmett?" I asked.

"OK. He's over there now." That was when I began to cry. I was crying for Emmett. I hugged my mother and buried my face in her shoulder. "Oh, Mom, I've been so scared."

Here is what happens when a star is born: From the streaming solar winds, from the gases blown off a dying star, from the dust swirling with atoms of carbon, nickel, gold, and iron, from the vapors of space, all of these are sucked in, to come together, compress, grow hot, then hotter, spinning and heaving and laboring as the core of a star is born.

Emmett told me once that every single atom in our body was once made in the hot core of a star. In other words, we are made of stardust. He told me that every carbon atom that ever was still is. "In the wings of a butterfly," he said. "In the rocks, in the leaves, and the petals of flowers."

For a long time after Phyllis died, Emmett didn't look at the stars. I thought maybe instead he was looking at the earth—our own backyard, or the grove, at the petals of flowers, the wings of a night moth. One night when I was sleeping, I heard the sound again: the *thwup-thwup* of a basketball on asphalt. It stopped, but I knew it wasn't a dream. I ran to the window. He was standing still, looking up at the sky.

"What are you doing?" I called down.

"I'm looking at the place where stars are made, thousands of them, a real nursery for new stars," he said.

"Where is it?"

"Orion," he answered.

"Orion?"

"Yeah, but to get the best view of the nursery, we should really wait until fall. October is the best time."

Chapter Forty-two

October would come, but Emmett would not be here to look for the star nursery in Orion. He would not be at Purdue, either. He would be in Korea. He joined up the day after graduation. He came home from Korea two years later and started college. That first summer Emmett was gone, my parents decided they wanted to go to the country. At first I thought they meant the farm with Grandma and Grandpa. But Mom and Dad had rented a cottage on a lake in northern Indiana for the summer. Dad would drive up on weekends. They let me swim in June and July. They seemed to think a freshwater lake with hardly any people was safer than a swimming pool. Evelyn came up and so did Grandma and Grandpa. If I had thought Grandma's corset was funny-looking, well, I had never seen her bathing suit. It had palm trees and parrots all over it and a skirt that came down to her knees almost.

We survived despite the swimming. No one got polio. I took a lot of Emmett's telescopes with me up there. And often Mom and Dad would join me at the end of the pier to watch as the constellations rose. It was a very solitary summer for me. Not many kids around the lake, but I didn't mind. I kept a sky journal and would send it every week to Emmett in Korea. Emmett had an important job over there and one that Mom and Dad hoped would keep him out of the line of fire. He was in charge of radar instrumentation maintenance.

That summer I preferred to do my sky watching alone. And even though there was no one to say, "Hey, Saint Georgie," I could recall Phyllis's voice so clearly. I read once that when the sound of someone's voice is kept in the deepest and most persistent part of memory, that a remembered face begins to fade before a voice.

Emmett always said that night reveals and light steals, that without darkness there is nothing. Night is a dark chink in the long day; only through this crack can we see the light, the ancient light and the places where stars are born and die. It is in the flow of the night that we discover who we are and that we are all of us made from the dust of stars.

Epilogue

Two years after Phyllis died, Dr. Jonas Salk discovered the polio vaccine. It was a happy day when Mom took me to the pediatrician's office to get my injection. The Korean War was almost over. Emmett had come home. He was at Purdue University. After he graduated from Purdue, he went on to work on his advanced degree in astrophysics at the Massachusetts Institute of Technology. It was while he was at M.I.T. that he began to pry open the treasure chest in the Square of Pegasus. Several years later, he made a startling discovery of an intense star-like source of light and radio energy. It was a very, very mysterious object. In fact it was one of the first quasars to be discovered, and it was beyond the far edge of the Milky Way galaxy. He called it Ph4-C112.

I went to college, Indiana University in Bloomington. I was a theater arts major and eventually became a set designer. Dr. and Mrs. Keller came to my graduation as they had to Emmett's, and Mrs. Keller tried to return the box I had made with the story of Orion. But I could see she wanted to keep it. It was a link with Phyllis. So I told her to keep it, and she kissed me and said, "Phyllis always said you were an excellent builder of small worlds."